I am

Mrs. Jesse James

I am
Mrs. Jesse James

a novel

PAT WAHLER

Blank Slate Press | St. Louis, MO

Blank Slate Press | Saint Louis, MO 63110
Copyright © 2018 Pat Wahler
All rights reserved.

For information, contact:
Blank Slate Press
an imprint of Amphorae Publishing Group
4168 Hartford Street, Saint Louis, MO 63116

Manufactured in the United States of America
Set in Adobe Caslon Pro
Interior designed by Kristina Blank Makansi
Cover Design by Kristina Blank Makansi

Library of Congress Control Number: 2018941568

ISBN: 9781943075461

For my family.
Without you, nothing makes sense.

Kearney, Missouri
April 6, 1882

A flash of sunlight glints off the polished coffin as four men, their skin dripping with sweat, bear his remains toward the grave. Zerelda walks next to me, a formidable figure dressed in black crepe. Yet even though she sniffles and mutters, her back is straight as an arrow. Two young children follow us, their eyes red and cheeks damp.

Life around me appears ordinary. Chickens peck the ground for bugs. Bushes unfurl new green leaves. Grass grows soft and lush. Yellow tulips fringe the porch, and white blooms dot my favorite dogwood tree. The rich scent of rain-dampened earth permeates the air while robins chirp and chase each other in their annual mating rituals. The beauty of such an uncommonly warm spring afternoon seemed oddly discordant with the occasion.

On such a day, how can I be burying my husband?

I feel the watchful eyes of the hundreds of people gathered within sight of the old farmhouse. Some sit on wagons, others stand in respectful silence. Most were drawn here, I suspect, by the lure of sensational headlines.

Perspiration glues my black silk dress against me, and dampness gathers on my forehead. I hold a handkerchief balled in one hand, but shrink against lifting my widow's veil to dab my face. The idea of exposing raw lines of grief to those who may have come to witness such a sight makes my stomach roil.

Our sad cortege moves slowly, until, finally, we stand at the burial site. Men have already dug a deep hole under the shade of a towering coffee bean tree. Zerelda peers into the darkness and nods.

She had ordered the men to dig the grave no less than seven feet deep, and in a voice trembling with anguish and rage, later told me why. "We must keep him safe from vandals and ghoulish robbers who would try to steal his body away from us."

That macabre thought had not occurred to me before. Yet remembering how others had scavenged through our home, I knew Zerelda was right to worry.

After she decreed he be laid to rest at the farm, the place where he grew up, rather than in a distant cemetery, I gave my assent without discussion. It would be a fitting place for him to sleep, for I knew Zerelda would defend his grave with the same passion with which she had defended his life.

The four men wrap thick braids of rope around the casket. Their forearms bulge as they lower it into the ground.

My brother, Robert, awkwardly pats my arm and whispers, "Zee, are you all right?"

I nod, and Pastor Martin steps forward, holding a Bible in one hand and fist full of mud in the other. With his graying hair and spectacles perched at the end of a long nose, he reminds me of a poster I'd once seen of a sad elephant from Barnum's circus. I can't bear to watch the clods fall from his hand, so I close my eyes and distract myself by trying to think of something, anything, else.

Memories materialize in moments, and I lose myself in the sounds of hooves thumping on a dirt pathway packed hard as stone. Fists pounding at a door. The crack and echo of a gunshot. Angry voices screaming for revenge. And the most fearsome memory of all—blood flowing in a dark, sticky pool of despair on the floor. If I'd spoken sooner, we might not now be standing beside a deep and dark grave.

My hands clench so tightly, the nails cut into my palms. I long for a different image to hold, one that will comfort me.

As though in answer to a prayer, the shadowy vision of a tall, sandy-haired young man appears. He walks toward me with the muscled stride of a horseman, then he laughs and reaches for my hand. His silver-blue eyes snap with youthful excitement from a time before anger and hate changed him into someone neither reporters nor detectives nor gossipmongers would ever capture accurately. The corners of my mouth turn up in a smile even though my lips are so parched they split when I move them. No one knew the man I married.

Truth be told, I never completely understood him either. Could it have been within my power to change destiny? For I know his past molded him into who he would become.

Just as my own past formed me.

1

*L*ove should blossom before marriage, not the other way around. My conclusion seemed so obvious, I turned to Lucy and repeated it out loud.

My sister, six years my senior, served as both a second mother and dearest companion. Her blue eyes sparkled at the prospect of a lively debate while she and I stirred a mountain of shirts, pants, dresses, and linens in a kettle of soapy water over an open fire. Without the element of diversion, washing the mountain of laundry from a large family in addition to dirty clothes our boarders paid us to clean, made for tedious work.

"How can you say that, Zee? You know how things are with Papa and Mama."

"That was different." I pulled a sheet from the kettle with a stick so it could cool. "Mama's parents were gone and she had to provide for her brothers and sisters. What choice did she have but to marry the man Uncle Drury picked for her?"

"Yes, indeed. And have you ever seen two people more in love than our parents?"

My sister knew I couldn't deny her question. I'd seen few marriages in my life as amiable as the one of John and Mary Mimms. Yet content as they were, I longed for a more adventurous future. Wringing the wet sheet, I opened it and snapped the fabric against a cloudless azure sky. The scent of soap mingled with sweet blooms from Mama's lilac bushes. "They were lucky. Not all arranged marriages turn out so well."

Lucy chuckled. "From what I've heard, even matches that start with honeyed affection can turn sour over time."

"Well, that won't happen for me." I slung the sheet over a line stretched between two trees.

Lucy ducked her head and tried, unsuccessfully, to hide a smile. "Now that you're fifteen and Mama lets you put up your hair, I imagine she'll soon allow you to be courted. Old Mr. Locke would likely make a suitable escort for you at the summer cotillion."

I pursed my mouth as though I'd bitten into a lemon. Our boarder, gray-haired William Locke, looked much closer to Papa's age than mine.

"You may have Mr. Locke for yourself, Lucy," I said. "I can scarcely abide to look at his face, especially when he spits a wad of tobacco on the ground. Soon enough I'll find my own beau."

I stared in defiance toward the boarding house. The large, two-story building sat anchored on flat ground between tall sycamore trees bursting with new green leaves. Their graceful branches shaded a wide front porch that stretched from one end of the house to the other. At some point, a kitchen had been tacked onto the side as though an afterthought. On its other side, a sturdy log barn stood near a pen housing chickens that fluffed their feathers and pecked busily on the ground. Beyond the yard a thick grove of trees hid the Missouri river from our view.

Wisps of burnished gold hair strayed around my face, and I pushed them away. At the age of fifteen, I'd begun to think about beaus. Over the past few months, any number of eligible young men in town had cast glances my way or hastened to hold the door for me when I entered the mercantile. They provided a much more appealing sight than Mr. Locke.

Lucy clucked her tongue and hung a striped cotton skirt on the line. "Papa and Mama may have something to say about that. You know they believe parents are in the best position to ensure girls are well settled."

"I know Papa won't force me to do anything without my consent." I turned to her and lifted my fist toward the heavens in dramatic fashion. "Lucy, I vow to you this moment that I will never marry for any reason other than true love."

Lucy rolled her eyes, but I thrust my chin forward. I'd never been more certain of anything. I knew what I wanted in life. Whenever possible, I stole away from the bustle of the boarding house to read, and the books I selected at the lending library or secretly shared with friends presented a much different picture than that of a farm wife or boarding house matron. Even though Papa wanted me to study Scripture, I preferred to escape from the woes of the day in my hiding place on the far side of the barn, well out of Mama's sight, where I could rest my bare feet in soft green grass before even turning the first page.

Any story that whisked me away and ignited my imagination became a favorite, but the most dog-eared book I acquired was one written by Miss Emily Brontë.

Wuthering Heights, the tale of tragic love and shocking madness, appealed to a side of me my parents would have been quite unhappy to discover. Many considered the book controversial, but I saw past the violence, stark cruelty, and obsession with revenge into the very heart of Heathcliff, and soon began to dream of finding a hero who would become my own Heathcliff, although I wrote for myself a much happier ending.

Lucy and I hung the last of the wet clothes, and then dragged the empty baskets back to the boarding house. She and my sister Nancy, would change bed linens while I helped Mama and Aunt Susan in the kitchen. I smiled and waved at my older brothers Robert, Thomas, and David, who were in the field behind the boarding house, preparing the ground for a plow. Not far from them, sunlight gleamed off the axes of Uncle Thomas and Papa as they chopped wood. Lucy glanced at me when I giggled. Sometimes even I struggled over names when we talked about a family member. Papa and Mama had chosen to baptize their large brood from names found within our extended family, which created no small amount of confusion.

That included my own name. Mama chose it to honor her sister-in-law, Zerelda, the woman who wed Mama's younger brother Robert James. Mama held a special affection for Robert and grieved for many months after he died of a fever while on a preaching mission in California. With no money to bring his body home to Missouri where Aunt Zerelda and her three young children—Frank, Jesse, and Susan—waited, Mama's beloved brother was buried in a pauper's grave, far from the people he loved. Even though my parents christened me Zerelda, they soon shortened the name to Zee, either to avoid confusion, or because no one would ever presume to give such a nickname to my formidable aunt.

But now, silly distractions over names were immaterial. While I secreted away my novels and dreamt of adventure and true love, talk of secession swirled around me, like wayward ripples on a quiet pond. I knew most of Missouri kept their loyalty steadfast with the newly elected President Lincoln, but his plans to grant freedom to the slaves created sympathy for the Southern cause in rural Harlem. Many of our neighbors had farms that relied on the labor of slaves. We had no slaves ourselves, but I remembered my early life in Kentucky. Growing hemp and tobacco required many hands and we could not have managed the farm without their help.

On the day Papa answered God's call to become a Methodist minister, he freed his slaves and then bought passage for our family on a steamboat bound for Missouri. The smell of river mud and fish made my stomach roil, and I didn't feel better until my feet were planted on firm ground in Clay County. We'd come to help Mama's brother Thomas and his wife Susan run their boarding house. No one dreamed the business would keep us bustling from daybreak to bedtime, although Papa reserved Sundays—his one day of rest—for preaching.

The endless supply of laundry, clothes to be mended, cooking, and cleaning made me long for the slower pace of life as a child in Kentucky. But if Papa and Mama taught us anything, it was the value of hard work and the sanctity of family obligations. And never more so, than at a time when each day brought greater turbulence.

The usual topics of conversation in Harlem—farming and the cost of supplies for the men, recipes and childbirth for the women—changed by 1860. Abraham Lincoln's election brought fear over what changes he might order. The possibilities were openly discussed everywhere, even at cotillions. On Sunday mornings, Papa preached, not only on Scripture, but on the foolhardy nature of the new president's attempts to force his will upon the people. Papa's parishioners—mostly poor farmers—came to the boarding house to listen. They stood under the shade of the sycamore trees and nodded in agreement when he spoke with such passion, birds in the trees grew silent. I listened to him but did not worry too much about the matter. Brave words from my father and older brothers were designed to convince me I had nothing to fear. They claimed the disagreement would not come to war. And if it did, I harbored a child's notion the matter would be settled sooner rather than later.

Yet unsettling tidings came to us through weary travelers and the few newspapers Uncle Thomas could obtain. First South Carolina seceded from the Union, followed in short order by Mississippi, Florida, Alabama, Georgia, Louisiana, and Texas. A shadow of doubt flickered in Papa's eyes, while Mama's darkened with fear over what might happen next. In an eerie sense of foreboding, I wondered if we were teetering on the edge of a precipice.

2

ithin months of South Carolina's exit from the Union, news arrived that Major Robert Anderson had marched his small regiment from Fort Moultrie toward Fort Sumter in the Charleston harbor. They didn't leave even when the Confederate states ordered them to vacate. General P.T.G. Beauregard answered Anderson's refusal by raining fire and brimstone on the fort until a white flag of surrender raised. Southerners rejoiced at the nearly bloodless victory, but Papa and my brother David had differing ideas about what might come next. They discussed the confrontation while I helped them clear the ground and break up the soil for planting our garden.

"That'll be an end to it," David crowed as he punched his shovel into the dirt. "The Federals will slink away and leave us in peace. They won't force the matter if the people don't wish to remain in the Union."

Papa sighed. "I hope you are right. Yet I am not sure the Union will let the South slip away so easily."

Something I'd seen in town that morning prompted me to jump into their conversation. "When Mama and I were at the mercantile, we heard Mr. Smithson and Mr. Kerry shouting at each other about treason. Mr. Kerry drew back his fist, and the clerk took hold of his arm just in time to stop a fight. What could make them so angry?"

"Daughter, we live in a state that voted not to secede. But no state can control the opinions of its citizens. Some of our neighbors are loyal to the North. Others believe the South is right."

I kicked a clod of dirt. "So people who were our friends are now our enemies?"

"In many cases, I fear so."

David straightened his shoulders. "Missouri should have seceded with the other states. Abe Lincoln's got no right to tell us what to do."

"He does as he sees fit, even as we must do the same," Papa replied while tugging hard at a stubborn weed. "But in case the conflict comes to war, there are things we should do to prepare." He straightened and squinted his brows together. "In my childhood, what I remember most of war is being hungry. We must shore up a supply of food and squirrel it away in the woods."

Papa and Uncle Thomas lost no time in preparing for the worst. They set aside a portion of our supplies and hid them deep in the woods. And it wasn't a day too soon. Newspaper headlines announced that President Lincoln had called for seventy-five thousand volunteers to put down the Southern rebellion. In response, some of the young men of Harlem decided to march away and join the president's Federal army. Others followed Governor Jackson's call to be in Missouri's state guard, which had a decided leaning toward the Confederacy. Their choices divided neighbors and deepened the rift in our community.

The number of people who came for preaching fell to a handful. Most were women and children, along with a few white-haired gentlemen, who huddled together in a grim knot. Papa spoke of keeping faith in God no matter our fears, but I began to wonder at his faith. So many prayers had already been sent to the Almighty, yet still we were facing war. I suspected similar prayers had been offered in Federal homes, yet all our petitions had gone unanswered.

I thought of the war in a detached way—as though reading a story—until the true meaning of it fell upon my family. Months earlier, Robert had returned to his sweetheart in Kentucky, but John and David tossed a plan to join the Confederate militia back and forth like a ball, while grinning and slapping each other on the back. They were eager to leave and strike a blow for tyranny, and their greatest fear was that the war would be over before they had a chance to go. All the young men of my acquaintance chafed to leave home and fight. They spoke of the conflict as if it were nothing more than a thrilling horse race they couldn't wait to win.

When Lucy and I ventured into town, even the women who purchased supplies at the mercantile spoke with confidence of triumph. Papa cautioned us to be careful what we said, although most of our friends were sympathetic as we were to the South. Yet as best I could tell, neither side considered the possibility of losing. Only my best friend, Catherine, whispered to me she heard if the Federals beat the South, they would swoop down, confiscate our property, and force loyal Southerners to pay the debts the Northerners, themselves, had incurred as reparation.

"Intolerable," I whispered back.

All our friends agreed, yet despite the fever-pitch of patriotism, the day John and David rode away, I trembled with fear for them. Mama kissed her sons and prepared a small bag of food to tuck into their saddlebags, white-faced but stoic as any soldier. Papa shook his boys' hands and murmured a prayer.

David saw me dab my eyes and gave me a swift hug. "Don't worry, Zee. We'll lick the Federals in no time and be back home before you even noticed we were gone."

I prayed this would be truth. Nightmares of cannon balls, homes burned to the ground, and cruel despotism haunted my sleep. I resented President Lincoln's goal to preserve the Union at all costs and wondered why anyone would willingly set such a fire.

We watched my brothers whoop and wave their hats as they galloped out of sight, horse hooves kicking up clouds of dust that drifted and then dissipated in the air. When we could no longer see them, Mama's upraised arm dropped to her side, and she took to her bed. Muffled sobs soon followed. I couldn't bear to hear her sorrow, and left the house to walk past fields green with new growth. A path accented by purple prairie clover and bright red butterfly weed calmed my spirit as weariness eased my body. Yet nothing could still my brain. Even opening a book didn't soothe me. Papa said the times called for faith, but my own faith seemed to be sorely tested.

We were just learning to navigate around the hole left by my brothers' absence when stories came of bandits trampling across the border from Kansas to Missouri. They appeared to care not a whit for the life or property of anyone considered a Southern sympathizer. Some called them Jayhawkers, and they were indeed corrupt desperadoes. I heard Mama whisper to Aunt Susan about them looting and burning the entire town of Osceola in St. Clair County, leaving every building in smoldering ruins. That terrible act against innocents became a catalyst that compelled even more men to ride away and fight for the cause.

Southern men answered Jayhawker attacks by forming their own guerilla groups. The Federals learned to fear Bushwhackers, men who operated in small squads from forests and backcountry areas. Cunning strategies and fast horses helped them ambush Northern sympathizers. They disrupted mail and interrupted war communications. Bushwhackers made it their business to exact bloody revenge for Jayhawker atrocities.

In a letter dated May 1863—hastily scribbled by Aunt Zerelda from nearby Kearney, and delivered through a passing friend—we learned that my cousin Frank had joined the Bushwhackers under William Quantrill. She wrote of pride in her eldest son and desperate worry over young Jesse's impatience to follow in his older brother's footsteps.

"I hope Zerelda can keep Jesse at home. He's far too young for such a dangerous life." Mama shook her head. "Why matters cannot be decided in peace instead of by fighting, I will never understand."

As skirmishes near us became more frequent, Lucy and I came to call the simple act of going outside a fearsome adventure. When sitting on the porch to catch a cool breeze, we could sometimes hear the faraway pop of gunfire. Once a cannon exploded so loudly we both jumped and craned our necks, hoping to discover what had occurred. Some of our neighbors were curious enough to climb upon a rooftop, hoping to catch a glimpse of a battle.

Papa sternly forbade us to try anything so foolish. "Men are dying. It is our duty to pray for them, not watch what happens as though they fight for our entertainment."

I thought of my brothers, John and David, somewhere far away and understood.

Although most of us believed the war would not last long, each day and week that passed told us we were wrong. Thanks to our hidden supplies, we always ate, although not as heartily as before. Since we did not own slaves and were far from town, Papa thanked God we were not considered worthy of attack, although a few of our things mysteriously disappeared, such as food growing in the garden, most of our chickens, and all our livestock except Lully, our old swaybacked mare. Yet this was a small inconvenience, and we were grateful no harm came to our us, our boarders, or our home.

Some of our neighbors were not so fortunate. A note came that my friend Catherine's sweetheart had been killed in Tennessee. Our neighbor's son, Benjamin, died in Kentucky. A young man named Philip, with whom I once shared a waltz, was reported missing in action. I lived in terror of hearing similar news about my brothers or cousins.

Those were the days when I first understood the truth of events that were like twisting winds or trembling earth. I could do nothing but learn to endure them or madness would surely follow.

By the time the war began, all of our boarders had fled Clay County, except Mr. Locke and a widow woman named Mrs. Parkinson. Neither of them complained about the less hearty meals, for we knew Our Glorious Cause required sacrifice from citizens as well as soldiers.

As I approached the age of eighteen years, Mr. Locke

began to stare at me in a manner more bothersome than the sound of gunfire. I charitably conceded that if he shaved off his tobacco-stained whiskers, he'd look remarkably like a portrait I'd once seen of George Washington, although our first president had keener eyes and a much kinder face. My cheeks flushed every time Mr. Locke's bespectacled gaze narrowed and followed me, for I held fast to a young girl's dreams of one special beau. So far my hopes had come to naught, for all our young men had gone away to fight, and I could only dream about what the future held.

Mama came to me one afternoon when I was washing dishes, her eyes hard with purpose. "Mr. Locke spoke to Papa. He has no family near and needs a companion for his old age. Mr. Locke is impressed by your energy and intelligence and would very much like for you to become his wife. He is willing to build a home for you or even to stay here after marriage, if you wish. Papa and I discussed his offer and believe this would be a good match. He has sufficient money for security and is a reliable man who would make a good husband for you."

I'd often considered what it would be like to have a husband kiss me, but the thought of William Locke's lips on mine made me shudder. "No, Mama. I don't wish to marry anyone for the sake of convenience or comfort."

"Zee, we did not raise you to be disrespectful. Your papa and I know what's best. We'd like to see you make a match with someone dependable who will take good care of you."

Rebellion burned in my soul. I lifted my chin to Mama and told her exactly what I thought. "You married Papa at your uncle's bidding. That was fine for you, but no one shall make me marry for any reason other than love."

Mama glared at me, two spots of color burning high

on her cheeks. She opened her mouth to say more, but as though considering her approach, she took a measured breath and then walked away. Yet even though Papa told me he spoke to Mr. Locke of my refusal; the persistent man continued his bold stares. I hoped Papa hadn't led him to believe I would ever change my mind, and I did my best to ignore his attention. To my other daily supplications lifted to God, I added the boon of a man entering my life who would sweep me far away from the terrors of war and the loneliness of isolation. For now, even Lucy had fallen in love, and she spent her time dreaming of a wedding, carrying the precious letters her soldier sent to her.

On a late summer night with air holding the promise of rain, a single rider thundered toward the boarding house, silencing the cicadas and tree frogs. Uncle Thomas and Aunt Susan were away, so Papa put Lucy and Nancy in charge of hiding Mama's silver, while he went outside with a loaded pistol clutched in his hand. Unnerved by such a sight, I stood next to Mama at the door and peered into the darkness.

When the tall rider dismounted, Papa's shoulders loosened. He embraced the man, and I followed Mama outside. My cousin, Frank James, stood before us, coated in dust from hard travel, his eyes hooded. Heavy stubble covered a face much thinner than I remembered.

"The Federals just raided Ma's farm. They whipped Jesse senseless and made a game of hanging Reuben."

Zerelda had married Dr. Samuel Reuben five years before the war began. Such a deed as Frank reported shocked me even more when I remembered the kindness I always found in Reuben's eyes. "Is he dead?" I blurted out the question.

"Not dead, but hurt bad enough. They let him dangle from a tree limb, lowered him down, and then hung him again over and over until he was gasping for breath. They're after information on where to find any of Quantrill's troops. The Federals watched Reuben choking from the end of a rope until Ma took Jesse's Bowie knife and cut him down." Frank's mouth turned up in a weary smile of admiration. "Then she gave the Feds bloody hell before tending to Reuben."

"Oh, no!" Mama's hand went to her throat.

"There're bruises and rope burns all over his neck, but at least he's alive. Jesse's young. He'll heal in time, but now he's more eager than ever to ride with me. I don't think Ma can hold him back much longer."

Papa shook his head in disbelief. "It seems there are no honorable boundaries in war. Did they finally leave Zerelda in peace?"

Frank snorted. "There's no such thing as peace with Federals. They arrested Ma and Reuben and hauled them both off to jail. Kept them in a cold, stone cell until they signed the Oath of Allegiance to the Union. God knows what will come next. I wanted to tell you, so you could keep your eyes open."

"We will pray for them and for you," Papa said.

I scurried inside the house and returned carrying a bag filled with Mama's fresh biscuits for Frank. He took it, thanked me, and then jumped back up into the saddle, tugged on the reins, and urged his chestnut gelding into a gallop. I watched as he disappeared through the distant woods.

Mama put her head on Papa's chest, and his arms went around her. My own head buzzed as I contemplated the viciousness of war. I feared for the safety of Reuben, Jesse, and Zerelda, and wondered if someday, a troop of nameless soldiers might descend upon our home and do whatever they wished.

None of us were surprised a few months later when word came that Jesse had run away from home to fight with Frank. After what he'd seen and endured, no one could blame him.

With the arrival of 1865, our world had become war-weary. Optimism had long faded. Early advantages gained by the South disappeared and supplies dwindled to a trickle. Hope for victory dimmed as each day passed. To avoid feeling completely helpless, I took on the ritual of praying over everything I did, whether scrubbing clothes worn thin and well-patched, boiling potato dumplings until they were soft, or beating the dirt from a braided rug. Maybe if God grew weary of hearing my entreaties, the fighting would end. I'd abandoned any opinion over who won or lost as long as our men could come home. We'd heard nothing from my brothers in many months and didn't know whether they lived or were lying by the side of a road.

Near the end of April, our neighbor, Mr. Hickman, rode to see us. His horse cantered to the barn, and he reined it in long enough to speak a few moments to Papa before spurring the animal away in a cloud of dust. I saw Papa bow his head and drop to his knees in the dirt. Fearing new evil tidings, I ran to him and rested my hand on his shoulder. He looked up with anguish carved deep into the lines on his face.

My mouth dried up like an afternoon in August. "What is it, Papa?"

"The war is over. General Lee has surrendered."

And suddenly I was crying. I thought about the past four years and how many men would never return to their mothers, sweethearts, or wives. Those lucky enough to come back would find their homes burned, crops trampled, property destroyed, and livestock stolen. The cost in lives and property—and pride—had all been for nothing. War brought many things, but none of them were glorious.

Yet a glimmer of hope stirred in me. I knelt beside Papa in the dirt. "I pray this means we will soon see John and David back home."

"As do I, daughter, but anger runs deep." His voice softened to a whisper. "There is more to tell. Not long after surrender, Lincoln was shot and killed by an assassin, a Southern sympathizer. I fear what the Federals will do once they reclaim the South and seek their revenge."

3

Only a few weeks after we received the news that ended the fight for states' rights, Mama and I were in the yard, pulling dry clothes off the line, when we saw two men with heavy beards trudge along the road toward the boarding house. Mama straightened and shaded her eyes to stare toward them.

I threw down a clean shirt, poised to flee. "Shall I find Papa?"

"No, I don't think they mean us any harm. Look how slowly they move, as though they've been walking a long time."

We watched until the men grew closer, and we recognized the faded uniforms as ragtag Confederate butternut. The toes of their boots were worn clean through, and one had an empty jacket sleeve pinned up high.

The taller man addressed Mama. "Are you Miz Mimms?" At her nod, he continued. "A friend asked me and my brother to deliver this message to you."

"Thank you, sir." Mama took a piece of dirty paper folded to a small square and slipped it in her apron pocket.

"Would you like to sit and rest a spell? We can get you some food if you're hungry."

"Thank you kindly, ma'am. We are right hungry. Thirsty too, and that's a fact. Been walking a long time, clear from Kentucky, but we're almost back to home."

Mama and I sliced bread and brought a dipper filled with cool water for them to share. The men sat in the shade of the porch and stretched their legs, wolfing down the bread as though ravenous.

"Have you run into any trouble on your way?" I could not keep the thought of my brothers traveling alone and in such a bedraggled state from my mind.

"Mostly just folks tired and hungry as we are. Everybody has the same idea. They all want to get back to their families, and there ain't much food to share along the way."

The shorter soldier nodded. "There's a lot of homes and barns burned to ashes. We're hoping things will be steady back at our farm."

"I hope so too, and wish you both Godspeed in your journey," Mama said.

The taller man swiped a sleeve across his mouth and nodded before he and his brother pushed themselves to their feet and set off to continue their determined trek.

When the men were out of earshot, Mama pulled the paper from her pocket and carefully unfolded it. Her brows pinched together as she read aloud.

Dear Aunt,

I write these words with a heavy heart. Jesse was riding in to surrender with the other men of his troop in Lexington when Federals started shooting. One of their bullets caught my brother in the chest. He's bad hurt and too weak to make the trip to Ma and Reuben

*in Nebraska. I'm counting on you to take care of your
nephew until he gets well enough to go home. We'll be
coming from Lafayette County, though I don't know how
long it will take us to get there.*
This from your nephew, Frank James

She lowered the paper. "We need to prepare a sickroom."

I chewed my lip. How badly was he wounded? Then it
occurred to me. Jesse must be in mortal danger indeed, for
him to be moved to us rather than his mother's new home
in Nebraska. Zerelda and Reuben had been forced from
their farm in Kearney after the General Order was signed
in January. It banished anyone giving aid to the guerilla
rebels. Zerelda's outspoken approval of her sons' activities,
and the shelter she offered them and their friends, put
the Samuel family near the top of the list of those sent
into exile. Zerelda, Reuben, my cousin Susan, and the
Samuel children fled to Rulo in southeastern Nebraska,
not far across the border from their beloved farm. In a
letter filled with venomous rage and anguish, Zerelda had
begged Uncle Thomas and Papa to check on her property
whenever they could, declaring they would return to
Missouri as soon as the Federals allowed them to do so.

I burned with curiosity while tearing linen cloth into
bandages, all the while keeping an eye on the road leading
to our home. Adding to my sense of unease, William
Locke continued his thinly veiled efforts to be closer to
me than I wished. One day he went so far as to touch my
arm, allowing his moist fingers to linger on my skin. I
stepped away and froze him with a stare before marching
from the room. His gaze made bile rise in my throat and
reminded me of the way a buyer examined a milk cow. I
prayed he'd grow weary of waiting for me to change my

mind and take leave of the boarding house once and for all.

As days passed, the razor-sharp edge of anticipating Jesse's arrival dulled. I kept myself busy in the kitchen with Mama and Aunt Susan, and with the endless chores of housekeeping. Once the sun set and the evening cooled, Lucy and I walked outside, where we could speak freely.

A full moon high in the sky lit our path while grass cushioned our feet and silenced our steps. Crickets chirped their summer song, and trees smelled of damp wood near the pond where a bullfrog bellowed mournfully for a mate.

"Zee, do you suppose Frank and Jesse could have been intercepted? I heard the Federals will look for any reason to hang a rebel."

I shook my head. "Frank knows how to be cautious. He'll be sure not to take any chances."

Unspoken words hung between us. As kin to the James boys, the possibility of the Federals knocking on our door and ordering us into exile made the small hairs on the back of my neck rise. I lifted a thick braid that hung halfway down my back and allowed a cool breeze to caress me. Lucy's skirt swished as it brushed against a bee balm plant, lifting the fragrance of lemon to my nose.

"Mama and Papa are eaten up with worry not knowing what may come next," I said. "I wish we'd get news. I feel as though we're balancing on a narrow log trying to cross a wide river."

"I fear what may come, too. Nothing is certain. I suppose all we can do is occupy our minds with other things and wait."

We walked a few more steps in silence before I spoke again. "I can't help hoping that when Jesse arrives, Mr. Locke will have something else to think of besides bothering me. He gets bolder every day."

Lucy grinned and fanned her face. "Mama will be sorely disappointed if you refuse him again. I'm sure he must have a few good qualities. I know Mama and Papa are certain he'd be a perfect match for you."

"Perfect if I wish to live the life of an old woman long before it's time for me to be one." I shot a sly glance at her. "Perhaps I should tell Mama to consider you for Mr. Locke instead, since you're more smitten with his charms than I. He might make a better husband than your young soldier, Boling Browder."

Lucy's muffled snort told me all I needed to know. We laughed and turned back to the house.

The next afternoon, while hanging wet laundry on the line, I heard horse hooves on the road. My heart jumped, and I stared in the direction of the sounds, worrying whether soldiers or other scoundrels could be on their way to raid our home. But all I saw was a small buckboard pulled by a thin old horse. A much younger animal, saddled and tethered, followed. The wagon squeaked and rattled, one wheel shimmying as though ready to fall off. A bearded man on the driver's bench hunched over the reins.

When I recognized him, I called out to Mama and Aunt Susan, who were sitting on the porch cutting vegetables. "It's Frank!"

"Thank the Lord," Mama said, jumping up to greet them.

Frank looked thin as ever. A heavy, dark beard partially obscured his face, but his blue eyes were still sharp and alert. Frank motioned toward the back of the wagon as Papa and Uncle Thomas joined us. "My brother's life hangs by a narrow thread. There's a bullet in his lung. He'll need every bit of attention you can give him."

Jesse's head rested on a folded blanket, his body wrapped

so tightly, he looked like a babe swaddled in a quilt. He appeared to be unconscious, face flushed and gaunt with small beads of moisture gathered across his forehead. Despite the stubble of a beard, he looked very young. I touched his cheek to check for fever, and his eyelids flickered. They opened, and I saw the same strikingly pale blue I remembered from times spent years ago when we played together as children. Then, his eyes had reflected a mischievous sparkle. Now they looked empty, whether from pain or the effects of hard living, I wasn't sure.

Frank spoke again, his voice thick with emotion. "Thank you for this. We had to take him someplace safe where he can get the care he needs. There're too many who want nothing more than to see one of the rebel gang swing, even though he lawfully surrendered and took their damned Ironclad Oath on his sickbed so they'd let him leave." Anger simmered beneath Frank's pain.

Mama squeezed his arm. "Try not to worry. Jesse is our kin, and we will do whatever we can for him." She motioned for Papa and Uncle Thomas. "Can you get him inside, please? Be gentle as you can."

They tugged on the pallet and lifted Jesse from the wagon. We followed them into the house, and though my father and uncle moved in a slow and cautious manner, Jesse's jaw clenched and he groaned in a way that made my breath catch.

Once they got him settled on a bed, Mama turned to me. "Zee, you sit with him for a moment while I speak with Frank. I want to find a way to get word to Zerelda so she knows Jesse is here. Then I'll be back. Perhaps later we can try to give him some soup. He needs nourishment to build his strength."

"Yes, Mama."

Jesse's chest rose and fell in a halting way, as though his lungs could not fill completely with air. I brushed aside the shock of sandy hair that covered his forehead.

At my touch, his eyes opened and darted around the room before he focused on my face. "Zee?" he whispered, his voice barely audible. "Is it you?"

I took his hand felt the calloused palms of a horseman. I'd already learned from Mama that reassurance must be one of the first treatments given to a patient. "Yes, Jesse. You're safe. We're going to take care of you until you're better. Rest now, and very soon you'll recover your strength."

My words appeared to bring a small measure of comfort. His eyes closed, and his body relaxed into the mattress. As he slept, I took the opportunity to study my cousin's face.

He was nearly eighteen, two years younger than me, yet he struck me as much older and harder than the last time we'd been together, five—or was it six?—years earlier. His family had stopped by to visit us on their way to a funeral. Jesse and I were walking together in the yard when he grabbed my arm and threw down a challenge. "Unless you give me my first kiss, Zee, I'll climb up to the hayloft and jump right out to the ground."

The foolish comment reminded me of a melodramatic story I'd recently read, and I laughed at his blatant impudence. But I tilted up my head to lightly touch my lips against his. Now that same young man lay before me, still and quiet with the dust of travel settled over him and a gleam on his skin that hinted of fever. I decided not to wait any longer for Mama. If I fetched the water myself, I could at least cool him down and sponge him clean.

But when I attempted to pull away my hand, his fingers tightened around mine.

4

*W*ater sloshed from the basin Mama carried into Jesse's room. She wetted a muslin rag and squeezed the cloth before wiping his face. Then she dipped and wiped again, running the cloth up and down each arm in turn. "I will stay here with him through the night, and you can take over in the morning. Frank plans to leave at dawn. He'll try to get word to Zerelda that Jesse is in our care. She must be frantic with worry by now."

My cousin's face was as pale as the sheet that covered him, and his sunken eyes frightened me, but I nodded and went to my bed. I closed my eyes, but sleep would not come. The responsibilities and risks that had arrived at our door consumed me, even as pride curved my lips into a smile. No one in the family had spoken of turning Jesse away.

When the soft light of dawn gleamed through the window, I tiptoed from my bed and hurried to Jesse's room, wondering how he had fared during the night. Mama dozed in a chair, her chin drooping toward her chest. A white pitcher and basin stood next to the candle, which had burned down to a nub, melting soft wax from the holder to the tabletop.

Jesse slept with no sheen of perspiration that might indicate fever. When I stepped closer, Mama lifted her head and yawned before she noticed me standing next to her.

"Good morning," she said.

"How is Jesse doing, Mama?"

"He seems to be holding his own. I gave him some broth last night, and he fell asleep soon after. Rest and nourishment are what he needs most to help his body mend." She smoothed a gentle hand over his shoulder and sighed. "I will clean the wound again, then I must see what food I can gather for Frank before he leaves us. You can go from the room while I change the bandage if you want. His injury is not pleasant to see."

"No, I'll stay. I've helped you before with illness and wounds. I can do so again."

Mama nodded approvingly and worked loose the buttons on Jesse's shirt. Pushing aside the edges, she exposed bandages streaked dark with blood and wrapped thick over the middle of his chest. Mama pulled the soiled cloth away piece by piece, using her dampened rag to loosen places that stuck to the wound.

When the entire lesion was exposed, I clapped a hand over my mouth. The open hole was red and swollen, and the sweetly sick odor of infection reached my nose. Jesse flinched under Mama's hand as she ran a damp cloth over crusts of dried blood to wash them away. With each swipe, fresh blood oozed to take the place of what she had removed, and its metallic scent filled the room. Mama worked until satisfied the wound was clean, then placed fresh bandages against Jesse's chest.

"Frank said two doctors saw him in Lexington right after the injury occurred. They both found it best not to remove the bullet. It's better to leave it there than to poke about in his lung. This is his second chest wound in less than a year's time." She shook her head. "Our work will be to keep the wound clean, give his body time to heal, and hope the bullet does no further damage."

"Shouldn't our doctor see him? Traveling could have caused more problems."

"Once Frank is safely away, Papa will arrange for Dr. Lykins to visit." She sighed. "I think your cousin could use some prayers in addition to good nursing care."

"Of course," I murmured. "He shall be in my prayers every night."

"You and Jesse always got on well together, didn't you? I know that made Zerelda happy."

"Jesse had a way about him that made me smile. Even if we had a disagreement, he always made sure to put things right between us. I'll do whatever I can to help him get well."

"I know you will. In spite of your stubbornness, I must confess you are a good daughter." She patted my cheek before picking up the basin, now filled with blood-stained water.

I smiled as she left the room. It wasn't common for Mama to bestow compliments, and I knew she'd been unhappy with me since I continued to refuse Mr. Locke's attentions.

I busied myself smoothing wrinkles from Jesse's blanket and scraping melted wax from the table. The pink light of dawn peeked through the window with the promise of a sunny day, and it drew my gaze for a dreamy moment. When I glanced back at the bed, I was startled to discover Jesse's eyes were open. He looked brighter and less exhausted than he had a few hours earlier.

"Good morning. Would you like some water?"

He nodded, and I poured from the pitcher into a cup. Lifting his head with one hand, I rested the cup against his lips. He took two sips before his head sank back into the pillow, his breathing ragged from the effort.

I waited for it to steady before asking, "How do you feel today?"

The muscles in his jaw twitched. "Like an ornery mule kicked me in the chest." His voice was raw, his tone petulant.

"I'm not surprised. Between your injury and being bounced for miles in that buckboard, it's a wonder you're alive. Would you like to try eating something?"

"Maybe later. Let's see how the water sits first. I haven't been able to keep much of anything down in a while." Jesse turned his face toward the window, where the low clouds of early morning held a brighter shade of pink and blue. He blinked rapidly.

"If the light bothers you, I can close the curtains."

"God, no. Don't do that. It would make me feel like I'm in a tomb. I don't want to lay in darkness any sooner than I have to."

"You're well on the path to recovery. All you need do is concentrate on resting and getting back your strength."

His lips turned up slightly at the corners. "You sound like Ma. Willing me to get well like one of those miracle-working preachers."

"I don't believe miracles are necessary. You just need time."

Jesse closed his eyes, apparently spent from the effort at conversation. The chair squeaked as I leaned back to watch him and wait. Within a short while, Frank clomped into the room, making no effort to be quiet. Jesse's eyes popped open.

"Well, Dingus, I'm leaving you in Zee's capable hands, so behave yourself."

My brows lifted and I looked at Frank. "Dingus?"

"It's a nickname our troop gave him. Last summer, he was loading pistols when one exploded and shot off the tip of his middle finger. The pain would've made most men cuss a blue streak, but my little brother yells out, 'That's the dod-dingus pistol I ever saw!' The men who heard him laughed so hard they were crying like babies. We've been calling him Dingus ever since."

I shot a glance at Jesse's hand, now laying atop his blanket. I'd been so consumed with his current injury, I hadn't even noticed the older one. Dingus. What kind of word is that? I shook my head at the strange story and excused myself to give my cousins privacy.

A few minutes later, Frank joined me in the hallway. Brow wrinkled, he reached for my hand. "Take good care of him, Zee. You're exactly what he needs. With your sweet ways, he'll do what he can to please you. A pretty young girl is the best medicine in the world for any man."

"You know I will." I kissed Frank's cheek. "We'll try to send word to your mother on his progress."

"And I'll find a way for you to get word to me, as well."

I gave him a hug and whispered, "Take care of yourself, too."

Frank nodded and turned toward the door, moving with lean grace. I didn't follow him. Instead, I went to the kitchen, where Mama had broth heating in a kettle. I took a slice of roasted chicken planned for the midday meal, and I cut it into small pieces, throwing them into the broth. Perhaps meat would tempt Jesse to eat more and help him gain back some of the weight he'd lost.

When I picked up the bowl and turned, Mr. Locke stood before me. "Miss Mimms, I would be honored if you would walk with me after dinner this evening."

I held my ground and looked up at him. "I'm sorry, sir, but one of our guests is very ill and I need to sit with him."

"Yes, I've heard about that young man. He's been operating outside the law, hasn't he?"

My back stiffened. "Indeed not, Mr. Locke. The man is a patriot and fine soldier in need of our care. I advise you to never again slander his character in my presence."

With heat in my face, I stepped around him and left the kitchen before anything more could be said. Lucy was just coming from Jesse's room, her arms filled with soiled sheets and bandages. She looked at me and raised a brow when we passed each other. I thumped Jesse's bowl of soup hard on the table next to the bed and some of the broth splashed out.

Jesse looked at me, squinting his eyes. "Your face is bright red. What's wrong?"

"Nothing you need concern yourself with." I forced myself to unclench my fisted hand and smile.

"Nothing? I don't believe you." He paused a moment. "Wait, I know what's going on. It's that old buzzard your mama's pushing as a suitor who's bothering you, isn't it? When Lucy changed the bedding, she told me about him."

"Sometimes my sister talks too much. It's nothing to worry over. From time to time he does things to devil me, that's all."

"Listen to my advice and stick to your guns. Don't ever let anyone push you into doing something you don't want. That'd be worse than a hangman's noose."

"Good advice from one who so often tempts the hang-man." Jesse barked out a laugh and then winced.

I gave him a schoolmarm's measured look. "Perhaps such levity is not good for your injury."

"*You* are good for my injury. And your remarks are as tart as I remember them. I guess you're not so overly fearful I'm at death's door if you can joke about it."

I held up the bowl of soup, and said, "If you're wise enough to do what I say and eat every bite I give you, your chance of survival will be even greater."

With a slight wince, he raised the arm with the injured finger and gave me a crisp salute. "Yes, ma'am."

I lifted the spoon to his mouth and he took the soup in the determined way of one doing his duty, rather than with any real sense of hunger. It didn't matter. A small sense of victory fortified me with each bite he swallowed. Once he emptied the bowl, I wiped the corner of his mouth with my apron.

His hand moved to his middle. "I can't remember the last time I had such a full belly. Now let's hope the soup will stay put."

"It will settle better if you try to sleep. Close your eyes, and I promise to be here when you wake."

His eyes drooped, and his voice betrayed his weariness. "I'm beginning to think the whole rebel army would have fared better if you were the one looking out for them."

Before long, Jesse's eyelids closed, and he did not speak further. I waited until his breath came steady, and watched him sleep for a few minutes, before carrying the bowl to the kitchen.

Mama stood at the window, staring outside. When she turned, there were dark crescents under her eyes. "This morning, a Union soldier cornered Papa and Uncle Thomas when they drove into town to make arrangements for Dr.

Lykins to visit. He wanted to know who we had in the boarding house and said they were keeping track of any rebels who had fought against them. Papa thought it best to say nothing of Jesse."

"Do you think Federals would ever ride out here to look?"

"I pray not, but in times of such high suspicion, it's impossible to predict what might happen."

The door to the kitchen creaked open, and we both jumped.

Mr. Locke sauntered in. "Good morning, ladies. I'm looking for a spare bit of biscuit to tide me over until we eat. May I take one?"

My heart thumped as Mama smiled and handed him a cold biscuit, a slight tremble in her normally unwavering hand. He took it and nodded in my direction before taking his leave.

I touched Mama's arm and whispered, "Do you suppose he heard?"

She sat down as though her knees had gone weak. "I hope not, but in any case, I don't believe he would try to cause trouble. I do think it best though, if we confine any talk of Jesse or Frank to the ears of our own kin and no one else." She took a steadying breath. "Did he eat anything?"

"Yes, and I even added a few bits of chicken to the broth. He swallowed everything in the bowl then fell asleep."

Mama nodded. "Perhaps Frank was right. Maybe you are Jesse's angel." She stood and squared her shoulders.

"Did he say that?" I tried to hide the blush in my cheeks, but Mama was looking back out the window. "My hope is he recovers quickly, so we can send him home to Zerelda. I'm afraid of what may happen if he's discovered here."

I returned to Jesse's room, pondering the danger the Federals could pose to us and our kin. The war might be over, but the course of our lives remained perilous as ever. My parents were right. Truly, in such times as these, our only security lay within the unbreakable ties of family.

5

As each day passed, Jesse's face regained color and began to lose its hollow, haunted look. My other chores had been abandoned so I could stay by his side, cooling his forehead if he felt too warm, cajoling him to eat, tending his wound, and reading aloud stories from the newspaper whenever he grew restless. Mama didn't scold, and my sisters voiced no complaint about the extra work falling to them. We all knew it was imperative we see Jesse healed and on his way home—for his safety as well as our own.

For nearly a month, Jesse lay in bed. His wound didn't ooze as much as before and he didn't sleep as much during the day. Mama posted a long letter to Aunt Zerelda, describing his progress and her belief he would soon be strong enough to go home. His departure would lighten Mama's shoulders, but it surprised me to realize how much I would miss him. Jesse had become the focal point of my days, and I found it nearly impossible to imagine life once he left for good.

My promise to stay close to his side provided another source of pleasure—it kept me far from Mr. Locke. I sensed his eyes on me, but had found ways to avoid him, until the day he had the audacity to wait for me right outside Jesse's door. I was carrying in a tray of food, and Mr. Locke blocked the threshold, moving his face so close to mine, I could see tobacco-stained teeth and smell the stench of foul breath.

"It would be a shame if anyone found out the name of your kinsman staying in this very house. The Federals might want to come out and ask a few questions about what's going on. If they don't like what they hear, there's no telling what might happen." When my chin lifted, he added, "Of course, if I became part of this family, it would be in my interest to provide protection from outsiders, would it not?"

"Keep your voice down, Mr. Locke. Our guest is sleeping." My face warmed with anger. "You've made your intentions plain enough, but you know my answer. If you believe I will bend to blackmail, you are most sadly mistaken."

His mouth twisted into a sneer. "I think you would be wise to consider my words carefully, Miss Mimms. If you're as smart as I think you are, you will make the right decision. After all, everyone needs security these days, don't they?"

I kept my eyes down and pushed past him into Jesse's room, closing the door quickly behind me so Mr. Locke could not see in. My hands were shaking so hard the dishes on the tray clattered together. I set it down near the pitcher and took a deep breath to compose myself. When I finally turned to Jesse, his eyes were blazing.

"Has something happened to inflame your wound?"

"That old blowhard dares to bully and threaten you right outside my door? Damn his eyes, that man is nothing more than a traitor."

"Please calm yourself. Nothing so dreadful happened.

I'll speak to Papa, and he'll take care of the matter."

"If I weren't weak as a kitten, there wouldn't be any need for you to speak to anyone. I don't abide threats made against me or mine."

I would have liked to explore his words further, but Jesse fisted his hands in such distress, I touched his arm instead. He struggled to sit up against his pillows, but I kept my hand on him, then sat in the chair.

"Listen to me. Forget what you heard. It is of no consequence." I lifted the bowl. "Here, I've brought your dinner. Let's talk of other things so you can calm yourself. Dr. Lykins will be here soon. You don't want him to see you in such a state."

As I fed him the soup, I chatted without pause about every inconsequential thing I could conjure until the rage had faded from his features. As he swallowed the last bite, Mama led Dr. Lykins into the room.

I moved aside, and the doctor put down his bag. He pulled Jesse's nightshirt open. Under the damp bandage, the wound remained raw and the skin around it red and puckered. I kept my eyes on Jesse's face and flinched when I saw how he pressed his lips together in a white line as Dr. Lykins worked on him.

After the doctor pressed a new bandage in place, he turned to Mama. "The wound appears to be healing, but not as fast as I'd like. There are still a few signs of infection, which is something we must guard against. Keep it as clean as you can. I'm afraid the bullet has done some damage to the lung and could complicate a full recovery. Healing will take a long while."

I voiced the question I knew Jesse wondered most.

"When will he be himself again?"

The doctor picked up his bag and regarded me. "You must be patient. Any lung wound is quite serious. I cannot predict with certainty what will occur, but I can say that much depends on two things: good nursing care and his will to recover. The rest is in God's hands."

The news sobered me. I had hoped for a declaration that Jesse's health would soon be restored, but I straightened my back to face the tasks ahead. He would receive the best care anyone could give. And as far as Jesse's will to recover, I held no doubt on that score at all.

Mama walked from the room with Dr. Lykins, whispering words I could not hear. Jesse looked at me, and I saw pleading under the pain that clouded his eyes. When he spoke, his voice was so soft I had to lean in to hear it.

"Do you suppose God wants me to die?"

My eyes widened. "Of course, he does not think something like that. What could ever make you think he would?"

"I've done a lot of bad things, Zee. Most of them I would never have dreamed possible. Ever since I left home, the war gave us permission to break every single commandment. Stealing, killing, revenge, and other deeds you'd disown me over if you knew of them. I've been part of it all. Does that shock you?"

His face appeared so openly pleading, I could not allow myself to show any emotion. I had no doubt he'd been involved in terrible acts, but I also knew terrible things had been done to him, and to his family. War made all manner of atrocities possible, and whether a person viewed the same act as heroic or despicable depended on the side to which they claimed allegiance.

Yes, Jesse had reason to hate. As to what he described,

I could not sit in judgment of him. I kept my voice soft. "What you have done is of benefit to the South and its people. It wasn't for yourself, but for others. That's what makes the difference."

The reassurance seemed to soothe him, although his eyes were achingly sad. I put a few drops of the laudanum Dr. Lykins left in Jesse's water, and held the cup to his lips. He drank it all, and within a short while he fell fast asleep.

I stood and arched my stiff back, unused to sitting for so long. On a normal day, one task after another seized my attention. Rarely did I have time to read or wade in the pond beyond our garden. Stillness didn't normally suit me, yet the quiet I found near Jesse's bed gave me strange comfort. I picked up the empty water pitcher and went to refill it.

Mama and Aunt Susan sat at the kitchen table. They stopped speaking when they saw me. Mama nudged Susan. "Would you leave us so I can speak with Zee for a moment?" My aunt nodded and kept her eyes down as she swept from the room.

"Lucy will take your place nursing Jesse. You have grown far too pale sitting for weeks by his bedside."

"But, Mama, I don't mind sitting with him."

As soon as the words left my mouth, I wanted to pull them back.

Her eyes narrowed. "You are becoming too attached to him. It will hurt you when he leaves, and mark me, he will be going soon. Last week I sent a telegram to Zerelda telling her he has improved enough to travel. She will send Susie to pick him up for the trip to Rulo."

My hands fisted. Mama had said nothing to me about sending such a message to Zerelda. I bit my tongue hard before speaking. "If he's leaving soon, there's no reason to have Lucy care for him. When the time comes for Jesse to go, there will be no interference from me. You needn't worry. I only want to help him."

"You have always had a tendency toward dreaminess and feeling too deeply. Keep in your mind that Jesse is your cousin and friend. He cannot be more to you than that."

"These are things I already know, Mama."

She gave me a sharp look and then nodded. "Very well. You may continue as long as you do not forget your promise."

Given Mama's desire to see Jesse gone, I half expected to hear a wagon heralding Susie's arrival any day. This knowledge shadowed each moment I spent with him—bathing his wound, coaxing him to eat, or teasing him to smile.

Finally, on a hot afternoon in mid-July, the dreaded time arrived. I had been reading next to Jesse's bed while he slept, and the sound of a horse approaching caught me up short. Carefully, I closed my book and set it on the table, my shoulders slumping as the reality hit. Soon Jesse would be gone. In slumber, his face looked even more boyish. I'd shaved him two days earlier, resulting in a tiny cut on his neck, and he'd laughed, calling me his executioner. I watched his chest rise and fall with each measured breath, and only turned when the door to his room swung open. But instead of seeing Susie, a tall man in dusty, faded clothes appeared. A large bushy beard hid most of his face, but when he removed his hat, I leapt to my feet and ran to hug him.

"Frank! I thought your sister was coming."

"She's here, but it made Ma feel easier for me to escort her at least part of the way." He looked at his brother. "I've heard what good care you've taken of him."

Frank didn't bother to soften his voice, and the sound caused Jesse's eyes to blink open. He saw Frank and grinned.

"Hello, Buck." The affectionate nickname made me smile. Zerelda had called Frank "Buck" ever since he turned fourteen and had grown as tall as a white-tail buck.

Frank took the seat I'd vacated. "I've come with Susie to take you home, Dingus. Ma was fit to be tied over not coming herself, but it's too dangerous for her to travel here when she's under orders to stay away. Reuben practically had to hold her in place so she wouldn't jump in the wagon. She's frantic to see you."

Jesse shot a glance my way. "Would you mind leaving us for a few minutes, Zee? Buck and I need some time to talk."

With a hot face, I pulled the door softly shut behind me. Susie stood just outside the threshold, wearing the same impish smile as her brother. Even though we hadn't seen each other in years, she stretched her arms wide, and I stepped into her embrace.

"It's so good to see you, Zee. I'm relieved Jesse is doing so much better. Ma is anxious to tend him herself now. We know he's got a lot of healing yet to do, and it'll be hard for him to let Frank head out without following. But such is the way of things."

"Perhaps being in Nebraska and far from everything that's happened in Missouri will help him heal faster. How is everyone doing in Rulo?"

"Ma is the same as always. She writes letters to any person she thinks can help us get back home. Reuben is still not himself. Ever since the Federals tortured him, he's been fearful, and now he's growing more so every day. A doctor told Ma the hanging may have damaged his mind. Said it's likely he'll never be the same as he was before."

My thoughts turned to Zerelda, Reuben, and their children waiting in Rulo. Despite her exile, Zerelda's defiance toward the Federals had not dimmed. When her young daughter was born, Zerelda had christened her Fannie Quantrill Samuel, in honor of the man who led Frank's troop of bushwhackers. She flatly announced to anyone who asked that she was proud to count a Quantrill as part of her family. Her words exemplified my aunt's lion-like courage, or as Papa sometimes said, her way of stirring up feelings that could later come back to haunt her.

A short while after he had arrived, Frank rode away without much more than a swift farewell. Papa explained if Frank stayed too long, it would increase the odds of bringing trouble to our door. The idea of never staying in one place for any length of time made my heart heavy, for that sad fate would also apply to Jesse. I scolded myself for the dark observation. His health had improved, and I should rejoice, rather than fret. But the idea of his departure still saddened me in ways I found hard to understand.

Papa and Uncle Thomas carried Jesse to the wagon in much the same manner they'd brought him into the house. Aunt Susan filled a bag with bandages, food, and some laudanum to ease his pain on the journey. I tucked a quilt around him with special care.

He captured my hand and kissed it.

"Thank you for all you've done. I know how hard you worked at pushing me so I wouldn't give up."

I wanted to tell him it wasn't burdensome at all, but Mama's presence made me change the words to something more proper.

"Please write when you can. Let us know how you're doing."

"I will," he promised.

"Good-bye, Susie. Both of you take care," I told them.

Susie laughed at my words. "Don't you worry. Frank plans on staying nearby. He'll keep an eye on us until we make it to the boat."

She waved before slapping the reins to move the horse forward, and the creaking wagon lumbered away. I picked up a broom from the porch, determined to resume my old chores before Mama had the chance to complain. I swept the sickroom floor and stripped away the dirty sheets. When I finished, Jesse's room seemed very empty. I didn't realize it then, but soon the house would become emptier still.

One week to the day after Jesse left us, William Locke disappeared.

6

*I*t was blazing hot the afternoon Mr. Locke told our other boarder, the frail Mrs. Parkinson, that he planned to walk to the pond for a swim. It was customary to extend such a courtesy in the event anyone else considered the same idea. After he set off, Aunt Susan joined Mrs. Parkinson on the porch. They watched him stroll away while Mrs. Parkinson commented on the dust clouds circling his boots.

By the time the sun rested against the horizon, Mr. Locke still had not returned. Even after I set the table with a dinner of boiled ham and potatoes, he did not appear. Papa saw Mr. Locke's empty chair, and his brow puckered. William Locke had never before missed a meal.

Papa slipped an arm around Mama's waist.

"Go ahead and serve dinner. Thomas and I will drive out to the pond. Perhaps Mr. Locke is ill. I've noticed he hasn't been himself of late. Or maybe he's been hurt."

Papa and Uncle Thomas left to harness Lully. They did not return until we were cleaning dishes.

"We saw nothing unusual on the road, but at the edge

of the pond, we found his clothes, folded up in a neat pile."

Papa held out a white linen shirt and brown pants that I'd washed often enough to recognize.

Aunt Susan's eyes widened.

"You don't suppose he might have drowned?"

Thomas shook his head. "The pond looked smooth as glass. A body would most likely float unless caught by a snag or weighted down. I'm not sure he even entered the water. The ground near the pond looks the same as everywhere else in July, baked hard as clay. It's as though William vanished without a trace."

"But a person cannot simply disappear." Mama's firm tone reined in my imagination. "What should we do, John?"

"In the morning, I will go to see Sheriff Wilson. He may send some men to search the area around the pond. I don't know of anything else we can do except say a prayer for William's safe return."

When Papa came back from town, he told us he'd made a report. The sheriff promised to launch an investigation when he could, and that he'd let us know if he found any clues. Uncle Thomas shook his head and declared a wandering marauder must have carried off William Locke, although none of us could come up with a reason for anyone to do so. Mama posted a letter to Mr. Locke's distant cousin, a woman named Janet. Whether the correspondence had been received or not, we never discovered, for no reply came.

After a few weeks, Papa and Uncle Thomas decided to empty the long-occupied room of Mr. Locke. Since he owed money for rent, they determined it fair to retain his remaining possessions, along with a small amount of money left in a wooden box under his bed.

Mr. Locke's absence didn't distress me. In fact, freedom

from the burn of his lingering glances made me smile for the first time since Jesse left. I had not yet shared with Papa the threats Mr. Locke made, and I decided not to worry him now that the information no longer mattered.

Any questions over the strange fate of William Locke disappeared when my brother David trudged back to us, thin and ragged but with the same warm hug. We were thrilled beyond belief when he told us he'd heard Thomas, too, would soon be allowed to make his way home. At that news, Mama fell to her knees and we all cried and bowed our heads, praying most fervently in thanks to the Almighty. As with every Southern sympathizer, both Thomas and David had been required to take the Ironclad Oath of Allegiance to the Union before they could return. This mattered not a whit to me. I only wanted them both back home with us.

With renewed vigor, I threw myself into work at the boarding house, trying to occupy my mind with things other than the four weeks spent in a small room nursing Jesse. I'd severed myself from anything but him, and now that he'd gone, my thoughts were muddled as if I'd just come to the surface after swimming underwater, oblivious to what had happened around me.

On a quiet Sunday afternoon, Lucy and I took the old buckboard out for a drive. I welcomed the fresh air and time away from the boarding house. We traveled toward town, and the farther from home we went, the more appalling the sights.

"The Campbell house is gone." Lucy said.

"Yes, and look at the Johnsons' barn."

I wondered at knowing so little of our neighbors' fates as trees and houses—charred and blackened, some fully burned to the ground—came into view. Tobacco crops were trampled, leaving scuffed holes behind. Much of Clay County had been damaged, although I noticed some newly hewn lumber had been lately hammered into place. People were working to pick up the broken pieces of their lives, despite the guerilla attacks that still continued. The war had officially ended, so why should raids go on? I found such actions harder to understand than the war had been.

As we rolled into town, Lucy pointed toward a man who had a pistol strapped on each hip and a rifle balanced on his shoulder. "Look at how well-armed he is. They say these days even ladies should carry a weapon."

"You know Papa would never hand over that old pistol of his to us. I'm not even sure it works. And don't say anything about this, whatever you do. He won't allow us to leave sight of home again."

In spite of the disorder and fear we witnessed, the image of Jesse remained in my mind. I composed a note to him and a long letter to Zerelda, begging her to tell me of his progress. Once the letters had been posted, an even more impatient wait began for a response.

It took a few weeks before a messenger delivered a telegram from Zerelda. The short and carefully worded missive turned my blood cold.

His condition is critical. Doctors give us no hope. His last request is that he not be allowed to die on Northern ground. We are bringing him home.

- Zerelda Samuel

From the time the news came, I crept around the house, pale and silent as an abandoned waif. When not working, I walked as far from the house as I dared to go and reread Zerelda's telegram, trying to find a shred of hope hidden in her words. Papa gravely told me to accept God's will, whatever it may be. Mama did not scold as much as before, and her shadowed eyes told me she, too, dreaded the notion of Jesse's death. Lucy tried to make me smile with teasing and a small joke, but she only succeeded in prompting tears.

It was the first week of September when a wagon arrived at the boarding house with Reuben, Zerelda, and the children. I ignored their calls to me and flew straight to the wagon bed, where Jesse lay on a pallet with his eyes closed. I touched his face and called to him, but he didn't move. Zerelda came to stand beside me and I looked up at her face. Deep lines of sorrow marred her forehead, but I could sense a simmering anger in her blue eyes.

Mama joined us and hugged her sister-in-law. Zerelda spoke forcefully as a man. "He's too weak to go all the way to the farm, Mary. We must leave him here with you again."

Mama glanced at me, swallowed, and then nodded.

As they had a few weeks before, Papa and Uncle Thomas lifted Jesse's pallet and carried him back into the house. This time, no sound escaped his lips.

Zerelda put her arm around my waist to prevent me from following them.

"His wound will not close. Infection has taken hold, and he is delirious with fever. Reuben and every other doctor who has seen him believe he has little chance of recovery."

My chin snapped up. "No. He was improving when he was here. He will live. I know it." I surprised myself at the vehemence of my tone.

Zerelda turned and studied my face, weighing my words before speaking. "Yes, my dear, I do believe if there is a chance for him, it lies with you. I'm giving my son to your care. Since the government tells us the war is over, I've decided we're going home. The Federals can be damned, and I swear to shoot any one of them who tries to stop us. I intend to stand on my own soil again. Or at least what's left of it," she added bitterly.

"I promise by all that's holy, Jesse will return to you, hearty and well. I'll see to it."

Zerelda kissed my cheek, and we walked arm in arm to Jesse's room. With tenderness, she smoothed his rumpled hair and placed her lips against his pale cheek, whispering a mother's words of endearment.

She straightened and took my hand. "I will be back within two weeks to see if you have performed a miracle. If anything should happen, send word at once." Her shoulders straightened before she stepped from the room.

I immediately went to work on my miracle. Fighting back tears at the sight of Jesse's emaciated frame, my fingers fumbled to open his buttons, as heat burned through the fabric. I drew aside the shirt's edges and took a deep breath to prepare myself for what lay beneath the bandages.

The flesh around the wound burned red and swollen. A foul-smelling thick discharge oozed between the ragged edges of open skin. My brow creased with indecision over what to do first, but Mama appeared in the doorway with a basin of cool water and a pile of bandages. She set them down without a word, resignation dimming the sparkle in her eyes, and left me to my work. I dipped a cloth in the cool water and wrung it out. And for the next five days, unless nature called me away, I did not leave Jesse's side.

7

I swiped the back of my hand across my damp
forehead and blew out a breath. Thunder rumbled
in the distance. We'd had no rain in a month, and
the thought of moisture to settle the dust and cool the air
made me almost sick with longing. Soon leaves would turn
color and the unrelenting heat of late summer would fade,
but for now, Jesse's sickroom was thick and stifling, ripe
with the putrid stink of infection. I imagined our pond, and
its soothing ripples of water.

Jesse still had not opened his eyes. I dozed in fits and
starts whenever his condition permitted. If he tossed and
turned, it meant a spike in fever. When he slept without
moving, my own eyes drooped. As each day passed, his
fortitude fed the fire of my hope. He had a core of great
strength. Many had succumbed to less within days, but
Jesse continued to fight, and so would I.

With my eyes closed, I fanned myself with a rag, trying
to forget the room's sticky discomfort. Just as my head began
to droop, a raspy voice called my name. The sound startled
me wide awake. For a moment, I wasn't sure whether the

voice had been real or come from a dream until I looked at Jesse's face.

He stared at me, blinking as though trying to clear his vision. Through cracked and peeling lips, he whispered a single word. "Thirsty."

I took a clean bandage and poured water from the pitcher over it. First, I pressed a wet cloth to his lips. Then I held the cup to his mouth with a shaking hand. He took a sip and swallowed. The sight heartened me more than anything. Dribbling liquid into his mouth with a spoon could not have provided for his body's needs much longer.

Jesse's eyes were clear, although he stumbled over each word as would one after waking from a long slumber. "What happened?"

"You've been very ill. Your mother brought you here so I could take care of you."

Though I could see the effort cost him, he nodded. My heart raced, hoping this might be the turning point in his recovery and an answer to my prayers.

Papa sent for Dr. Lykins, who arrived soon after. He listened to Jesse's chest, frowned, and pronounced him out of immediate danger. Mama sent a telegram to Zerelda in Kearney.

Jesse had turned a corner. From that day forward, he improved, and though he was eager to be well, he restrained his own impatience and followed the doctor's orders. He stayed in bed, although I saw his fingers pluck at the bedclothes and his gaze wander to the window.

Zerelda arrived at the boarding house one day short of the two weeks she'd predicted. Her elation at finding her son alive and lucid seemed to vibrate through every part of her being, and she hugged me in a crushing embrace.

"You've done it, Zee. You saved our boy. I knew if anyone could get him well, it would be you."

I smiled at her use of the word "our". Perhaps now he did belong, at least a little, to both of us.

At the sight of his mother's jubilation, Jesse's lips curved up.

"I wasn't ever alone, Ma. I could feel someone watching over me every minute. No medic on earth could have been as dedicated to an unruly patient as Zee has been."

Zerelda's eyes brimmed with unshed tears, and she patted my hand. "Thank you for what you've done. Your mother told me you stayed by his side day and night."

"I promised to do anything necessary to help him get well, Aunt Zerelda, and I always keep my word."

She touched a sunflower sitting in a pitcher next to Jesse's bed and sighed, looking wearier than I'd ever seen her. Something troubled her still.

"Tell us, Aunt, how did you find the farm when you went home?"

Her nostrils flared. "The grounds are overgrown with weeds and brush. Part of the house was burned and part of it torn to pieces. We need to repair the damages and there's work to be done so the fields will be ready for planting next spring. Yet it will lighten my soul to have Jesse back home with me."

An idea occurred to me and I cleared my throat. "Dr. Lykins says Jesse will still need a great deal of nursing care and a long rest before he can leave his bed. With so many other tasks for you to do, you may want to think about letting him stay here until he gains more strength."

I knew Mama would be horrified at my suggestion, but since she wasn't present to hear my words, it pleased me to plant the notion in Zerelda's head.

My aunt twisted her wedding ring and stared out the window. Jesse caught my eye and winked. "She's right, Ma. I can't lie in bed like a baby and give you more work to do than you already have."

Zerelda pinched the top of her nose before replying. "It's true enough I'm distracted by it all. I'm not even sure where we'd put you until the house is fully repaired. Yes. Much as I'd like to take you home now, I'll go ask Mary for a few more weeks. I don't want you to have another setback because we've moved you too soon."

Never one to hesitate after coming to a decision, she put one hand on her hip and marched from the room to speak with Mama. I knew their conversation would be brief. Not even Mama would consider refusing her request.

Jesse smiled and reached for my hand. "If I have to lie in bed, I'd rather do it here. You're more fun to talk to than Ma."

The awkward compliment brought heat to my face. "As you well know, there hasn't been much talking of late. You've been asleep a long time and have been quite spoiled, indeed. When you regain some of your strength, you shan't be mollycoddled another moment."

"I don't know about that. Something tells me you enjoy being the best nursemaid a man could have."

He laughed out loud at the look on my face and then winced, his hand clenched hard around mine.

At that moment, Zerelda bustled back into the room. Her eyes widened, and she lifted a brow before aiming a lengthy stare in my direction.

"Mary has agreed. We've arranged for Jesse to stay at least three more weeks. Longer if need be, depending on how he gets along. I'll be over to check on him as often as I can. I do not want my son to overstay his welcome."

Her tone was brisk, but I didn't stare at the floor as had been my practice in the past when she entered a room. In my childhood, Zerelda's commanding presence had tied my tongue, but today my eyes met hers before I excused myself so she and Jesse could visit in private.

The kitchen smelled of wood smoke and fresh bread. I sank into a chair at our battered oak table, famished and exhausted. Mama stirred a pot she had filled with tomatoes, carrots, and potatoes from the garden, and my mouth watered at the aroma of vegetables simmering in broth.

She turned from the kettle to me and placed her arms akimbo. "Zee, we need to talk about this. Papa and I are still concerned you are spending too much time with Jesse. Since he appeared close to death, we felt it best to say nothing. But now that his health has turned for the better, I will take responsibility for him and Aunt Susan will help me. I appreciate your deep concern for your cousin, but it's not seemly for a young woman to spend so much time alone with a man whose health is no longer precarious."

"Don't speak of him as though he has no name, Mama. I'm sorry, but I don't intend to put anyone else in charge. Jesse feels better when I'm with him, and the better he feels, the sooner he'll get well."

She took a deep breath at my brazenness and paused as though counting to ten before speaking. "Very well, but I insist there are things you must not do. Only Susan or I will bathe him and help him with the chamber pot. An unmarried girl should not touch the body of a man in such a way."

I refrained from telling her that I, not Aunt Susan, had already bathed most of Jesse's bare skin when fever took hold of him, and during times when he needed cleaning.

I'd been far too worried to concern myself with proprieties. In truth, being familiar with his body had become natural. But some things, I knew, were best not shared with one's mother. I wasn't even yet ready to talk about it with Lucy.

"Yes, ma'am. Whatever you say."

As I hoped, my answer satisfied her. She turned back to the stove and spoke in her usual brisk fashion. "You stay here and eat some soup. Then rest. It won't do to have two people in the house who need nursing. Besides, Papa will be preaching tomorrow, and he'd like it if you were there."

For once, we were in agreement. She placed a bowl of soup and a slice of warm bread in front of me, and I eagerly finished both. With a full stomach and the beacon of hope refreshed, I went to my room. Jesse would be in good hands with his mother. Zerelda could take my place until she left to go home.

I lay in my bed and remembered the look Jesse gave me. A prickling sensation raced through my body. My face, arms, legs, and even my toes tingled. I forced myself to ignore the strange feelings, closed my eyes, and tried, unsuccessfully, to sleep.

At some point, exhaustion took over. I woke in the morning, and the wisps of a pleasant dream lingered. But hard as I tried, I couldn't recapture any of its details.

8

Almost a month had passed since Jesse came back to our home. He'd turned an important corner, but he was not out of the woods yet. He would improve enough to sit up, then sink back into lethargic weakness. My emotions followed the path of his well-being, either bursting with elation or dropping into despair. Dr. Lykins cautioned that he fared as well as could be expected given the nature of his injury, and that our most important job was to make sure he rested so all his energy could be used to recover.

Jesse's conduct fluctuated as much as his body. On good days, he would gamely chew and swallow each bite I fed him. Other days, he seemed unwilling to even attempt lifting his hand. Yet difficult as his illness was for all of us, I knew Jesse chafed under his weakness more than anyone else.

One early October day, after a brief visit from Frank, Jesse became increasingly morose. "I could be out helping protect us from the Union's Reconstruction rather than lying around here like I'm older than Methuselah. Frank is doing his part. I want to do mine."

He pushed away the tray of food I'd brought him and fixed his gaze on the window.

"Jesse, it does you no good when you refuse to eat. How will you ever regain your strength without food?"

"It doesn't seem to make much difference. I'm tired of doing what I'm supposed to do and not getting better."

I set the tray on his bedside table. There were times when Jesse acted much younger than his age, yet I tried to understand. For such a young man, he'd lived an amazingly independent life, traveling in primitive forests and along backcountry roads. I knew the hard set to his jaw came from the experience of riding with border raiders, and I imagined it was torture for him to lie in bed and be reliant on others.

My musing sparked an idea.

"How would you like to go outside? I can help you to the porch. There's a comfortable rocking chair to sit in and feel the sun on your face."

His lips curved up, and I recognized a boyish gleam in his eyes.

"Can I? Would it be all right?"

"Eat your lunch, and I'll help you outside. If this adventure does as much good for you as I think it might, perhaps your mother won't be so angry when she finds out I let you leave bed against doctor's orders."

I had yet to see Jesse clean his plate with such enthusiasm. Once he'd finished every bite, he swiped his hand across his lips.

"I'm ready. Let's do it now before you change your mind."

I helped him swing his legs over the side of the bed. The edges of his lips whitened.

"Are you sure you feel strong enough? We could try again tomorrow."

"No. I want to go outside now."

I lifted his arm and draped it across my shoulders.

"On the count of three, we'll stand up. One … two … three."

Jesse struggled to his feet, leaning most of his weight on me. Despite how thin he'd become, I was still much smaller, but if sheer determination counted for anything, we would both stay upright.

In a shuffle step interrupted by a pause every few moments, we made slow progress outside the bedroom, through the parlor, and onto the front porch. Jesse dropped into the rocking chair, pale and winded, perspiration dotting his forehead. After my own breath returned to normal, I checked his wound and was relieved to see no fresh red seeping through the bandage. With a blanket folded across his knees against the cool autumn air, Jesse closed his eyes and turned his face toward the sun as though he'd forgotten its warmth. He sat that way in silence for several minutes until color returned to his cheeks.

When he opened his eyes, new hope stirred in them. "Thank you, Zee. This makes me feel as though there's a chance someday I'll be well again, sitting on my horse, and doing what needs to be done."

A long-absent spark brightened his eyes and lifted my heart higher than a thin summer cloud. "I'm glad. You needed to see what made you who you are. Lying in a bed for weeks has sapped your strength and your will. From now on, we'll venture outside as often as you wish no matter what anyone else says. It's what you need. It's what will save you."

Jesse took my hand, and his thumb brushed across the palm. "You're the one who knows me best. Not even Ma understands the way you do."

"Yes, and won't she be furious once she knows what we've done?"

Jesse laughed out loud. "Indeed, she will. But I wager she'll be pleased enough at the result."

In that moment, it didn't matter to me what Aunt Zerelda or Mama said.

When Mama discovered our adventure to the porch, she lectured me about responsibility and told me to obey the doctor's orders. After that, Papa drew me aside and in a gentle voice counseled me to have patience. I heard them both but paid no mind to their advice. Each day, Jesse and I ventured to the porch, and before long, he leaned less heavily on me, able to sit outside for longer periods of time. And during each outing, I could see his countenance sharpen as he absorbed the sunlight and inhaled the scent of a clean breeze.

Our continued treks to the porch meant Jesse stopped complaining about meals, and his appetite improved so much that he ate anything I served him. In the open air, he became much like the Jesse I remembered—lighthearted and happy. We ate together outside at least once each day and called the meals a picnic.

One afternoon, after settling him in the chair, I went inside to fetch our lunch of chicken and potatoes. I carried out the steaming food, my steps light. Jesse cleaned everything from his plate and washed down the food with a great gulp of water. When he leaned back and grinned, I raised a brow.

"What are you finding so humorous today?"

"I haven't felt this good in a long time. Every day is better. It won't be long until I can be back to fighting with Frank."

"I don't understand what fighting can change now. The war is over, and the Federals are in control. Papa says we must learn ways to soothe them rather than enflame tensions."

"I witnessed too much of Federal ways to think they can ever be soothed. I saw what they did to Southerners. Fine strong boys getting their brains blown out. Houses burned over people's heads. I once had a Federal hold a knife to my throat, and he would've cut me from ear to ear if a soldier named Archie Clement hadn't shot him dead. He's the one who taught me the way to fight is to show up where no one expects to see you. Then do what you have to do and ride away like the wind."

I shuddered at his words. "I can't imagine living through that kind of horror."

"And I hope you never learn the meaning of such horror. It changes someone to kill and see killing and wash enough blood off their hands to turn creek water red. No, I'm not worried one bit about enflaming Federals or anyone else who tries to betray me. The sooner I'm back at the work of making them pay for what they've done, the better."

I clamped my mouth shut to avoid saying anything I might later regret. My own feelings were at war, wondering whether I should champion Papa's position, agree with Jesse's, or succumb to my own sorrow at his eagerness to leave. I piled empty dishes on the tray, to avoid looking at him.

He viewed me curiously. "You're not pleased about something. What is it?"

"I'm not certain fighting is going to gain anything for anyone, but I am glad you're getting well."

"One thing is sure. Once I leave, there'll be much less work for you. It's a wonder you're not down sick in bed too, the way you've run yourself thin taking care of me. You've been my anchor, Zee. I'm only alive now because of you."

His words pacified me but did not take away the sting of his potential departure. Yet I had no right to voice such feelings, and forced myself to smile.

As Jesse's strength grew, he ventured farther from the house, although I insisted someone must always be with him. On the day we walked to the barn and visited with Uncle Thomas's mare, Lully, Jesse couldn't have been more lighthearted. The scent of sweet hay and Jesse's smile when the mare nuzzled his palm with her velvet nose, lifted my spirits.

"Mark my words, Zee, I'll soon be sitting on a horse again. That day can't get here soon enough. One of the worst parts of being sick for so long has been not riding. There's nothing I love better than being on the back of a fast horse, flying like the wind."

"I have no doubt you'll be in the saddle again. Whenever you have that stubborn look, you generally accomplish what you set out to do."

He picked up a brush to run down Lully's neck, and she tossed her head and nickered in response.

"Once I can ride, I'll be able to join Frank and see to it that justice is done."

"But your mother needs your help with the farm," I chose my words carefully. "Don't you think that's more important than exacting revenge?"

"Dirt has been done to me and mine, and whether the Federals want to call the war over or not doesn't matter.

Don't they still keep their boots pressed hard on our necks? Yes, they do, and I don't know if they'll ever stop. I don't intend to walk away from anyone who tries to take away my rights or who turns out to be a traitor."

Something about his words triggered a memory that sent a shiver down my spine. What was it Jesse had said?

Before I could answer my own question, his eyes softened, and he took my hand.

"You've done so much for me these past weeks. More than anyone ever has. I don't feel right unless your pretty face is the first thing I see every morning and the last at night. You know Ma plans for me to go home within the week, and quick as I can sit on a horse again, I'll be riding out to join Frank. I don't have any right to ask such a thing, but if I don't end up gut shot in some far-off place, when the time comes for me to go back home, I'd like it if you married me." He pressed my hand to his chest. "I need you, Zee."

My eyes widened. Jesse moved close enough that his breath stirred my hair. I looked up at him, searching for a sign that his feelings echoed mine. His hand cupped my cheek, and for once, it wasn't me who kept us on our feet. Had he not placed his arms around me, I would have fallen under the crush of emotion. Although I hadn't allowed myself to admit it, this was the moment for which I'd been waiting. This was the man I wanted to spend my life with. Jesse leaned down, and his breath warmed my face.

Just before our lips met, I remembered something Jesse said about Mr. Locke. The name he'd called him in an eruption of blistering fury.

Traitor.

9

When sorting through images stored in my mind of the time we spent together, the most bittersweet would be the day Zerelda came to take Jesse home.

The dark, smoky scent of fire filled the air as Papa and Uncle Thomas set to burning dry undergrowth in the woods closest to the house. Frost would soon sparkle on the ground, heralding the approach of a long winter. I ignored Mama's tight-lipped glance and threw a shawl over my shoulders to keep away the chill when Jesse and I left the house to stroll on a path near the heavy woods behind the garden.

With frequent stops to rest, this trek was the farthest he'd yet gone from the house. Dry leaves and twigs snapped and crunched beneath our feet. When we reached the point where no one could see us, Jesse took my hand.

I fumbled for the right words to say and settled on a simple truth. "I'll be sorry to see you go, Jesse."

His arm pressed against mine and he chuckled. "You may miss seeing me, but I do believe your mother is beyond ready to have me go."

Despite the slow pace, Jesse's breath came quicker than it should. When we reached a small clearing, I pointed at a large tree that had been toppled by the wind. The root ball was taller than Jesse's head, and its broad trunk afforded us a perfect place to rest.

Jesse inhaled a deep breath. "There's nothing like woodlands, the damp earth, the moss, the softening wood." A crow cawed and a woodpecker drummed against a nearby tree. "This is a pure slice of heaven." He turned and looked at me. "Pure heaven. Just like your face."

A blush heated my cheeks as he reached up and ran a thumb across my skin.

"Tell me the truth, Zee. Is it fair asking you to wait for me?"

"Fair? Of course, it's fair. I'll wait as long as you need me to. But I've been thinking, what if there's no need for delay? Why don't you let me go with you now? I could help your mother take care of you until you're strong again."

"You know your parents would never agree to that. Besides, they need you here, not traipsing around after me into God knows what sort of mayhem."

"I've already decided I don't care what Mama thinks. I intend to take the path that's right for me."

"As you should. But I don't want to shove our intentions in anyone's face. This is to be a proper courtship, at least as much as I can make it so. I plan to win your mother's approval. Maybe she'll be happier with me when I become well-known for my daring deeds. Just like the hero in one of those books you read to me."

His notion made me laugh despite the fear weighing down my shoulders. I decided it best to open my heart. "If we're speaking truth, I must confess something. I'm afraid once you leave, you'll forget all about me, and I'll never see you again. If that's the way of it, please tell me so now."

Jesse pulled me closer and whispered in my ear, "Zee, I love you. There is no one on Earth I love more. When I'm strong again and have found a way to support you, we'll be married."

"So, you're telling me this is truly an engagement?"

"Indeed, it is," he replied solemnly.

I looked at my lap, and Jesse lifted my chin. The strength of his gaze told me he spoke the truth.

Yet I wanted more. "With what will we pledge our troth?"

"I'm afraid I don't have a ring to give you." He wrinkled his brow then smiled. "But I've got this."

Reaching into his breast pocket, he pulled out a large, burnished token that he pressed into my palm. It had Lady Liberty's head on it, and I realized it was a one cent coin, the type that for years had been minted oversized until citizens complained about their pockets weighed down from cumbersome copper pennies. The metal held the warmth of Jesse's body.

"A penny?"

"Yes, but not an ordinary one." He pointed at the coin. "See the date? It's 1828. My pa's pa gave it to him on his tenth birthday. He kept it all those years and gave it to me when he walked out the door bound for California. I remember that day like it was yesterday because I cried so hard about him leaving. It's all I have left of him now." He smoothed a finger over the coin in my hand. "I always thought of this piece as lucky. I want you to keep it until the day we marry."

I shook my head. "Oh, no. You must keep your lucky coin. I want nothing to stand in the way of your safe return."

Jesse chuckled. "Knowing you're waiting for me is all the luck I need." He squeezed my fingers around the token, and his smile disappeared. "Let me speak plainly. I think it will be best if we keep our promise a secret from everyone. They'd try to convince us marriage would be folly. Let me prove myself before we even bring up the subject. Is that all right with you?"

I nodded, and he took me in his arms, sealing our promise with a kiss. I clung to his neck while the sun's warmth blessed us.

Finally, he pulled away. "Come along now. We'd better get back before your mama and mine send out a militia to find us."

I slipped the coin into the pocket of my skirt. Feeling its weight brought a small measure of comfort as Jesse took my hand and we walked home.

Zerelda sat in her buggy near the boarding house porch with my family gathered around. As though sensing my mood, no one smiled when Papa helped Jesse climb into the seat next to his mother. I bit my lip to see his wan face and the way he grimaced as he settled in. Jesse made the effort to smile at me, but the fact that he allowed his mother to keep the reins showed how weak he still was. I couldn't make myself smile back at him. His departure pained me like an amputation, another wound of war.

"I'll write to you, Zee," he said.

"Yes, please. I'd like to know how you're doing."

After my supremely inadequate words, Zerelda clucked to start the horse's plodding hooves. I shoved my hand into my pocket, wrapped my fingers around the coin, and thought of our kiss and our promise to each other. I was bursting with the desire to tell the whole world that Jesse and I were well and truly engaged, and that his absence would break my heart. But I was bound to silence. Tears spilled from my eyes. I pulled out my handkerchief and blotted my cheeks and nose. When I looked up, I realized Mama was staring at me.

"It's past time we returned to a normal life, Zee," she said, her tone stern. "Please make your cousin's sickroom tidy."

The fact that Mama didn't use Jesse's name did not escape me. She wanted all traces of him gone. Yet I nodded without a word of complaint and watched her walk to the house.

Lucy came to stand beside me and wrapped her arm around my waist. "I'm afraid Mama suspects how you and Jesse feel about each other. The expression on your face doesn't hide anything, you know." She let out a long sigh. "You glow like a firefly whenever you look at him. It's the same way I feel when I see Boling."

Lucy's beau, Boling Browder, had returned from the war and been patiently courting Lucy for the past few months. He planned to open a small mercantile in Kearney, and Lucy's shining eyes demonstrated her complete approval of the idea. He came to call often, with freshly picked flowers or some small confection. Mama took time to bake his favorite sweetbread, and Papa never failed to shake his hand. It was evident Lucy had our parents' blessing for her marriage. All I had was a secret promise.

Suddenly, my need to speak about what had happened outweighed my vow. Lucy, my sister and dearest friend, could be trusted over anyone else. I hoped Jesse would understand.

"I've tried to hide it, but … Oh, Lucy, something has happened between Jesse and me. Today we made a pledge to marry once he is healed and finished riding with Frank."

If my news surprised Lucy, she didn't show it. "I thought as much. What will you say to Mama and Papa?"

"It will be some time before anything can be settled between us, so we decided not to speak of our engagement for now. Besides, Jesse hopes to convince them by his deeds that our marriage would be a blessing rather than a curse."

"You know Mama and Papa don't approve of poking a hornet's nest. They fear further retribution from the Federals unless the South bends to every demand of the government. Authorities will be watching Jesse and Frank. In itself, that's problem enough, but there's more to consider."

"More? What else is there?"

"Mama and Papa love their kin and have always done anything they could to help them, but they've never approved of cousins marrying and find such a practice to be most ill-advised. I know they intend to push you toward someone they feel would be more suitable."

My hands knotted together. "As you well know, cousins marrying is nothing so extraordinary. Look at the Canfields. And the Morgans, too. I know Mama would like nothing better than for me to take a husband of her choosing, but she will not be the mistress of my fate. I still intend to be the one making decisions about my own future."

"I understand. An arranged marriage worked out happily for Mama and Papa, but these days it's a rather old-fashioned notion that often brings nothing but a cold and lonely union." Lucy linked her arm through mine. "Love is seldom decided through the workings of logic, is it? I hope Jesse can do as he says. If he pleases Mama and Papa, then perhaps they'll change their minds and things will work out as you wish. Come. Let's go inside. I'll help you clean out his room."

I followed Lucy with an aching heart. I already missed Jesse and wondered how he could possibly prove himself to my parents when they were so set against him. Pulling dirty sheets from the bed, I puzzled over what seemed an impossible situation.

There had to be some way to secure the future I wanted without separating me from my family.

10

*J*esse spent the next three months at his mother's
farm, twenty-five miles away from me, recovering
his strength and helping Zerelda rebuild. When
he wrote that his vigor had returned enough for him to
be back in the saddle, his bliss fairly jumped from the
page. He and Frank had been lying low long enough for
me to believe they had reconsidered their plans to wreak
vengeance against the Federals, but the emergence of a new
political party soon dashed my hopes.

They were called Radicals, and they seemed to take
pleasure in punishing Southerner sympathizers. Thanks to
them, some of our men found themselves unable to cast a
vote, retain their property, or even walk into town without
harassment. This fanned the glowing coals of resentment
and soon rumors abounded of former rebels looking for
their own justice through secret raids carried out under the
cover of darkness.

Occasionally, Jesse took the long ride from Kearney
to Harlem. He spoke in such an unfailingly polite way to
Mama and Papa, it made me smile, offering them help if a

fence needed mending or a wheel on the wagon had to be fixed. Jesse teased my sisters about their beaux until they blushed, before wandering outside to smoke a cigar with my brothers and refight the war. Once he'd done his duty with my family, he would slant a look at me, and we'd steal away for half an hour alone together.

"Frank and I have put in some long days. The old farmhouse looks better than it did before the war started. Who knows? We might even whitewash the place. I think Ma would like that."

"She must be well pleased, having her sons home and seeing all the things she loves taken care of."

"The timing's been good since Ma and Reuben's baby is due to come any time. She's chafing at the idea of not getting around to do as much as she wants."

"What about you? How are you feeling?"

"I still have pain in my chest. Reuben says it will probably always bother me, but I'm alive." He laughed. "I even joined the Mount Olivet Baptist Church. They convinced me to sing in the choir every Sunday morning. Can you imagine that? Me singing in a church choir? I guess there's no telling what wonders can come with time."

"I've heard you sing," I said with a laugh. "They must be in desperate need."

He took my hand in his and brought it to his lips for a light kiss. "Thank you kindly, miss, for saving me from the sin of conceit. I guess my biggest excitement these days is when a few of the boys I rode with during the war show up. We get to jaw about some of our old battles and what might be in store for us in the future. There's even been some talk of joining together once in a while and letting the Federals know we haven't quite forgotten what they did to us."

I blinked at him. "What do you mean?"

"Oh, I don't know. We'll get it figured out. But enough talk of that. I'm considering what I can do to make money and secure our future."

"I could be quite happy as a farmer's wife," I reminded him.

Jesse shook his head. "It's still too fresh and raw for me. On some days I can live with what's happened, but other times I think the war won't ever be over until we get back everything we lost. And there are plenty of people who feel the same way I do."

I reached in my pocket to touch the penny Jesse had given to me. "I hope you don't spend so much time living in the past that you forget about the future."

"The future's always in my mind. Can't you see how hard I'm working to get your mama's approval? It's about the toughest thing I've ever done."

I sighed. Jesse treated Mama as though she were made of cut crystal, yet every time she glanced at the pistol strapped to his hip, her demeanor cooled. It infuriated me to see her treat him so when I knew he was doing his best to win her affection.

"We must be patient for now," I said. "But I won't plan my future around Mama's wishes, and I've told her so."

My chin trembled and Jesse put his arms around me to kiss away my agitation.

After he left, I decided to take a walk before going back inside, lest I say something to Mama that would set back Jesse's efforts even more. While tramping near the woods to the chirps of sparrows, my temper cooled enough for me to decide it best to keep myself busy until Jesse or I could come up with a more tangible plan.

Work served as the best antidote for worry, and I had no trouble finding enough to do. I did all my old chores and some of Lucy's too, now that she spent more time with her beau. She had taken to humming at all hours, smiling dreamily when she hung clothes on the line, and pinning a flower on her dress when Boling was expected for a visit. In my view, there was nothing extraordinary about Lucy's beau. He was an ordinary man, of ordinary height, with an ordinary—albeit a bit stiff and narrow—moustache. But whenever Lucy entered a room, he leapt to his feet and smiled in a way that left no doubt of his feelings.

As weeks passed, I couldn't help but feel a pang of jealousy when Lucy talked of Boling. My last note from Jesse said he'd be leaving the farm for a while. He didn't tell me where he was going or when he'd be back, and as time went on, I had no way of knowing whether I entered his mind at all. Doubts clouded my thoughts, and I wondered if the engagement had been nothing more than a dream. My mood grew dark and morose. It didn't help the day Boling came to see Lucy, bringing news that left us reeling.

"According to the newspaper, bandits robbed the Clay County Savings Association in Liberty, right in broad daylight," he said. "They got away with over fifty-eight thousand dollars. While they were riding out on fast horses, the men let loose a valley of shots and a boy on the street got hit and killed. The sheriff sent a posse after them right away, but the desperados escaped by crossing the Missouri River."

Papa crossed his arms, leaned back in his chair and shook his head. "I don't recall ever hearing about a bank robbery that audacious before."

Boling nodded. "The authorities are calling it the first day-time bank robbery and claim the episode carries the mark of rebel Bushwhackers. The whole town of Liberty is up in arms." He took a puff of his cigar and blew out a cloud of white smoke. "Between the robbery and all the shooting and fighting going on between citizens who stand with the Federals and those with Southern sympathies, it feels like we're heading for another civil war bloodier than the first one. Some say the robber gang is most likely led by Arch Clement, so the state is bringing in Union officers to find him."

My back went ramrod straight. Jesse had talked about how much he admired Archie Clement's strategy and utter fearlessness during the war. I prayed his loyalty to Clement would not place him anywhere near Liberty. Papa must have had the same thought, as his face lost much of its color.

A sense of foreboding prompted me to rise and excuse myself. If anyone knew Jesse's whereabouts it would be Zerelda. Barely had I put pen to paper when Mama spoke from behind me. I covered the letter with my hand.

"It has been some time since Jesse sent any correspondence. I'm afraid you are letting your feelings for a young man who does not concern himself with you control your emotions. It is time to face hard facts and think of doing something to plan your own future. " Mama paused to inhale a deep breath. "Boling has spoken to us of his neighbor who is a widower. The man has three small children and is in need of a wife. Lucy finds him a pleasant man, and when Boling inquired, he said he would be most interested in meeting you."

I turned incredulous eyes on her. "I'm sorry, Mama, but you already know how I feel. I'd rather face the future alone than do as you propose."

She put her hand on my shoulder.

"My dear, you must remember that love can grow in time. And if not love, then surely companionship."

"No. I will not consider it." My voice was shaking as my feelings threatened to overwhelm me.

"Zee, your father and I insist—" I shook off her hand and fled the room before she could finish. Mama had voiced what I feared most—that Jesse had forgotten me. Once in my room, I fell onto my bed and let bitter tears soak my pillow.

I spent the next few days in bed. My head ached, and all I wanted was to sleep. Mama believed my state to be exhaustion, but Lucy knew better. She brought me a tray with warm broth and bathed my forehead in the same soothing manner I had done for Jesse. The reminder did not comfort me, though I was grateful for her presence.

Only upon Lucy's urging and Mama's threat to send for the doctor, did I force myself to get out of bed and put on a fresh dress. My hands smoothed the wrinkles from its folds, and I resolved to put the state of my relationship with Jesse to the back of my mind.

As though the timing had been planned, on the first of August, a letter came from Zerelda.

My dear niece,

I hope this finds you well. I'm happy to say Reuben and I welcomed a sweet blond-haired baby boy on 26, July. The child appears strong and robust, so we have high hopes he will grow into a fine man one day. Before Jesse left us, he requested a special favor. He said if the baby was a boy, he wished us to name the child after his most admired comrade. Thus to please him, our child will be christened Archie Peyton Samuel.

I am afraid I cannot answer your questions about my sons, as they do not tell me where they travel.

Perhaps they believe such knowledge would cause their old mother to worry overmuch.

Give our warmest regards to your parents. Without the comfort of loved ones, I do not know how we should survive these hard times.

Your faithful aunt,
Zerelda Samuel

Oh, how Zerelda must have leaped at the chance to grant Jesse's request. It provided another opportunity for her to trumpet her loyalty to her sons' Bushwhacker comrades. Yet her letter did not lessen my worries a bit, for newspapers soon blazed with the occurrence of yet another robbery, this time in Lexington. The bank turned over more than two thousand dollars to four armed bandits who easily eluded a posse sent after them.

When the leaves started to drop from our trees, I shivered to think of the frigid air that would soon come. I despised the confinement and dark silence of winter, and the thought of struggling through a deep blanket of snow to feed our chickens made me want to crawl deeper under the covers.

Still, preparing for the cold, lean months kept us busy. While Papa and Uncle Thomas pounded nails to secure loose boards on the house and patched a hole in the roof of the chicken coop, Mama and I spent hours in the kitchen, cutting up ripe tomatoes, squash, and green beans to simmer and put away for the bleak time ahead.

On a day swirling with snow just before Christmas, Boling came to the house dressed in a new gray suit. He and

Lucy sat together on the walnut settee. She kept her eyes cast down, while Boling slipped a finger into his collar as though it were pinching his neck. Aunt Susan stayed in the kitchen to clean while Mama carried in a tray of biscuits, still warm and fragrant from baking in the Dutch oven.

Papa took a biscuit and smiled.

"It's been a while since we've seen a paper, Boling. You keep up with the news. Can you tell us what's been going on?"

Boling placed a biscuit on a napkin draped over his knee and paused a moment before answering.

"As a matter of fact, there is some news that may interest you. I heard a large group of men who fought under Quantrill rode into Lexington a few days ago, saying they wanted to enlist in the militia. The sheriff let them sign up but then said they had to clear out of town. All of them did what he asked, except for their leader, that old cut-throat Archie Clement."

I kept my eyes on the floor as Uncle Thomas asked what I wondered. "Do they know who rode in with them?"

"That's what I wanted to tell you. Reports say there were about twenty-six men altogether," Boling's face reddened, "and two of them were identified as Frank and Jesse James."

I shifted in my chair and couldn't hold my tongue any longer. "But if they did nothing more serious than ride into town to enlist, what's wrong with that?"

"You're right," Boling hastened to add. "They rode out of town with the others as ordered. But Arch Clement didn't go. Instead he went over to the hotel and bought himself a drink. A soldier confronted him, and then the shooting started. Clement tried to run and was gunned down on the street. A reporter wrote a story that condemned his killing, and the next thing anyone knew, the Federals went and tore up the newspaper office."

A log from the fireplace popped, making me jump, and a glowing cinder flew out on the hearth. It hissed there until Uncle Thomas shoveled it back into the fireplace.

I put down the biscuit I'd been holding. I knew Jesse counted Archie Clement among his best friends and that news of his death would hit him hard. And I knew, too, that the news would stoke his sorrow into fury.

Papa sighed, his eyes grave. "It's not surprising resentment still simmers. With all that's happened, too many disagreements are settled by gunfire. All we can do is pray for reconciliation. I believe that is our best hope."

I held no illusions that prayer would make those still intent on fighting take a peaceful course. Heavenly intercession had not helped prevent war, so why would it help secure peace now? I threw my biscuit into the fire and shook the crumbs from my skirt. I decided to confine my own prayers to those of a woman for her loved ones. I would pray for my family. I would pray for Jesse.

11

*P*apa's knuckles were white on the packages he handed me. "We must be very cautious," he said, climbing down from the wagon. He and Uncle Thomas had been into town. Mama and I had met them at the barn to help with the goods they bought. "Today I heard of a Baptist minister with Southern sympathies who was beaten when he tried to resume preaching to his flock."

"Beaten for spreading the gospel?" Mama asked, incredulity making her voice high and thin.

Papa's face was grim. "Beaten for speaking his mind," he said. "Since the Federals have been ordered to stop any hint of rebellion, they'll be keeping a close watch over anyone they think is stirring trouble. There's been talk in town about Frank and Jesse. I believe some of these comments were made for our benefit."

I'd heard the tales of Federal outrages, of neighbors who—because of southern sympathies—were refused loans or had their property seized and sold for pennies on the dollar to benefit railroad expansion. Many of our friends shared Frank's and Jesse's anger. Their perspective was certainly not unique among those tired of living under Federal occupation, and I knew many wished they could take the law into their own hands. I shuddered to think of the Union man—an officer!—who'd taken advantage of a young girl in Lafayette County. When the Federals refused to arrest him, he was found hanging from a tree in his own front yard. Local gossips and reporters told many such stories of retaliation against Union sympathizers, including robberies, intimidation, and even cold-blooded murder. Jesse, Frank, and other guerilla rebels were often named as suspects, although, I noticed, with very little evidence.

We were all tired of the turmoil, but Uncle Thomas and Aunt Susan found the constant state of unrest unbearable. One day, they sat us down and said they planned to move to Kentucky within the month, since there was little money now to be made at the boarding house. Their sons had moved to Kentucky after the war, and my aunt and uncle now planned to join them, waiting out the uncertainty of Reconstruction—along with the hunt for Frank and Jessee—in a place distant from the constant state of tension in Missouri.

"I feel we're deserting you," Uncle Thomas said, "but we cannot live this way any longer. It's time for us to join our boys. Susan misses them, and so do I. They say life is quieter in Kentucky these days. Perhaps someday, we will return."

Just a few short weeks later, Mama hugged her brother and wiped the tears from her eyes. Then she turned to Aunt Susan and the two women wrapped their arms around each other, holding tight. "Have a safe journey," Mama whispered, "and let us know as soon as you're settled."

Papa held out his hand to Uncle Thomas who gripped it firmly. "I hope you find what you're looking for," Papa said.

"We'll do our best to keep the boarding house open, and I'll send you money when I can."

The fear of repercussions from Frank and Jesse's growing notoriety had wearied us all. As the number of robberies at Union-held banks mounted, the rumors multiplied and Jesse and Frank were nearly always in the middle of them. Although I knew Jesse wanted to make the Federals pay for their misdeeds, I couldn't imagine him being responsible for half of the things others accused him of doing. On one occasion, a newspaper reported the James gang robbed a Texas bank. The next day, another story claimed the gang had held up a bank in Tennessee. Even to my biased eye, such a crime spree could hardly be possible.

Jesse and Frank stayed far from their mother's farm, where the sheriff too often rode near. Nor did Jesse come to see me. Local authorities posted rewards and scoured the countryside. I even heard the banks might band together and hire the Pinkerton Agency to find the culprits. It infuriated Zerelda to know eyes were on her farm, and she told us how she despised the idea of anyone keeping her sons away. I silently agreed.

Sheriff Wilson even paid a visit to us. Fingering the edges of his battered hat, he looked almost as worn out as his horse.

"Mr. Mimms, I'd like permission to search your place."

Papa did not invite him in. "May I ask the reason?"

"You know we're looking for your nephews, along with a few of their cronies from the war. Seems they may be keeping a mite busy visiting banks across the region."

Papa's head lifted, and he fixed a stern gaze on the sheriff. "So you are planning to arrest them?"

"At the very least, they need to answer some questions. But right now, my concern is figuring out where they are.

I've got men searching the woods, but if it takes a court order to search your house, I'll go to the judge and get one."

"That won't be necessary. You may make your search. You will not find what you're looking for here."

The sheriff tromped through the house, peering in each room before ambling about in the yard to poke in the barn and chicken coop. He even opened the door to stare inside the privy. After his inspection, he nodded to Papa and climbed on his horse to ride with empty hands back into town.

Later in the day, Sheriff Wilson came back with a grim report. One of his men had found a decomposed body clothed only in tattered undergarments in a shallow grave not far from our pond. A single gunshot to the head had taken his life. Buried with him was a pair of shattered spectacles.

No one said a word until the sheriff left, then Mama grabbed Papa's arm. "Could it be?"

"William Locke. I suspect so." Papa glanced at me. "But in light of what's happened, the less we say, the better."

Later, Lucy and I talked about the strange discovery. "Why wouldn't Papa say anything to the sheriff about it? Jesse wasn't strong enough to lift a cup, let alone a gun, when he left."

Her eyes clouded. "I know. But Frank was."

My heart thudded and my stomach turned queasy.

On a cloudy spring day in 1867, two years after the war, Lucy married her soldier. Rain pattered down upon them as the couple scurried from our boarding house parlor to

Boling's carriage. He'd built a tidy, little home for them that stood near the store he operated in Kearney. I shared Lucy's happiness, but harbored a deep sorrow for my own plight. She had been my closest confidante, and, since my sister Nancy and I were more distant with each other, I would no longer have anyone with whom I could freely discuss my fears and hopes.

No sooner had the happy couple departed for their honeymoon, than two of the guests fell into a heated discussion. One declared loyalty to the guerilla gangs, while the other thought hanging would be too good for them. It took all Papa's considerable diplomatic skills to calm the men before the argument could erupt into a fight.

I fanned my cheeks and wished everyone would leave so I could think. Lucy was gone. Jesse could be anywhere. And from the stony look on Mama's face, I knew that what had happened to sully the wedding day would be another mark she held against him.

With a kettle on to heat the water, I pushed my rolling pin across the thick dough to flatten it for dumplings. The tip of my knife made the first cut, and I started on the second when Papa's voice rang out through the house: "Frank and Jesse are here!"

My knife clattered to the table. I wiped the flour from my hands onto my apron while I ran. Mama called after me, but I didn't hear what she said. Smoothing my hair, I stopped short on the front porch.

With his blue eyes shaded by a derby hat, Jesse sat astride

a pretty bay mare, dressed in a fine, new suit coat and wearing a wide grin. Next to him, Frank was on a prancing chestnut, his face nearly hidden beneath a full, dark beard, much longer than it had been the last time I saw him. Jesse's clean-shaven profile made an odd contrast to his brother's, and I was pleased to see him looking so healthy and strong.

Of the many things I wanted to say, now that he'd arrived, I uttered one word in a voice that squeaked an octave higher than normal. "Jesse."

He dismounted and walked over to take both my hands. "Hello, Zee."

"You look well." My voice sounded vapid and foolish, yet I didn't know what else I could say.

Jesse, however, had never been one to stand silent. "Thanks to you, I feel better than ever. Buck and I are traveling through on business and stopped to see Ma. We need to be on our way, but I told him I couldn't ride out without stopping here first, even if but for a moment."

Months of doubt melted away like April snow. He hadn't forgotten me after all. Jesse lifted my hand to his lips while Frank turned studiously away to speak with Papa. A tremor shivered through me, and I wished mightily that his mouth touched my lips instead of my fingers, no matter who might be watching.

"I'm glad you came. I must confess to fearing I would never hear from you again."

A line appeared between Jesse's brows, though his eyes were merry. "Do you really think that poorly of me?"

"So much time has gone by, I began to believe you had changed your mind. Or that I had dreamed our pledge. Do you still want the things we talked about so long ago?"

"Of course, I do. You won't be rid of me as easily as

you seem to think. I intend to come back for you. It may take a while to do what I must do, but until then, I'll visit as often as I'm able. I have ways of getting out a letter from time to time, too."

"You know I have no desire to be rid of you."

My gaze dropped for a moment, and when I looked up, the question I wanted to ask came tumbling out. "There's been so much about you and Frank in the papers, all of it associated with terrible deeds. Is it true?"

Jesse shook his head, and I wished I hadn't taken the light from his eyes.

"Don't believe everything you read. A lot of those stories are made up by the Federals still trying their best to tarnish our names." He shot a quick glance at Frank. "Just as we plan to undermine them any way we can."

Frank nodded, and then issued a gruff command. "We need to go now. The woods are full."

Jesse leaned toward me and placed a light kiss on my cheek. "Good-bye, Zee. Try not to worry. Take care of yourself, and remember I love you."

And then he vaulted onto his horse's back. He and Frank spurred their animals forward and galloped away, though Jesse did turn to give me a final wave. I kept my hand raised in a farewell salute until Mama came to stand beside me, lips thinned enough to disappear.

"What pledge?" she asked.

I turned to face her. "You were listening? Our words were private."

"Nothing you do or say is too private for me not to know. What sort of pledge did you and Jesse make?"

I considered lying, but my pride wouldn't let me. "We plan to marry."

The color drained from her face. "Under no circumstances will Papa and I ever permit such a thing."

"I'm sorry, but I'm afraid it doesn't matter what you think. I love him, and I want to marry him. There will never be anyone else for me."

"My girl, that would not be a good idea for many reasons, not the least of which is he is your blood cousin. He also has Federals searching the entire state for him. Jesse's activities have not endeared him to the North, and I don't want you to marry into such a life."

With feet firmly planted, my hands went to my hips.

"So you would rather I marry someone else and be unhappy than to choose my own fate?"

"Jesse is my own dear brother's son and I love him, but I do not want you to align yourself with anyone who has the law nipping at his heels and must forever be on the run. You deserve much more than that."

"You're right, Mama. I deserve to be with someone I love and who loves me in return."

She held up her hand to silence me from speaking further. "Enough. There is little point in any more argument. If and when the day comes that Jesse asks for your hand, decisions will be made. But remember this—he is young and walks a dangerous path. Who knows what the future may hold in store for him?"

Mama's ominous words were mitigated by my relief at newfound proof of Jesse's devotion. I didn't care about anything else. If he had asked me to climb behind him on his horse and ride away now, I would have done so. But until he was ready to make such a commitment, I could only wonder when I would hear from him again. I put my hand in my pocket and clutched the penny. For the time being, I must be content with as much as he was able to give me.

Over the next many months, more bold robberies were reported. The stories claimed the crimes were linked and laid the blame directly at the feet of Jesse and Frank James. I refused to drive into town. Curious stares from our neighbors had become too grating. By the end of 1869, even Papa seemed shaken.

"I cannot believe it." Papa waved a newspaper he'd brought home. "Jesse wrote a letter to Governor McClurg about the bank robbery in Gallatin. It's printed right here in the *Liberty Tribune*. He says he and Frank are innocent of robbing the bank and killing the cashier and that he can prove it, but he doesn't want to turn himself in for fear of being hung without a trial. Listen to his final lines:

> *But as to them mobbing me for a crime I am innocent of, that is played out. As soon as I think I can get a just trial I will surrender myself to the civil authorities of Missouri and prove to the world I am innocent of the crime charged against me.*
>
> *Respectfully,*
> *Jesse W. James*

Papa put the paper down, and I grabbed it to read the letter with my own eyes. Jesse had been bold to send it, but I understood why. Despite his thirst for retribution, I knew he didn't want to be a hunted man.

Later, the *Tribune* published letters from three people who swore Jesse and Frank were in Kearney, not Gallatin, when the robbery occurred. One affidavit came from a friend of the Samuel family, a merchant named Mr. Groom. Another came from Jesse's sister, Susie, and the final one from Zerelda. I could not believe Jesse would commit such a callous act as he'd been accused of, but even I knew it would have been better for him if someone other than friend or family offered proof of his innocence.

Yet much to my surprise, the letters did help his cause. Fewer accusations were flung about, and we heard almost no demands for either his arrest or for the snap and stretch of a hangman's noose. With passions cooling, hope stirred my heart, until a telegram came to us.

My dear family,

The boys left for Texas, where many of their friends are gathering. I do not know how long they will be gone, but I fear greatly for their safety, and most earnestly beg you to pray for them.

Zerelda Samuel

12

erelda didn't need to beg me for prayer. The fear in her telegram had infected me like a fever. I included Jesse and Frank in my supplications to heaven more times each day than I could count, hoping God listened to me more clearly now than he had done before. Some days my heart filled with such turmoil that I asked Papa to pray along with me. Seeing his calm and steady hands clasped together kept my thoughts from spinning beyond control.

The passage of time cooled gossip and virulent outcries against the rebels, returning our lives almost to normal as new settlers arrived in Harlem. Our empty rooms filled with guests. While this happy circumstance added to the family's pocketbook, it also multiplied the tasks to be done. Keeping busy didn't bother me, for when occupied, I had less time to mull over the question of when—or if—I would see Jesse again. Shrouding my worries with work, I sometimes forgot to eat. My clothes fit me looser than they had in years.

After a long day spent weeding the garden and scrubbing every floor in the house, my head drooped over dinner. Papa touched my arm, and I jerked my head up.

"Zee, you are exhausting yourself. Try to finish dinner, then go to bed." His eyes were gentle and his tone made me feel like a child comforted during a thunderstorm by her father's calm assurances. There were many times he had tucked me into bed years ago in Kentucky and his presence never failed to soothe me. I dutifully ate a few more bites, then pushed away my plate.

Mama peered at me and placed her hand on my forehead. "There aren't any signs of fever, but you need rest. Go to bed now."

I went to my room and slipped under the covers, trying to sleep, but my eyes simply would not close. I strained to hear the distant sound of a horse's hooves galloping down the road. But only the chirp of crickets and call of a whippoorwill met my ears. After long minutes of tossing and turning, I rose, threw a shawl over my shoulders, and tiptoed outside.

Sitting on the bottom step of the porch beneath a silent expanse of stars, I looked up and hoped that somewhere in Texas, Jesse studied the same pinpricks of light. A pack of coyotes howled a mournful chorus and I shivered, clutching the shawl tighter around me. The solitude relieved my aching heart, so I stayed on that step until the stars disappeared and the eastern sky blushed a pale shade of rose. Finally, I crept back inside. The next morning, Mama did not wake me. I slept until dinner.

Piling breakfast dishes in the dry sink, I poured a kettle of hot water over them. Thunder shook the house and thick dark clouds had gathered in the sky.

"Thank the Lord, it looks like rain is on the way. I will be out in the garden helping Papa before it starts," Mama told me, untying her apron.

Thank the Lord, indeed. The plants had become so parched; we'd taken to carrying pails of water out to the garden to keep them alive.

I washed each of the plates, and then whisked a towel over them. After they had been stacked on the table, I considered whether to put them away or get laundry off the line before the storm hit. Before I could make a decision, a woman's scream made me inhale a sharp breath. Heart racing, I dropped the towel and ran outside.

Near the garden, Papa lay on the ground with one arm outstretched as though reaching for something. Mama kneeled over him.

When she saw me, her hand went to her throat. "He's gone, Zee. Papa is dead!"

I dropped to my knees and touched him, hoping to find the sign of a heart still beating. But his chest was silent and still. Mama's hands were clasped around his, and tears flowed down her cheeks.

Our newest boarder, Mr. Ackerman, ran toward us, skidding to a halt when he took in the scene. His mouth gaped in horror.

"Please fetch Dr. Lykins," I said. "I can't leave Mama."

"Yes, Miss Mimms," he said and sprinted toward the barn.

I stared down at Papa's face, my eyes burning and my heart numb with disblief. But I dared not let myself cry. Mama needed me. My arm went around her thin shoulders. "Would you like to go inside?"

"No." She did not lift her head. "I must stay here." She smoothed his hair, her other hand still holding his. Mama moved her lips silently while I watched the road, willing the doctor to arrive. When the sound of carriage wheels finally came, my breath caught to see that Dr. Lykins had the coroner with him.

Both men examined Papa, then the doctor took Mama's hand in his. "I'm very sorry, Mrs. Mimms. It looks as though he was taken by a cardiac insufficiency before he even knew what happened." He turned to me. "Let us carry him into the house for you."

"Thank you," I said. "We'll make a place for him in the parlor."

They lifted him, and thunder rumbled again. A few drops of rain pattered on our heads as I helped Mama to her feet and we walked toward the house to prepare for what must be done.

The next two days were a nightmare of people coming and going. They spoke in quiet tones and brought more food than we could ever hope to eat, even if we had the appetite to do so. My brothers and sisters returned with their families. We wrapped our arms around each other and wept together. Our neighbors spoke kind words about how much they would miss Papa's sound and steady guidance. Even Zerelda, Reuben, and their young children drove from Kearney to witness Papa's plain pine coffin lowered into the ground.

The old cemetery smelled of weathered limestone. Flowers moldered on graves, with monuments standing in neat rows to mark the final resting place of a parent, a child, a sweetheart, or a friend. My chin trembled as the first clods of earth fell on Papa's casket, but I withheld my tears and gripped Mama's hand. I longed for the comfort of Jesse's strength, but he and Frank were far away and most likely not even aware of what had happened.

Once the pastor uttered his final words of prayer, we trudged away in a sad procession. A gentle breeze caressed my face, ruffling wisps of hair from my bonnet. Zerelda put her arms around me. "Your papa was a good man. We will miss him very much."

"Indeed, we will. Every day." My heart skittered at the thought.

She tilted her head and while Mama spoke to Reuben, she whispered to me, "You must be wondering about Jesse. I have no news of him or Frank. A few friends in Texas may know where he is. I will try my best to get word to him of your loss."

She left my side when Mama turned back to me, hand outstretched to take mine. The mourners bestowed a final handshake or hug before leaving us. They would return to their own lives. Ours would never be the same. Once everyone save my brother Robert and his family left us, we drove home in silence. Mama sank into a chair at the kitchen table. I put a plate in front of her, but she only pushed the food with her fork. It frightened me to see her so quiet.

"You'll become ill if you don't eat something, Mama."

She looked down at the plate and didn't reply.

Robert took her arm. "You must be worrying about how you'll manage with Papa gone. I want you to know I've saved some money since I moved back to Missouri. It's not a lot, but I'd like to buy the boarding house from you. I will run it and you can lay down your burdens and stay as long as you want."

Mama shook her head and tucked a persistent strand of graying hair behind her ear. When her chin lifted, I noticed the first spark since before Papa's death.

"No. He would not want me to give up. As long as I am able, I will run this place. I can hire a man for the outside work, and Zee can help me with the rest as she has always done."

With my own future uncertain, and new wounds so fresh, there seemed no reason to disagree with her. I nodded, feeling like an otter caught in a trap. Robert kissed her cheek.

"Very well. But remember you can send word any time you need me."

Mama's back slumped as soon as Robert gathered his family and left.

"You must go and lie down now, Mama. You haven't slept in days."

She let me lead her to the bed she had shared with Papa. I tucked a well-worn quilt around her, and she brushed her hand across the soft faded fabric. Her eyes squeezed shut, and I tiptoed away.

The parlor seemed quieter than a tomb. I thought of Papa and wondered idly how the sun could still rise and set without his smiling face. Sunbeams from the window fell across his Bible, sitting as always on the table near his favorite chair. Over the years, I'd seen it in his hands countless times. I picked up the heavy gilt-edged book, and discovered a card Mama had embroidered and sewn onto a faded blue ribbon that marked a place. I opened the book.

Breathing in the scent of decades-old pages, my finger moved down to where Papa had underlined a verse, Psalm 30:5. *"For his anger endureth but a moment; in his favor is life: weeping may endure for a night, but joy cometh in the morning."*

I closed the book and hugged it to my chest as tears rolled down my cheeks.

13

We did not celebrate Christmas that year. Mama had no desire to visit anyone, nor did she feel up to having family come see us. Much as I would have enjoyed the diversion of my sisters and brothers, and the chance to smile at the antics of young nieces and nephews, I respected her wishes to keep our first Christmas without Papa reserved for quiet reflection.

After the holiday passed, we entered 1871, a new year that I hoped would bring happier times. At least we were blessed with mild weather. Snow dusted the ground less than half a dozen times over the worst months of winter, swiftly melting into a slushy muck. Even though we didn't need to shovel deep snowdrifts, the loss of Papa, coupled with the short days and dreary lack of sunlight, dampened my spirit.

When February arrived, it held the promise of spring close enough to touch. I threw grain to the chickens and smiled as they clucked, scratched in the dirt, and flapped their wings at each other. A rooster preened and strutted near his harem. Soon, fluffy yellow chicks would follow the

hens, adding their peeps to the brash cacophony. When the chickens abruptly grew silent and lifted their heads, I looked up. The sound of a horse's hooves rang on the road. I saw a rider urging his mount straight toward me. I stared for a moment at the apparition, and then the empty bucket dropped and my hand went to my throat.

Jesse.

As soon as his horse reached me, he pulled back the reins sharply enough that the animal reared, her front legs slashing the air. He settled her, and then dismounted, his steed dancing in place without bolting, even though he had dropped the reins. I ran straight into his waiting arms, dampening his dusty shirtfront with my tears. He held me tight against him.

"I couldn't get here sooner, Zee. I'm sorry. You know I loved your papa as if he were my own." He pushed me away to look at my face. "You look pale. How are you holding up?"

"I don't think I've ever been so tired. Mama barely speaks and keeps herself busy all day until late in the evening. Now only she and I are left at the boarding house." I closed my eyes for a moment. "It makes me feel very alone."

Jesse pulled me back against his chest.

"But you're not alone, Zee. I hope to stay closer to Kearney for a while, and I'll come to see you often as I can. I want to do a better job of planning for the day we marry."

I pulled away to look at him.

"Do you mean we will be wed soon?"

"Very soon, I hope. I need to get a few more dollars together before we can set a definite date."

He glanced toward the house. "I don't suppose it would do any good for me to speak to your mother?"

"No. Now isn't the time. She still buries her grief in work. Perhaps when she's able to recover herself more fully."

Jesse nodded and brushed a hand against my cheek. "I haven't even been to the farm yet. I wanted to see you."

His arms surrounded me again, and I leaned into his warmth, absorbing his strength, like water to a dry sponge.

"I wish you didn't have to leave at all."

Jesse kissed me before pulling away. "There are still a few things that must be done before that can happen. Until then, promise me you'll take good care of yourself. I'll be back very soon."

He kissed me again and then leapt onto his horse's back in a move worthy of any performer, urging the animal into a ground-eating canter. Turning away from the path, he sent his mount over our split-rail fence, and I laughed out loud. Jesse was home, and it sounded as though he might be ready at last to set down roots.

In June, news hit of another bold robbery at a bank in southern Iowa. Hadn't I just seen Jesse a few days before? It seemed no matter where trouble happened, the blame landed squarely on my cousins. This time, they were paired with Cole Younger and his brothers. Swiftly following the robbery, another letter from Jesse appeared in the newspaper, proclaiming his innocence. Jesse blamed Radicals for the accusations against him, and his letter contained more political observations than any he'd ever expressed before. He even went so far as to endorse Horace Greeley for president.

I knew in light of this robbery and another one occurring a few weeks later, that the publicity would require Jesse to

avoid travel and keep away from the people he loved. I tried my best to ignore the mounting rumors and let myself bask in the luxury of Jesse's brief, surreptitious visits.

On one such occasion, we sat in the cool shade of the porch. His loose-limbed posture belied the fact that he kept his horse tethered no more than five feet away. He had two guns on his saddle and a pistol strapped to his hip, a habit that still infuriated Mama. But I reveled in his company. We talked and laughed, even though Jesse kept a vigilant watch on the trees beyond our house. I poured fresh cider into his cup and he lifted it to me.

"Here's to some good news. I've made a friend in John Newman Edwards, the editor of the *Kansas City Times*."

I looked at him with my brows lifted. "You've actually met with him?"

"Only a few times, but enough to know he understands me. John's a Southerner, too. He rode with General Shelby and wrote about some of the ablest and most gallant fighters in the Confederacy. He knows the things I do against Union-held businesses strike another blow for the South and tells me any letter I send him, he'll publish, so my side of the story can be told."

Such an alliance reminded me of a dance with the devil, so I cleared my throat and searched for the right words to say. "Would it not be best if your name stayed out of the papers? It seems to me such attention could stir up more anger against you."

"Not from any true Confederate. What do I care what Radicals have to say about me? If they hate me, then I know I'm doing my job well."

I wasn't so sure but didn't wish to waste our limited time together engaging in an argument that would prove futile.

A hawk soared overhead in the clear blue sky. We watched its flight, and I searched for a neutral topic.

"Jesse, do you remember when we talked about raising horses? It sounded like a fine idea. Is that something you would still like to do?"

He shrugged. "I think about it once in a while. But there's still work to be done here. With John's help, I think we can make the Federals understand Southerners won't lie down and be bullied. I don't care how many guards they post in their banks. I'll make them pay for what they've done until everything that's been lost is returned in full. I can't run off to pursue a dream before I've finished."

The determined jut of his chin froze my heart. "It sounds like you've turned this into a quest. Don't you know dreams, not revenge, are the foundation of a happy future?"

"Sometimes I think you read too much, Zee. Don't you know life doesn't always go along smoothly until there's a happy ending?"

I bit my lip and Jesse reached out to take my hand. We sat in silence a few moments more. Then, as though he sensed my mood, he kissed me lightly on the cheek and strode to his horse, mounted, and set the animal galloping away to continue his personal quest against the Federals. Although I knew he'd return when he could, I took a deep breath, wondering how many days or weeks before he appeared next. My back ached with weariness.

Mama came outside to pick up our empty glasses. She sighed and shook her head at me. "I hope you're coming to realize the folly of a pledge to a man on the run. You spend your life waiting for someone who may never do the things he promises. I've seen you take to your bed with a vacant stare in desperate sorrow. It is as though you live for nothing but Jesse."

My jaw set stubbornly. "He will someday be my husband. Why should I not feel sorrow when he's away from me?"

"I tell you again, we do not know if that event will occur. It has been years since you two promised each other marriage. Despite his vow, you are still here with me. He may promise the moon, but nothing he has done has brought your union closer to fruition. Instead, he rides in, holds your hand and whispers his promises, and then rides right back out again."

My eyes filled with tears at the sting of Mama's words. Her face softened. She put her hand on my arm and sat beside me.

"I've asked the doctor to come visit with you. Between pining over Jesse, Papa's death, and worrying about me, you have had too much on your shoulders. Perhaps there is something he can offer to make you feel better."

I had no strength to argue. Blue spells did seem to come more often than before, sometimes leaving me so weak that all I could do was lie in bed. When my spirit sank so low, Papa had advised me to read from Scripture to fill my mind with messages to uplift my soul, rather than fall prey to the work of the devil. With a guilty pang, I realized that I hadn't opened the Bible since the day we buried Papa.

Life had become so different from my girlish hopes. My brothers and sisters had all started families of their own. Even Lucy had urged me to consider whether I should remain as a spinster help-mate for Mama or leave the boarding house to find a different life. If talking to a doctor could help me regain my energy and optimism, then I wouldn't refuse.

When Dr. Lykins arrived, he spoke for a long while with Mama before he came to see me. He listened to my chest and asked a list of questions, writing down my answers. When finished, he took off his spectacles and gravely diagnosed me with melancholia. Then he prescribed camphor and one blue pill of mercury to clear my body of black bile.

I followed his instructions, although Jesse's presence was the tonic I needed most. Even a simple letter from him lifted my spirit.

Jesse wrote regularly to friends, his family, me—and the newspaper. I usually received at least six letters from him over the course of a year, always delivered through one of his most trusted friends. Mama told me to burn them lest they be found in our home by someone who might use them against us, but I couldn't bear to destroy the few tokens of his affection and hid them under my mattress instead. Since I never knew whether he'd be near or far away, I treasured every word.

I'd read his most recent message so often, the paper wore thin and a tear appeared on its folded edge. Even if it should dissolve and crumble, the words had been permanently etched on my heart.

Dearest Zee,

We have been riding day upon day. Frank and I are mostly of the same mind. We will make a strike against the North as long as we are able and not roll over in defeat like so many other Confederates have done. Of course, I have my own ideas on how to handle things, so there are times when we ride our separate ways. Frank is growing weary of this life. He talks about coming home and settling down.

You will be much surprised to learn my brother found a sweetheart in Kansas City. Her name is Annie, and Frank met her at the horse races. She's a pretty thing, though not as pretty as you. It makes me laugh to see old Buck slick back his hair and blow the dust off his hat to impress her. He even considered shaving off his beard until I told him he'd look like an old man pretending to be young. I argue there is still much work to be done and we are the ones to do it. He grunts back, which you can imagine is not a very satisfactory response. For myself, I will fight on in every way I can until the Federals permanently remove their boots from our necks.

I'm sorry to tell you that for what I've done, and what I must continue to do, I asked the church at Mount Olivet to strike my name from the rolls. It's no longer worthy to appear there. I hope you will not think harshly of me, for I'm only doing what I must.

I hope this letter finds you well. I miss your soft voice. Without you, Zee, I wouldn't be here. I owe you my life and give you my heart. If any ten-cent man comes around courting, let him know you belong to someone else who will soon, God willing, be back. Hold fast to the coin I gave you. Perhaps I will soon be in a position to exchange it for a ring.

Affectionately,

J.J.

My chest tightened at the notion Jesse intended to continue a life that made him feel he wasn't worthy to be on the rolls of a church. Papa preached about a God who granted forgiveness. Had Jesse forgotten it was never too late to seek it? More than ever, he needed someone to stand by him. Someone who could steady him through the bloody horrors of his past.

Fear that he may have sought mooring in his new friend, John Newman Edwards, made me press my lips together in worry. Mr. Edwards published another series of articles featuring the rebel warriors, words that glorified the bold and daring men who led a crusade against a Union government intent on keeping the South in its iron fist. His words were flowery, but at least they promoted understanding rather than condemnation.

Jesse believed the course he had chosen was noble and right, but I feared what he might do next with John Edwards encouraging him. Would he ever end his reckless mission of vengeance? And what would it take to stop him?

Yet despite my unsettled feelings, I followed Papa's advice and looked to Scripture for comfort, praying Jesse would abandon his wandering ways and reckless deeds. I wanted him to choose a new course for his life, one that would include me.

Soon, whether from Dr. Lykins's tonics or the comfort found in Papa's old Bible, I slowly began to emerge from darkness and resume my full duties helping Mama at the boarding house.

14

esse's visits dwindled as the newspapers reported another series of robberies. Any time a reporter named Jesse as a suspect, Jesse would send the paper a letter claiming his innocence, or an article written by James Edwards would appear, who minimized the event and said the men were only continuing a daring war to avenge the South. In one such story, published in November of 1873, Mr. Edwards claimed to have interviewed Jesse and Frank. He wrote that Jesse spent a long convalescence at our boarding house in Harlem.

Had Mama read it, she would have collapsed in horror, but unlike Papa, she, thankfully, chose not to seek out information on what latest outrage her nephews may or may not have committed.

I read the newspapers that came my way, but secluded myself at home and abandoned any effort to see Catherine or the other women who had once been my friends. The thought of answering questions about my cousins, now so blatantly made public, would be more than I could stand. I found myself meeting each day with a fevered energy that did not burn out until sleep claimed me at night. I could not allow even a moment for my mind to be unoccupied. But after days of operating in such fashion, darkness arrived within me again, this time bringing such a heavy weight that I once more retreated to my bed.

Mama brought a bowl of broth to me. "Dr. Lykins is coming. I am worried your illness may overcome you."

I rolled onto my side away from her to face the window. Gray clouds billowed in the sky, and a few raindrops spotted the glass. "There's no need to leave the broth. I'm too tired to eat."

She did not respond, and I heard the door to my room shut. Within the hour low voices murmured in the parlor. Soon Dr. Lykins entered my room, took my hand, and gazed at me with kind brown eyes.

"Zee, I know you have been through much, but you must make an effort to free yourself from worry over things you cannot change. Such musing is not good for your mind. Instead of burying yourself here, you should see people with whom you can develop friendships." He nodded. "It might be wise to consider someone who could make you a loving husband."

His words brought my head from the pillow. "It sounds as though Mama has spoken to you of things she wants for me rather than my own desires."

Dr. Lykins laid a calming hand on my arm. "It's true your mama has wishes for you, and since you're a woman grown, I will speak frankly. Your mother fears your attachment to your cousin will harm you. You must remember Jesse James is a hunted man and will never be able to lead a normal life. I am sorry to be blunt, my dear, but I've seen cases such as yours, where a woman who has lost a love pines away until death. If you don't forget about him, this situation could even affect your nerves to the point that someday you might be committed to the state insane asylum."

My eyes widened at his harsh words.

"Now then, Zee, before things become so difficult, I believe it is in your best interest to leave the boarding house and its memories. If you think about what I've said, you'll soon see I'm right."

He patted my arm as though comforting a child and prescribed more of the same tonics as he had before.

The next morning, through long habit, my thoughts turned to Jesse. I counted the time since we first pledged to marry. Nine years! It shocked me to realize how long it had been. Rubbing my aching head, I considered the possibility that even if he wanted to, Jesse might be unable to abandon the notorious life he led. The thought made me want nothing more than to curl back under the covers, but I remembered Dr. Lykins's words and forced myself to rise. My hands shook as I fastened the buttons of my dress, and I tried to think past the fog that gripped me.

Work had always been my consolation, and I used it again to make sense of my conflicting emotions. Upon considering Dr. Lykins' words, one thing stood out to me above all else. At the age of twenty-nine, I needed to leave Mama and be out on my own. I'd already been hoarding whatever money she gave me and kept it wrapped in a handkerchief hidden in my dresser drawer. If there would be no wedding, at least I could use the money to help me go—but to what destination, I had no idea.

In the kitchen, a kettle bubbled while Mama peeled skin from potatoes.

"I need to speak to you, Mama."

She paused a moment before her knife moved again. "Yes. What is it?"

"I've been thinking about looking for work. Perhaps as a teacher or governess."

Mama put the knife down and turned to me with brows arched. "What did you say?"

"I said I'd like to find a job."

"Have you not enough duties here?"

"I'm stifled and close to losing my mind, as Dr. Lykins has been so eager to tell me. I need to leave this place."

Mama's eyes softened. "If you could find the right man to marry, your life would soon change. It's a joyful thing to have a reliable man and children in your life. You and your husband could stay here with me and make a decent living. After I am gone, the boarding house would belong to you."

"We've been over this many times already, Mama. I have no intention of marrying merely for the sake of gaining a husband."

"But I'm afraid I cannot manage this place alone." She rubbed her forehead. "Perhaps if you had a little time away, it would refresh your spirit. Let me consider the matter."

Mama picked up the knife and continued to peel potatoes, her back straight as a poker.

I sighed and went to the garden, where I could sort my muddled thoughts. A mockingbird scolded while I pulled weeds with my bare hands until my back ached, and my nails were stained with dirt. I pulled and tossed and pulled and tossed, until a row of scraggly weeds were left to wither on the ground.

There were few options open. Nancy and her husband weren't sympathetic to my plight and I didn't want to beg from my brothers. The thought of going to Lucy tempted me more than anything else, but the stern hand of reason stayed my impulse. Lucy and I saw each other so rarely now. Boling feared my relationship with Jesse would bring trouble to their door. If I begged to move in, he would be apoplectic, and I couldn't ask Lucy to intervene on my behalf. Her loyalty belonged to her husband. Yet there had to be a way.

On a morning so cool and wet with dew I needed a heavy shawl over my shoulders, I went outside to sip my coffee. The grass sparkled as though someone had sprinkled it with diamond dust. A train whistled, and I remembered the tracks ran both east and west. Either direction could bring a new life for me. It was then that I noticed the buggy traveling on the road moving slowly toward the boarding house. A large figure held the reins of a horse that plodded. I stared as they came closer. My mouth dropped when I recognized the driver.

Zerelda. The bonnet shading her face had wilted, and her clothes were damp and rumpled.

Mama joined me outside, a line puckering her brow. Zerelda drove the rig to the porch before she pulled back on the reins. I helped her step down, and her scowl deepened.

"I can't stay for anything more than a sip of water before I go on my way. The Pinkertons have been sending men all through the county to hunt down my boys. Some brown-suited fool came to the farm asking questions, but left soon enough when he caught sight of my rifle. Others have been nosing around with the neighbors. You need to take care. It would not surprise me if a stranger came here pretending to be someone else. Mark well that such a person could be a rattlesnake in disguise."

Mama nodded, her eyes shadowed. "We never talk to anyone outside family about the boys. You can trust us to help in whatever way we can."

"Yes, I know that, Mary, and I thank you. We have always been able to depend on you, and that fact will never be forgotten. As for you, Zee," she added gruffly, "you hold a special place in my heart. I give you credit for saving Jesse's life. He's spoken to me often of his deep affection for you."

It was a bold statement to make in front of Mama, when Zerelda surely knew of Mama's opposition to our relationship. A small part of the weight on my shoulders lifted at what I deemed to be her support, and my lips turned up.

She spared me a brief smile before fixing a sterner eye on Mama. "I hope sometime soon my boys will be free from persecution and able to live a normal life without the harassment that comes my way and theirs. Nearly every day someone is watching at the edge of the farm or trespassing on my property. They're keeping my family from me. I want to see Frank and Jesse without worrying one or both of them will be hung from a tree like the Federals did to Reuben."

"I understand your feelings." Mama pointed at the porch. "You look exhausted. Perhaps you should come and sit with us in the shade for a while. I can fetch you something cool to drink."

Zerelda shook her head and turned toward the wagon. "Never mind. I can't linger here any longer. There are other places to stop before I can take the train for home."

My brow furrowed. Given Frank and Jesse's increasing infamy, I wondered if Zerelda's dream would ever be possible. She nodded briskly toward Mama, and I helped her climb back into the wagon. Zerelda moved stiffly as

Mama sometimes did. She had aged so much in the last few years. Perhaps we all had.

She lifted the reins, and the horse broke into a trot, wagon wheels drawing ruts in damp earth. I knew she would spread similar warnings to our neighbors. It wouldn't surprise me if she sharpened her warnings with implied threats for those less sympathetic to her cause. Mama glanced at me and then trudged into the house.

The increased interest of lawmen fanned my fear for Jesse, and for us as well. An odd prickly feeling settled on me that I couldn't shake—as though someone had walked on my grave.

Within days after Zerelda's warning, a rider approached the boarding house. I half-turned, wondering whether to run inside for Papa's old pistol, when I recognized our neighbor, Jim Lindell. A sigh of relief left me.

He reined in his horse. "Zee, can you get your ma? I have news for you both."

Mama must have heard the horse hooves because she stepped outside, wiping her hands on her apron. "What is it, Jim?"

"The town is buzzing with news from Independence that I knew you'd want to know. A Pinkerton detective got himself killed in a shootout. I hear John Younger was shot dead, too. I reckon Zerelda was right when she came by to warn us trouble was coming."

Heart skittering, I couldn't keep myself from asking, "Mr. Lindell, was anyone else wounded?"

"One other detective got hurt pretty bad, but it sounds like he'll live." He scratched his stubbly chin. "They say the war's over, but it sure feels like the fighting is never going to end."

My fears deepened, and sleepless nights returned. More often than not, I left my bed to count the stars. In light of the latest round of violence, the thought of leaving Mama alone to cope with whatever might come next made my stomach clench. I couldn't desert her now. Until I knew more, I decided to delay making any final decision about my future. Surely after so much time already had passed, a few more months wouldn't matter.

As it happened, news came sooner than I expected. On a day when Mama drove into town with Mrs. Lindell to buy supplies, a solitary messenger rode to the house. Even after he stopped his horse, the animal pranced about as though he were accustomed to running. The rider had a silver-striped beard and a hat sat low on his forehead, keeping his face hidden. The horse blew heavily when the man leaned down to hand me a small piece of paper.

"A message for you, miss," he said.

I took the note, and the man loosened his reins to let his animal charge away. I watched until he was out of sight, and then my fingers fumbled to open the paper. I scanned the few words scribbled on it and inhaled sharply.

Dearest Zee,

I cannot bear to wait any longer. It's time we fulfill the pledge we made so long ago. Be ready, for I will arrive very soon so we can make a plan to start our new life together.

With love and much anticipation,

J.J.

15

One moment my eyes burned with tears, and the next it seemed as though I could float away like a basket under a hot air balloon. Fearful of Mama's reaction, I kept the contents of Jesse's note secret, tucking the paper into the pocket of my dress, next to the coin he gave me. At night, I hid both under my pillow. Over the years, it often seemed unlikely that a life with Jesse was even possible, but with the note as a talisman, a renewed sense of hope buoyed me.

I stood at the dry sink to wash dishes from the breakfast meal, and sung a wistful war-time song I hadn't thought of in years:

> *Beautiful dreamer, wake unto me,*
> *Starlight and dewdrops are waiting for thee,*
> *Sounds of the rude world, heard in the day,*
> *Lull'd by the moonlight have all passed away.*

Mama came into the kitchen, with a full laundry basket. I closed my mouth, and her eyes narrowed. "Take this and start heating the water, please."

"Yes, Mama."

I dragged the basket outside. In the yard, chickens squawked as I walked past them while the man Mama had hired to help us, hammered a board on the coop. The old red rooster flapped his wings at the unwelcome disturbance to his kingdom.

Flower buds had begun to tease with hints of the yellow and pink that would soon follow, and I filled my lungs with clean air. Never had I seen a bluer sky. Only yesterday, I didn't notice the beauty bursting around me. Today, I worked the pump handle and added my song to that of the birds.

Mama spent her time in the kitchen while I pulled dirty linens from the beds and swept floors. We had no time to speak until the sky darkened and Mama filled our plates for dinner. We'd made a habit of taking our final meal of the day together after the boarders had eaten, so we could speak of things that could not be safely mentioned in front of others. It was a practice Papa had established once news of Jesse and Frank began to appear in newspapers. Now with Papa gone, and my brothers and sisters on their own, Mama and I sat across from each other, speaking politely of our day's work.

Mama folded her hands to bless the food and then looked at me. "I am pleased to see you are following Dr. Lykins's instruction. It has been a long time since you were so lighthearted."

I dismissed our differences of opinion as though they hadn't happened. "Yes, indeed, Mama. I'm very sorry to have grieved you."

She passed a warm biscuit to me and smiled. "I have come up with an idea that I hope will please you. Would you like to go visit Lucy for a week or two? I can manage things here until you return, and I know she would be very happy to see you. She has been quite lonely during her confinement and would enjoy your company."

Spending time with Lucy in Kearney would be a balm to my long-battered soul. I'd missed having a confidante. And with Lucy's house lying only a few miles from Zerelda's, such a visit might also make it easier for Jesse and I to see each other. I paused so as not to appear overly eager.

"Thank you, Mama. I'd love to spend time with Lucy. How soon can we make the arrangements?"

She patted her lips with a napkin and beamed at my words. "I proposed the idea a few weeks ago in a letter. We will send a telegram to say when you are coming. I think such a visit would benefit both of you."

The corners of my mouth lifted, and I could feel my heart hammering with excitement. "Can we send the telegram tomorrow?"

Before Mama could answer, someone rapped softly at the kitchen entrance. We both jumped at the unexpected sound. She looked at me and then at the door before scooting back her chair. I wished my fingers were wrapped around Papa's pistol as Mama walked toward the door and waited a heartbeat before pulling it open.

The damp scent of evening wafted in, tree frogs chirping a crescendo on the breeze. A man wearing a wide-brimmed slouch hat and long dark frockcoat stood in the doorway. I squinted until the glow of our kitchen lamp illuminated his face. He swept off the hat in a courtly manner to expose sandy-colored hair and a familiar grin. My breath caught, and I leapt from my chair to run toward him.

The wait had been too long to care what Mama thought. I thumped against Jesse like a ship reaching harbor. His arms went 'round me, and his chin rested on my head. I melted into his warmth. We stayed that way for a long moment before he stepped inside and pushed the door shut. His pale eyes shone with a sparkling intensity.

"Aunt Mary, I've come here tonight to tell you I love Zee and cannot live any longer without her by my side. I have enough money to provide a secure start for us. We've waited a long time and want to get married as soon as we can. Will you give us your blessing?"

Mama backed up a step and clutched a chair near the door. Her hands were white-knuckled, holding on as though to keep herself from falling. Her cheeks flushed a deep scarlet.

"Jesse, you know the life you live even better than I do. There are stories of robberies and murders and a price on your head. Detectives chase you everywhere you go. So do bounty hunters. You cannot expect me to allow my daughter to go with you when it means she will suffer the same dangers. A plan such as this is not wise. I am sorry, but I cannot with good conscience give you my blessing."

Jesse's face fell, and for once, he seemed at a loss for words.

But I didn't intend to keep silent and starched my back. "You know being with him is all I've ever wanted. Jesse and I love each other, and we intend to be wed. I would like to have your blessing, but with or without it, I'm telling you we will be married."

Mama lifted her chin, and her voice frosted.

"Zee, your disrespect does you no credit. You must listen to reason. I want only what is best for you."

"If you don't mind, Mama, I'd like to make such a decision for myself."

"Daughter, do not be foolish. You and Jesse must not marry, if for no other reason than your agreement to help me run the boarding house. Would you leave me here alone?" Mama's voice faded, and she swallowed hard. "Please pray about this and think carefully before you do anything you will come to regret later. At the very least, take a few months before plunging into such a marriage."

I stared at my mother and noticed how the lines in her face had deepened and her lips had thinned. She looked older and wearier than I'd ever seen her, even on the day we buried Papa. In an instant, I realized the depth of her feelings. No matter how long or hard Jesse tried, time would not soften her heart. She would never agree to our union.

I turned to Jesse. "Give me a moment to pack my bag. I'm going with you tonight."

Mama drew a sharp breath. "I cannot believe you would consider leaving under such circumstances. Think what your papa would say if he were still here."

"I have prayed and thought and worried for many long years and know full well what I'm doing." My gaze stayed on Jesse. "Let's leave right away, please. Now that I think on it, there's nothing I need to take with me after all."

I saw a spark of admiration in his eyes, and his lips curved up in a half smile.

Mama shook her head and blew out a long, low sigh. "I had hoped with time you would come to your senses. Marrying someone who could be here to help us in our work would provide a secure future for you."

"You seem more worried over the boarding house than my happiness. I've stayed here longer than any of my brothers or sisters. You can't force me into a life I don't want because it benefits you."

She raised her hand, and I thought she might slap me. But her arm dropped, and she lowered her shoulders.

"If nothing I can say will dissuade you from this foolishness, at least consider the consequences of running away with a man in the night like a thief. Such unseemly behavior would bring shame to your family and to your papa's memory. If you insist upon marriage, a proper wedding would be preferable to an elopement."

Mama's eyes glittered with unshed tears, but her features looked cold as if they had been carved from stone.

"Very well, Mama. I won't leave tonight. Beyond that, I promise nothing."

I moved away from the censure I saw written on her face. Jesse and I left the kitchen to walk outside where the chirp of crickets rose and fell in a soothing nighttime serenade. His pretty bay mare snorted and tossed her head.

"Easy, Kate. Steady, girl," he said.

She quieted with the soothing sound of his voice, and I remembered Jesse's way with horses. As I touched the mare's sleek neck, the import of what I'd done struck me. I began to shiver.

"Would you like my coat, Zee?"

"No. I'm all right."

He sighed and lowered his voice. "If you've changed your mind about marrying me, I want you to know I understand."

"No. I couldn't ever go back to my old life." The words blazed from my mouth. "That's finished for good. I want nothing more than to be with you. But where will we go? Mama will never agree to host a wedding of which she disapproves."

He pulled me against the warmth of his chest. The sound of his heartbeat steadied mine.

"We could go to my mother's farm. She'd be happy to welcome us."

The thought of what Zerelda might say about the nature of my exit from home made me squirm. I shook my head as another idea occurred to me.

"Lucy. I know she'd let us have our wedding at her house. She's already expecting me to visit."

His brows wrinkled together. "Are you sure about that? Boling's always feared any attention being brought to them because of me. A wedding might be more than he'd be willing to allow."

"Lucy understands how it is with us. And as long as we move quickly, I don't think Boling would mind."

He shrugged his shoulders. "Whatever it is you want, I want, too."

I thought of Mama waiting in the kitchen, and my stomach clenched.

"The way things are now, the sooner I go, the better. I'll be on the first train to Kearney tomorrow morning. Can you manage to see me at Lucy's after I arrive?"

His cocky grin returned.

"You know I can manage whatever I set out to do."

Brushing dust off the sleeve of his coat, I smiled. "Yes, I do believe you can."

16

*T*he next morning, Mama kept her head bent over a dress that needed mending. She punctured the fabric so hard with her needle that I could hear every stitch. She did not look up or even acknowledge me, but I couldn't leave with no words between us. "Good-bye, Mama. Remember to send word to Robert. He'll help you with whatever you need." Her needle paused only a few seconds before it resumed a steady *plunk, plunk, plunk.* I sighed and carried my bag outside to where our hired man waited to take me to the depot.

The money I'd been saving bought my ticket with a comforting amount left over. Taking my seat, I stared out the window and watched green fields appear and disappear as the train brought me closer to Lucy. My mind seemed at war. I didn't know whether to feel sorrow at the rift between me and Mama or joy at the notion of marrying the man I loved.

After the train made it to Kearney, I scurried past the people who strolled on the depot platform to rent a horse and buggy. By mid-morning, I'd arrived at Lucy's small home and tethered the sad-looking gelding's reins to a fence post under the shade of an elm tree. An azalea bush near Lucy's front porch bloomed with ruby-colored blossoms, and a rooster crowed from the backyard.

Brushing dust from my clothes, I took a deep breath, and rapped on the front door. A few moments passed before it opened.

My sister, swollen with child, stood in the doorway. When she saw me, her eyes rounded. I sobbed her name and my arms encircled her in a tight hug. We laughed through our tears, and in an instant my fears fell away as though I'd returned home after a long absence.

She stepped back and held me at arm's length. "Mama wrote you might come to visit, but I didn't expect to see you so soon."

I swallowed hard and looked away. "I left this morning because of a disagreement with Mama. Last night Jesse and I told her we were going to be married. She took a strong stand against us and refused her consent for us to wed. I threatened to elope with him and she told me such a thing would shame the family. So, I've come here in hopes you'll let me stay until Jesse and I can be properly married."

Lucy's mouth dropped open in surprise, but she swiftly pressed her lips together.

"Come in and sit down. You know you can count on me. Boling is at the mercantile now. I'll speak with him tonight, but I feel sure he won't object as long as we're discreet."

"Let him know Jesse and I plan to marry within the week," I said, linking my arm with hers as we walked to the small settee in the parlor.

"It's finally happening. I can scarcely take it in. Have the two of you spoken of where you'll go after you marry?"

"No, we haven't had time to talk about that. I'm sure Jesse will have ideas on what's best for us."

Lucy placed her hand over her rounded stomach. "Zee, you know I love you and Jesse very much, but I confess to being worried. It sometimes seems as though he has no concern over himself at all."

"Don't you think he would have been captured long before now if he wasn't careful? I'm not afraid, and you shouldn't be either."

Lucy smiled at me, but her eyes were troubled.

When darkness fell, Jesse came to see me. He kissed my cheek and hugged Lucy before nodding at Boling, who kept his face arranged in stiff lines. At Lucy's urging, Boling had agreed to host our wedding. We decided on a simple ceremony without any frills or frippery. April 24, 1874. The date took residence in my brain like a favorite hymn. I wanted to sing it aloud. Jesse rose from the table where we'd made our plans and shook Boling's hand.

"I must leave now, but not before thanking you. I'll never forget this." Then he turned to me and grinned. "Tomorrow morning at nine o'clock I'll meet you at Uncle Billy's, and we'll ask him to perform the ceremony."

Mama's younger brother, the Reverend William James, was a Methodist minister, and a man we knew we could trust. But the next day when we arrived and discussed our intentions with him, the whiskers on his chin quivered with outrage. "How can you consider such a thing, Zee?"

Uncle Billy used every argument at his disposal to dissuade me from marrying Jesse, citing the many accusations against him, but I remained firm in my resolve. He finally conceded when I used the statement that won any argument I'd ever had with myself about Jesse.

"He's not half as bad as the newspapers make him sound, Uncle Billy. Most of what they say isn't even true."

Once Uncle Billy finally agreed, he turned to Jesse and lectured him at length on the error of his ways and the wisdom of placing his feet on a new path. Jesse uncharacteristically stared at the floor and suffered the scolding with no reply other than a flushed face and curt nod.

Lucy and I made preparations for the wedding. I didn't feel at all cheated, and loved the idea of a simple affair with only our closest family members present to witness the moment I'd envisioned for so long.

As I expected, Mama declined to attend, but my sister, Nancy, and three of my brothers planned to come with their families. Frank wasn't in town—Jesse suspected he was courting—nor could Uncle Reuben and Aunt Zerelda make the trip without raising suspicion among bounty hunters who were vigilant in their search for clues. Jesse promised Zerelda we'd visit her at the farm soon after we were wed.

My nervousness and excitement grew in equal measure. At last we would have our own special day. And once we were wed, no one would ever separate us again.

On the morning of the wedding, Lucy and I gathered late-blooming tulips and displayed them in arrangements of yellow, red, and orange throughout the room. She even loaned me the white silk gown and veil that she had worn a few years earlier. Jesse wanted me to have a new dress, but I preferred Lucy's. It made me feel secure, as if I'd been wrapped in her love.

While the guests arrived, I peeked out the bedroom door and saw Jesse in a new dark-gray suit and well-polished black boots. With a lily blossom pinned to his lapel, he looked dashing enough to be a hero in any storybook.

Over in a quiet corner of the room, Uncle Billy stood silent with a heavy Bible tucked under his arm. He looked so glum the guests might have mistaken the occasion for a funeral rather than a wedding.

I shut the door and Lucy helped me hook up the back of her beautiful silk gown. Then she pinned my hair into a chignon, and tucked a short lacy veil under orange blossoms that sat like a crown on my head. She took my hand and squeezed it.

"You look lovely."

I hugged her and then we walked together into the parlor. All eyes turned toward me, and my heart swelled with emotion. Jesse's eyes widened. I realized he'd never seen me in anything but everyday calico, and smiled. I took my place next to him, while the soft warm glow of lamplight illuminated our faces.

Uncle Billy opened his Bible and cleared his throat. "We are gathered together this day—"

The sound of hoof beats and shouts halted his words. Jesse patted his hip reflexively for a gun that wasn't there, then dashed to the window. He stared a moment before holding up a hand to our startled guests. "It's Bill Fox!"

My heart pounded. Why was one of Jesse's comrades coming here now? My brother, David, opened the door and Bill ran into the room, puffing with breathlessness.

"Two detectives got wind you're here. They're not far behind me."

Jesse nodded. "Good work, Bill. Best you ride out now. Wait in the woods for me."

Quick as a blink, Jesse grabbed my arm. Our guests looked around the room as though deciding whether to stay or flee.

"Everyone be calm. I'm going to hide Zee then ride out for a while. When the detectives come to the door, just say you're here for a family party."

With only four rooms in Lucy's house, I wondered where Jesse could hide me. Our guests stood open-mouthed, too shocked to respond, and Jesse whisked me to the bedroom, lifting a fat feather mattress from the bed.

"Lie down here. I'll leave a space at the top for air."

Numbly, I did as he bade.

"Don't worry, just stay quiet as you can. I'll let you know when it's all right to come out."

He kissed me and settled the mattress on my body. I lay there, listening to my heart gallop until enough time passed that my forehead dampened. Voices mumbled from the parlor, and I strained to hear the words.

Uncle Billy's voice rose above the others.

"He is not here. Please leave my niece's home."

My ears buzzed when the staccato rhythm of boots clumped across the wood floor. I held my breath and waited. Would someone burst into the bedroom and find me? But no one did, and soon the hum of many people speaking at once reached my ears.

A horse whinnied and I heard the high-pitched rebel howl. "Yaooow!" I turned my head, trying to make sense of what was happening.

An unfamiliar man's voice boomed out.

"I see him. It's Jesse James! Let's go."

Feet scuttled, and more hoof beats met my ears. Seconds ticked by, and then minutes. No one came to fetch me, and I knew I would go mad if I didn't find out what was happening. I pushed the mattress off, tiptoed to the bedroom door, and opened it. The women were huddled around a small parlor window and I called out to them.

"What's going on outside? Where's Jesse?"

Lucy came to me and put her arm around my waist.

"When the detectives came to the door, Jesse rode past the house and jumped his mare over the fence, yelling at the top of his lungs. The detectives ran to their horses and rode out after him."

I closed my eyes and shook my head. It seemed not even after years of waiting would the fates allow me the happiness of a wedding.

Lucy bade me sit down and brought a glass of water. "Drink this, dearest. Please don't think the worst. I'm sure Jesse will be fine."

I smoothed the wrinkles that had been pressed into her wedding gown and tried to blink away the tears gathering in my eyes.

David patted my shoulder. "He'll be back. I know he will. We must give him time. His horse is fast, and he knows the woods like no one else."

Boling, clearly shaken by the events that had transpired, retrieved a small bottle of whisky and poured two swallows for all the men except David, who was studying to become a Baptist minister and never took a drink of liquor.

The clock ticked. We waited a full hour, and it nearly brought me to tears wondering whether we should send everyone home. Lucy patted my hand and I tried to swallow my disappointment. This couldn't be happening—and yet, it had. I took a breath to speak when the sound of a horse brought me to my feet, ready to race for the bedroom to hide.

David sprinted to the door and peered into the darkness. Finally, he spoke. "It's all right. He's back."

A few minutes later, Jesse ambled through the door. His

suit wasn't even rumpled and he grinned as though he'd just won the Derby. He smoothed his hair and straightened his black silk neck tie.

"It must not be overly difficult to become a detective these days." Jesse's eyes twinkled. "Those fellows were riding plugs, and I'm sure they're now so turned around in the woods it'll take them two days to find their way out."

He slapped David's back and guffawed.

Uncle Billy fixed a keen eye on me. "Zee, I ask you again. Are you sure you want to go through with this?"

A niggling doubt cast a shadow over me. Was this an omen of how I'd spend the rest of my life? I studied Jesse's face and saw a hint of vulnerability beneath the veneer of his triumphant smile. I could not deny my feelings for him, and even though my heart was in my throat, I spoke one emphatic word. "Yes."

Moments later, my family watched as Jesse slipped a narrow gold band on my finger, and Uncle Billy pronounced us husband and wife. Jesse placed his firm but gentle lips on mine to the sound of applause. I knew my smile matched Jesse's as he went around the room shaking hands. Lucy tearfully embraced me before I hugged each person who'd come to witness our marriage, from my youngest niece, to Uncle Billy. All the while, I kept glancing toward Jesse to assure myself he hadn't disappeared.

"One drink of punch, Zee, a toast with our guests, and then we must leave without delay," Jesse told me. "Where there's one detective, it's likely another will show up."

Boling toasted our union, and glasses were raised. I clinked my goblet against Jesse's and sipped sweet black-berry wine.

While Jesse went outside to fetch the horse and buggy from the barn, Lucy helped me unbutton the gown and change into my dark green traveling dress.

"You've chosen a difficult life, Zee. I hope Jesse will make you happy." She smoothed my hair. "Take care of yourself."

I hugged her. "Don't worry over me. Thank you for everything you've done for us. Tell Mama that despite our differences, I love her."

In the parlor, Jesse waited for me, thumbs hooked in his belt. I went to stand next to him, and Uncle Billy bowed his head over us.

"Oh Lord, may you bless and grant safe travel to these young people. I ask that you keep them always in your hands. Amen."

Jesse had already loaded a small trunk with the trousseau he'd purchased for me. After tying his horse to the back of the buggy, he lifted me into the seat. We both smiled and waved as would any newlyweds, and he set us on a course to the one place he'd always gone for haven—his mother's farm.

As we slowly moved from the lights of Lucy's house, the stars twinkled in the sky like a million grains of sand. The buggy's wheels rolled across the rutted road, muffled by dampness and the chirps of crickets. Despite the cover of night, Jesse didn't relax, and his eyes relentlessly searched this way and that around us.

I sighed in contentment and reached into the pocket of my dress. "I have something for you."

He glanced at me with a raised brow. I opened my fingers and showed him the large copper penny on my palm.

"You said I should keep this until the day we marry. Now I'm returning it to your care."

Jesse took the coin and chuckled. He slipped it into his breast pocket.

"You've kept it for a long time. Now I think this penny will bring luck for us both."

I nodded then yawned.

"Put your head down and try to rest a while, Zee, until we get to Ma's. I'll wager she'll want us to tell her all about the wedding before she lets us go to bed."

My cheeks warmed at his words, but exhaustion had a stronger claim. I leaned against Jesse and let my head droop on his muscled shoulder. He put one arm around me, and I fell asleep. Some time later, his body jostled against me, and my eyes opened. The old farmhouse stood before us, one light gleaming from the parlor window.

"Let's go in and see Ma."

Jesse helped me down. My legs were so stiff that I stumbled and had to take his arm. Zerelda opened the door before we could even knock, as though she had been waiting.

"My dear daughter," she said before kissing my cheek.

Reuben hugged me. His face wore the same vacant expression it had acquired since the day the Federals hanged him from a tall tree near the farmhouse. His cheekbones were more sharply outlined than ever but his eyes were as gentle as I remembered them

"Tell me everything," Zerelda commanded in a soft voice, so as not to wake Sarah, John, Fannie, or little Archie, who were already in their beds.

I spoke to her of dresses, flowers, and our family. Jesse described the nighttime raid, making it sound as though the event had given everyone a good laugh.

Zerelda's face darkened like a thundercloud. "The Pinkertons again. They sniff around too much for my taste.

I wonder at the wisdom of you staying here any longer than one night."

"Don't worry, Ma. John Edwards is putting a story in the paper saying we left right after the ceremony to live in Mexico. It's a wedding gift from him to me. The detectives and reporters will be so busy checking for a couple heading south that we can lay low here for a week or two before I put Zee on the train to Susie and Alan in Texas."

I looked at him and the mantel clock chimed the hour. "We won't take the cars together to see your sister?"

"The last thing we should do is travel anywhere together. It would raise suspicion."

I chewed my lip and wondered at his reasoning. I wanted to be with my husband, yet his plan did seem the slightest bit exhilarating, like a secret rendezvous.

Zerelda interrupted my twisting thoughts. "Well, tonight is your wedding night. I don't suppose the two of you would care to share a bedroom with the rest of us, so I've made up a room especially for you with a nice soft bed."

Her eyes gleamed with mischief as she gestured toward a closed door. Then she took Reuben's arm. "Come along. Let's go and let the two lovers be."

My face flushed as Jesse opened the door. The room glowed with luminous warmth that flickered from three taper candles. I saw a dresser and mirror with one bed. The mattress had a patchwork quilt folded over it. The bright colors made me smile, for I recognized Zerelda's firm stitches holding all the pieces together.

Jesse thumped our bag on the floor. He turned and tenderness softened his expression as his arms went around me. I closed my eyes and lifted my chin, waiting for his lips to find mine.

17

In the morning, sunlight streamed through the bedroom window, casting light across the bed and over my face. My eyes opened and I stretched languidly like a cat. Only a shallow indentation remained in the spot next to me where Jesse had fallen asleep late in the night. Gathering the quilt around my body, I got up to peek out the window.

Great puffy white clouds hung suspended in the blue sky. Birds twittered from the stout branches of Zerelda's favorite coffee bean tree, and golden blossoms on the forsythia bushes danced with an errant breeze. The scent of ham and biscuits reached me, and my stomach reminded me I hadn't eaten dinner.

Jesse strolled into the bedroom wearing a white cotton shirt and brown vest over dark pants. His clothes showed no sign of wear, making him look like a prosperous landowner headed for town. He leaned over the bed and gave me a lingering kiss. When he pulled away, I sighed. "Good morning, husband."

"Good morning, wife," he responded with a smile. "Ma

and Charlotte are cooking us a breakfast that I swear would beat anything served in a high-class hotel. Are you rested enough to get up?"

My cheeks burned when I remembered what had passed between us during the night. I should indeed be tired, but instead, my body filled with an airy dose of happiness. I stretched again. "Yes. I'll get dressed and help them with breakfast."

Jesse put his hand on my bare arm. "Ma says this morning you are not to lift a finger. She and Charlotte will take care of everything. I'll wait for you in the kitchen." He touched my cheek and grinned.

I jumped out of bed and picked up clothes scattered haphazardly on the floor. Another whiff of food and my stomach rumbled again. Both Zerelda and her former slave, Charlotte, were skilled in the kitchen, so I knew a feast awaited me. I wiggled into my chemise and drawers easily enough, but hooking the corset took more time. A new blue flowered dress looked festive enough to wear for my first day as a wife, so I put it on, smoothed the skirt, and glanced into the mirror.

The glass reflected wide blue eyes and a tangled mass of hair. I pulled my curls up into a sedate bun and secured it with ivory pins, allowing a few strands to wisp around my face. Then I pinched my cheeks, took a deep breath, and walked to the kitchen.

There were two plates on a table that held a small pitcher filled with yellow daffodils. Jesse pulled out a chair for me with a flourish as though we were at a fine restaurant. I blushed and sat down. He took his place beside me.

Charlotte carried in a tray with steaming biscuits, ham, and a pot of thick, hot gravy. She poured coffee into our cups, then grinned. "Miz Zerelda says you are to have breakfast alone. Call out if you need anything else."

I reached for the cup. "This looks wonderful. Thank you, Charlotte."

We filled our plates and emptied them almost as fast. Jesse heaped his plate with a second helping of food and drowned it in gravy. When he'd eaten every bite, he lifted his coffee cup.

"A toast to my beautiful wife. May we always be as happy as we are today."

I clinked my cup against his, resisting the urge to suggest we return to our bed.

The next few days flew by faster than I could have imagined. We walked trails near the farm, held hands without a second thought over who might see us, and talked about the times we'd shared and our dreams for the future. Jesse's steps were light as he moved along the path.

"We have no ties and can go wherever we want. Doesn't that sound like a fine life?"

"The idea of visiting new places is appealing," I admitted. "The boarding house kept us so busy, we could seldom ever leave it. I've only been on a train three times in my life."

He laughed and ran his fingers down a strand of my hair, making me shiver in spite of the warm sunlight.

"There's a world of things to see, and I hope to show you much of it. Going from one place to another is something I've always enjoyed. Never the same view twice."

"Yes, that does sound wonderful. Yet at some point"— my cheeks grew warm— "we might have children to think of. Will we settle somewhere then?"

"Ah, Zee. Let's worry about that when the time comes. Now we should just enjoy being together."

He kissed my hand, and I forgot the silly notion. Jesse tickled me and I dashed away from him, giggling like I hadn't done since childhood.

Yet too soon, the morning arrived when we were to depart. My bags were packed, but I dreaded the long ride to Texas without my new husband beside me.

Jesse had the buggy hitched and Reuben sat in the driver's seat, dangling the reins from his hand while Jesse loaded my bags. His bay mare stood nearby, saddled, and waiting.

Eight-year-old Archie, Jesse's youngest half-brother, played a tuneless melody for us on a wooden flute Jesse had given him. The other children hooted and erupted in laughter at his attempts. The child's crestfallen face prompted me to whisper in his ear. "That's beautiful, Archie. Thank you for such a sweet tune."

His small chest expanded with pride and I hugged him, before saying good-bye to the other children and Reuben. Then I kissed Zerelda's cheek. "There aren't words enough to thank you for all you've done for us."

She patted my arm. "I ask you both to take care. Stay far away from anyone who means you harm."

Jesse nodded and kissed his mother, agreeing dutifully to what she asked. From the look on his face, I suspected this must have been a frequent exchange between them. He helped me into the buggy, and then handed me a small stack of paper currency that he'd pulled from his bulging coat pocket.

"This should be enough for your ticket and anything you may need until I join you. Remember though, when you make your purchase, use a name—any name you want except your own. Then send a telegram to Susie and let her know when you'll arrive. She'll meet the train and take you to her house. It won't be long before I join you."

I clung to his hand, unwilling to have him leave me.

"How long will we stay in Texas?"

"For a while, I think. Even a month in Texas wouldn't be enough to show you everything. We'll spend some time with Alan and Susie before heading to Galveston. Just wait until you see the coast." Jesse winked. "Did you hear my little sister is teaching school now? Imagine Susie running a classroom!"

He laughed out loud at the notion, and I knew he'd find a dozen ways to devil her over it. Jesse went to his horse and lifted himself into the saddle. Leaning his weight into the stirrups, he touched his hat once to me before digging in his heels to send the horse galloping off toward the woods. His mount lifted like a bird over the split-rail fence and disappeared from my view.

Reuben stared after him. I touched his arm, and he clucked to the horse.

"This will be the longest train trip I've ever taken," I said. "I hope I don't get off at the wrong city."

"Ask the porter to help you. He can let you know whenever you need to switch to another train and when it's your final stop."

"I hadn't thought about changing trains. Thank you, Reuben. That's good for me to know."

My stomach fluttered over the thought of traveling so far away, but I couldn't stop smiling. I had once thought my life dull. Now it seemed anything could happen.

The depot bustled with passengers strolling the platform near the train. I hugged Reuben and carried my bag to the clerk. Then, with eyes downcast, I bought the ticket.

"Passage to Texas for Mrs. Edgar Warren, please." I used the first name that came to my mind, waiting for the clerk to eye me with suspicion and call for the sheriff. But he only took my money and passed the ticket along to me with a few dollars' change. After I sent Susie a telegram, I boarded the train and nodded politely at the other passengers, until I found my seat. The air in the car was heavy and warm with the pungent odor of many bodies in a small space. I leaned back and heard the whistle blow. The scent of dark smoke and coal-powered steam reached the car.

My hands smoothed wrinkles from my skirt before I opened the painted folding fan my sister Lucy had given me as a wedding gift. The vigorous fanning did little more than move stagnant air around and muss my hair as the train clacked along.

I put down the fan and let my eyelids drift together. Train travel soothed me like a lullaby. Throughout the trip, I dozed off and on, letting thoughts float through my dreams like pleasant ghosts.

The porter woke me when we arrived in Sherman. The scene outside surprised me. I thought the town would be small, but there were men in suit coats strolling on the train platform while women lifted parasols to shade them from the afternoon sun. Houses stood beyond the depot and the road was congested with wagons and buggies. I stepped from the train and looked one way then the other until a woman's voice caught my attention.

"Hello! I'm over here."

Susie waved a gloved hand at me.

I lifted my bag with both hands and weaved my way toward her to avoid jostling anyone else.

Even though it had been more than two years since I'd

seen her, Susie hadn't changed a bit. Her blue eyes sparkled, and her dark-blonde hair gleamed in the sun. I dropped my bag and she pulled me into a hug. Then she stepped back and tilted her head to study my face.

"You've never looked better. Marriage to my scamp of a brother must agree with you."

My cheeks flushed and I smiled. "Yes, I suppose it does."

Susie took my arm, and we moved with the crowd's flow. She waved at a few of the ladies we passed, and they nodded. "Quite a few of our friends from Missouri have settled here," she said. "Texas is a friendly place for those who fought for the South."

"I thought Sherman would be a quiet little town."

"It used to be, before wheat and cotton buyers flooded the area. When we first arrived, the people still struggled under the government's idea of forcing southerners back into the Union. But look at us now." She pointed at a construction site where men were pounding boards. "See over there? The town can barely keep up with building enough places for everyone to stay."

I recalled Susie's marriage in 1870 to Alan Parmer, one of Frank's former comrades under Quantrill. Not long after their wedding, the couple had relocated to Sherman, Texas, where Alan got a job managing the Stone Land and Cattle Company. Jesse had told me he and Frank made frequent visits to see the Parmers and other former rebel fighters who preferred a looser interpretation of how Reconstruction ought to look.

When we reached Susie's tidily whitewashed home, an idea struck me. I decided to test it out on her.

"Has Jesse ever spoken to you of moving to Texas?"

Susie frowned and pursed her lips.

"I know my brother enjoys spending time here, but he's never mentioned staying. I'm not sure if he'd be eager to leave Missouri, where he knows every creek and valley like the back of his hand."

She opened the front door. I stepped inside, and my gaze was immediately drawn to a large Confederate flag hanging over the fireplace. It dominated the room like a prized centerpiece.

Susie noticed my open-mouthed expression and laughed. "Alan is quite proud of that flag. It went through several skirmishes with him and Frank when they fought under William Quantrill."

"At home, we must be careful of such displays, lest authorities claim we were violating the Oath of Allegiance."

Susie nodded. "You'll find there's not much worry over the oath here." She pulled off her gloves. "You must be exhausted after your trip. Let's get you settled into a room."

18

I enjoyed spending time with Susie and Alan, laughing at their stories and admiring the fine life they'd built for themselves. Yet it had been nearly a week since I'd been with Jesse. I peeked outside more than once each day, longing for the sight of him.

Susie and I were in the kitchen stacking dishes when she looked out the window and smiled. "I do believe you have a visitor, Zee."

She wiped her hands and went to the door. I followed her, smoothing my hair with a thumping heart.

"Well, it's about time you got here. Your bride has been worrying," Susie said and gave him a soft slap on the arm.

Jesse bent to hug her, but his eyes stayed on me. He released his sister and walked across the braided rug to put his arms around my waist, his face lit up with nearly palpable desire. He pressed his lips against mine until Susie coughed.

"Time enough later for that, my dears. How was your trip?"

"Fair enough, I suppose, though it would have been nicer to have my wife with me."

He kept his arm around me and I leaned against him. His gaze lifted to the Confederate flag.

"Well, I see it's still here." He looked down at me, pride written clearly across his face. "Zee, did Susie tell you about that flag? It means a lot to Alan. To all of us."

"Yes, she did. It must bring back memories."

"I'm sure you're hungry, Jess," Susie said, heading toward the kitchen. "Let me get you something to eat, then we can talk. I'm so glad you're both here, though seeing you reminds me how much I miss my family and home."

"Speaking of home," Jesse said with a grin, "I couldn't believe it when Ma told me my little sister is now a schoolteacher. Well, ma'am, tell me, just how many students have you made wear the dunce cap this week?"

"For your information, I have ten children in class, and none of them have done a thing to deserve such treatment. They're not at all the reprobate you were. As I remember, Ma had to take much sterner methods than a dunce cap to keep you learning your lessons."

He threw back his head and guffawed. "And I have the pinched ears to prove it!" He winked at me and turned back to his sister. "Where's Alan?"

"He should be home soon. He's looking forward to spending time with you again."

"We'll stay a few more days, then be on our way to Galveston. Can you believe Zee's never seen the ocean? I'd like to spend a good long while enjoying it before we take ourselves back home."

I smiled at their lighthearted banter. Texas and its beauty, or even exotic Mexico, seemed like an adventure waiting to happen. I wanted to speak of places we might go and things we would do, yet I stayed silent, unsure of what Jesse might want shared or kept secret. I had already learned the intricate details of my new role as the wife of a hunted man.

After helping Susie clean up the dinner plates, I walked outside with Jesse, our fingers entwined. The ground was hard and cracked as stone. Trees and flowers were brown and crisp from heat. Yet in the distance, the sky had darkened. A flash lit heavy clouds, followed a few seconds later by the rumble of thunder. I took a deep breath of air that held the promising scent of rain.

"Susie says it's been weeks since they've even had drizzle. It looks as though a storm is heading our way. That will be a blessing."

"Yes." Jesse lifted my hand and touched his lips to it. "Do you know how much I missed you, sweetheart?"

"I only know how lonely I've been waiting to see you again."

He pulled me closer, and his lips nuzzled my hair.

I seized the moment of tenderness to speak aloud what I'd been thinking. "Texas is a beautiful place. I can't wait to see more of it. And Mexico. Wouldn't it be heavenly to explore together? Perhaps if the day comes when we want to settle down, Alan could find a job for you here in Texas and we could live far away from those in Missouri who chase after you."

Jesse raised a quizzical brow.

"I like it well enough here, I suppose. Spending time in Texas is something I enjoy, though I've never considered staying. But one thing I can say for certain is I don't aim to settle for a job herding someone else's cattle."

"Dearest, going anywhere with you will make me happy. You've given me a reason to anticipate each new day. My worry is over detectives and men who are after blood money."

His hand stroked my back. "Let me ease your mind. Do you know how many times I've ridden through a town bold as you please in broad daylight? If there's one thing I've learned about lawmen, it's that none of them ever think to look for me in obvious places. You worry too much."

"Perhaps you don't worry enough. You've been lucky so far. Someday your luck might run out."

He stepped away from me and pulled the penny I had returned to him from his pocket. The coin flipped in the air, and he caught it neatly when it fell.

"My luck is here to stay. Have a little faith. I promise no detective or bounty hunter will ever find me unless I aim for them to."

I chewed my lip, unwilling to disagree further on the first day of our honeymoon. He was so self-confident, it frightened me more than if he took threats seriously. I reminded myself I'd gotten what I wanted, and knew wherever we went, my life would not be tame again.

The next day, Jesse drove me around town. He pointed out the brick office where Alan worked, and a tiny schoolhouse made of chinked logs where Susie taught her young students.

When we reached a wooded area, he stopped the buggy and turned to me.

"How well can you shoot a gun?"

"I haven't handled a gun except for a few times when one of my brothers let me shoot their hunting rifle at a tin can."

"That's what I thought. I want you to learn how to use a pistol. It's the best way to protect yourself during times when I'm not around."

He yanked a weapon from the holster he'd secured around his hip faster than I could blink, and sun glinted off the barrel.

"This is my Colt. You can't get a better gun." He pointed it toward the trees. "Look over there. See that blackbird sitting yonder on the branch?"

I nodded and Jesse aimed the gun, pulled back the hammer, and fired. The bird dropped from the branch, dead as a stone. Then he aimed and fired again at a knot in the tree's trunk. Another pop, and the bullet hit its mark.

He handed the pistol to me.

"Now you try. Look down the barrel to aim at what you want to hit."

I held up the gun with two hands and aimed at a tree branch. When I pulled the trigger, the gun fired but the bullet missed. Jesse laughed and told me to try again. After I puffed and sweated over firing nearly a dozen shots, one rang true, and Jesse nodded.

"Good job. But remember, you'll need to practice, and don't expect to hit a target from too far away, though you don't want someone who means you harm very close either. Aim for the chest. It's the easiest target to hit."

I gave the pistol back. "Jesse, I'm not sure I could ever shoot anyone."

"Yes, you could," he told me, his eyes suddenly grim. "When it means your life or the life of someone you love, you'll find you can do just about anything."

Later that evening, we spoke over dinner of a letter Susie had received that day from Zerelda.

"Ma wrote that she's never seen anything like it," Susie said. "Grasshoppers swarming in black clouds and dropping from the sky like hailstones. They ate up everything. Crops and grass and leaves, and even the clothes hanging on the line. Hundreds of miles of ground were hit. She says there'll be nothing much left for anyone to harvest come fall."

Jesse arched a brow and looked at Alan. "I've heard of such things happening, but never witnessed it. Sounds like a plague straight out of the Bible. Ma sure doesn't need any more trouble than she's already got."

After dinner, Jesse kissed me and said not to wait up. He and Alan planned to rehash old battle strategies with their friends. Susie's two-year-old son, Robert Archie, climbed on my lap and I forgot to worry over Zerelda's letter. Susie fussed over her sweet blond baby and I remembered that she'd suffered several miscarriages before he was born. The child's round rosy cheeks and precious smile captivated me, and I wondered how soon it would be until I held a baby of my own.

Alan returned home within a few hours, but Jesse didn't come back until early the next morning, smelling of stale whiskey and cigars. I raised a brow when I discussed with Susie his late night, but she only shrugged in amusement as though we were talking about a high-spirited child. Jesse slept until dawn, then rose in a petulant humor to load the buggy with our bags. His lack of sleep from the previous night had drained him, and he looked as though he'd rather be back in bed still.

I hugged Susie and promised her we'd soon have another visit. My heart had lightened when Jesse told me we would travel together on the train to Galveston. It would be our first official trip as man and wife. I put on the dress he claimed deepened the blue of my eyes and pinned on my favorite hat, tilted forward, with silk ribbons trailing down the back. Jesse looked at me and blinked the exhaustion from his eyes. His mouth tugged a little as he offered his arm. I dropped a small curtsy and took it, like a queen.

The depot smelled of damp wood, dirt, and too many people. While Jesse purchased our tickets, I waited next to a stack of penny newspapers. With a smug look, he requested passage from the balding clerk for Mr. and Mrs. William Campbell. I stared at the papers to keep from smiling, until a headline caught my eye. A daring late-night stagecoach robbery had taken place outside Sherman. I backed away from the papers as though they were on fire and watched Jesse make small jokes with the clerk.

Tickets in hand, he led me to the train. We squeezed past a crush of other passengers, excusing ourselves as we went along.

When we found our seat, Jesse put his hand over mine. "I'm still played out. Do you mind if I sleep for a while?"

"Of course not. But Jesse," I couldn't resist asking, "when you went out... where did you go?"

"Just jawing with the boys. Went on a lot longer than I realized, and I'm sorry. You won't hold it against me, will you, sweetheart?"

I shook my head, and he sighed, leaning back and pulling his bowler hat low. I turned to the window that framed countryside pretty enough to be a painting and considered what he said. My mind had become as suspicious as a detective's. It would be folly not to trust my own husband. So, I turned my fears into anticipation over trips we would take, dreaming of adventures like those in the stories I'd read. My lips curved up when I thought about little Robert Archie and opened my fan to wave air toward my face.

Someday, children would come to us. Then we'd settle in a place of our own, as my sisters and Susie had done. He'd stop running, and we'd put down roots. I half-closed my eyes and in a prickle of nervous longing, I pictured a beautiful baby with eyes like Jesse's, lying in my arms.

19

My first sight of an endless horizon of water made me forget everything else. I tasted salt on the breeze that blew across the waves and cooled the air. Hungry seabirds pecked in the wet sand, searching for a tidbit that might have washed in with the tide. They screeched and scattered as I strolled by to pick up small pink shells while entire families dressed in bathing costumes waded into the water. I wished I could do the same.

With my arm looped through Jesse's, we walked past a marina where waves swept against fishing boats, making them rock from side to side in the water. The boats had piles of fish bigger than any string of catfish my brothers had ever caught, but the scent of decaying sea life and wet rope made me put my handkerchief to my nose. My eyes widened when I spied the most unusual creature I'd ever seen waving all eight of its arms in the sun.

Jesse laughed. "That's a young octopus. They grow up to be a lot bigger than that." He pulled me away from the strange sight. "Let's get ready for dinner. We're going to celebrate being in Galveston, so I'm taking you someplace new."

I smiled up at him. "That shouldn't be hard. Everything here is new to me."

After we changed into our dinner clothes, Jesse hailed a carriage and had the driver take us to J.H. Forbes, an oyster saloon near the harbor. We moved past tables filled with customers who shouted to each another, unlike the restaurants I knew, where the patrons spoke quietly as if in church. Jesse strutted like a rooster, and a few people waved at him. He held up a hand, acknowledging their salutation, and whispered to me that they were some of his old friends.

Our waiter, a brusque man in a white shirt with sleeves rolled to his elbow, took us to a table.

"Bring me a bottle of your finest champagne, sir, and a plate of oysters," Jesse told him.

Wide-eyed, I looked around me. The room clamored with the sounds of dishes rattling and voices that competed to be heard.

"This is unlike anything I've ever seen before," I said. "And now oysters and champagne too? I've never tasted either one."

He laughed and ran a finger down my cheek. "Then its time you do."

We'd been in our seat for only a few moments when two men sitting at a table near us began to snarl at each other. Their voices boomed louder and louder, until both men leapt to their feet, raising fists as though ready to fight. I stared with my heart in my throat, but Jesse watched mildly, his hand resting against his hip where I knew he carried a pistol.

Within moments, a man with arms like a blacksmith came to their table and roared at them.

"You men can either shut up or get out."

The combatants glowered, but then recovered themselves and sat down to swill more of the foamy beer.

"What was that about?" I asked Jesse when I caught my breath.

"Probably too much drink. If it were any real problem, they wouldn't have talked, just started punching … or worse."

"I've never seen such behavior in public, or anywhere else for that matter."

"That's mild compared to what's happened here before. Men have drawn knives or even guns when tempers grow hot enough. That's what I like about this place. You never know what might happen."

I scooted to the edge of my chair, wondering if I might need to jump up and run. Jesse put his hand over mine and squeezed.

"Stop worrying. I'll make sure you stay safe." He poured another glass of champagne. Sipping the bubbly liquid soon helped me relax enough to ignore my surroundings and grow giddy as a young colt.

When the plate of oysters arrived, I stared at it dubiously.

"Tip the shell to your mouth," he said, "and let the oyster slide in. A bite or two, then swallow. Here, I'll show you."

I watched him first and then picked up a shell and bravely put it to my lips. I grimaced at the taste, gritty and salty as sand and sea. The second one went down easier. By the third oyster, I'd either grown to like the flavor or the champagne had convinced me the slippery seafood had turned to ambrosia. I ate until my stomach grew tight with food. Then Jesse paid the bill, leaving a tip that made me suck in my breath.

By the time the buggy got us back to our room, my legs were so wobbly, Jesse had to carry me to our bed.

Much later, after he had fallen asleep, I sat up and wrapped my arms around my knees, wishing we could go on this way forever. But I'd noticed Jesse scanning the newspapers with brows knitted as though searching for something. A week later, he confirmed what I feared.

"It's time we leave for home."

"And where would home be?"

"For now, we'll go to Kansas City."

I pushed back my hair and regarded him with a wistful smile. "I wish we didn't have to leave Galveston."

He put his arm around my waist and squeezed. "We'll come again someday. There're a lot of other places you'll like just as much. But Ma's been on my mind. I need to figure out what I can do for her. From the sound of her letter, she could use some help taking care of the farm."

"Will we be able to take the cars together?"

"Not when we're traveling to Kansas City. I'll make arrangements for someone to meet you at the station and get there soon as I can."

We didn't speak much on the way to the depot. He handed my bag to the porter and kissed me. "Good-bye, sweetheart," he whispered. "I'll see you very soon."

I settled into my seat and leaned back. My eyes closed and I fell into a deep sleep, dreaming that Jesse bought us a small cottage in Galveston that stood so near the sea, we could watch the waves flow to the shore. He took out a fishing boat to search for treasure buried under the water, while I cooked a fat mackerel for dinner.

When the train reached Kansas City, the whistle blew and I rubbed the sleep from my eyes and stretched. I'd been dreaming for hours.

The depot held its usual crowd of travelers. After

stepping to the platform, I searched for a familiar face among them, realizing I had no idea who Jesse planned to send. When I saw a tall man with a long beard, I laughed in delight before I could speak a word. "It's been too long. How I wish you could have been with us at our wedding."

Frank picked up my bag and grinned, leading me away from the crush of people. "I'm sorry to have missed your nuptials, but it just so happens that while you were gone, I had a wedding of my own."

I stopped walking and my mouth dropped open like one of the fish I'd seen in Galveston. "What did you say?"

"I married a young lady by the name of Miss Annie Ralston."

My hand flew to my chest. "I heard you were courting, but nothing of an engagement."

"We had to keep it a secret from everyone. Her father doesn't approve of me, so when he put his foot down, she packed and left home. We met up in Omaha and got married there on June sixth."

"Well … congratulations. Does Jesse know?"

"Not yet, but he will soon enough. I expect him to arrive within days."

I absorbed this new information. "When will I meet your wife?"

"Very soon. But for the time being, we have other business to take care of. Jesse asked me to take you to the rooms he rented until he can figure out the best place for you to go. He says I'm to remind you about never using your real name. You two will be John and Josie Howard, so it's important you remember that."

I said the new names out loud, tasting them on my tongue until the words were natural rather than forced. But even such an odd exercise could not take away my joy at the possibility of seeing my brothers and sisters who lived near Kansas City. I had no idea how long it would take for Jesse to return and feared the specter of loneliness. I knew such a state of mind brought the risk of a blue spell and fiddled with a button on my dress.

Frank drove us to a wood-clad house with a "For Rent" sign in front, not far from the depot, and settled me inside before kissing my cheek and leaving. I looked at the sparsely furnished rooms and pushed up my sleeves to set about making it into a home, albeit a temporary one.

By the next afternoon, I'd been to the mercantile for supplies, and not a single speck of dust could be found in the house. Even the gray film on the windows had been scrubbed away. The only thing left to do was to wash the floors, so I dropped to my knees and dipped a rag into the bucket of water. I'd finished half the floor, when the front door opened. Pausing, I waited with my heart pounding, until Jesse called out to me. I threw down the rag and ran to my husband, wrapping my damp arms around his travel-dusty neck. We kissed as though we'd been separated for months rather than days.

When we drew apart, he looked at me and grinned.

"You get prettier every time I see you."

I tucked the hair wisping from its pins and wished my dress wasn't wet with perspiration and dirty mop water.

"I've been cleaning and must look a fright, but thank you for being gallant enough not to mention it. Can I fix you something to eat?"

"Not just yet. I went to the farm first to take care of some things for Ma, then came straight to you. Frank and I have a meeting today. We're planning a new business venture. I shouldn't be away long, but when I get back, you can be sure I'll be hungry enough to eat a horse."

I nodded and tried not to let my disappointment show. At least the pantry was well stocked, so I could easily impress him with my cooking prowess. I thumped an iron skillet on the table and hoped there would be time to make myself fresh as a new bride before he returned. I intended to make the first meal in our new little house one he would remember.

20

Over the next few weeks, Jesse spent most of his days and nights with me. Our relationship deepened in ways I hadn't dreamed possible. He brought home flowers for no reason, and I happily seduced him with his favorite foods. Not even the bothersome requirement of assumed names could dim my pleasure at being Jesse's wife.

August arrived, thick with heat and humidity. I sweltered near the fire in the kitchen, when Jesse came in and announced that he and Frank planned to leave to investigate some opportunities for investment.

"We both have families now and must support our wives in the manner they deserve," he said.

I wiped my sleeve over my forehead. "Where are you going?"

"There are several places we mean to check out, but you shouldn't worry. I'll be back soon. Go stay with your sister if it makes you feel easier, but I don't foresee any trouble. Just in case, I've cleaned and loaded one of my old pistols to ease your mind. It's in the bedroom. Use it if you have to."

"Why can't I go? It's been so wonderful being here together."

His lips pursed before he shook his head. "I can't take a wife along with me when my mind has to be focused on business." He put a finger under my chin and gently tipped it up it. "I promise not to be gone long. A bee doesn't stay away from a flower, does he? No, because he needs its nectar to live."

Jesse pulled me close, and my breath left with a gasp. He rubbed his hand up and down my back and nuzzled my hair.

"Just remember you're Josie Howard and I'm John Davis Howard, although in case you wonder, Frank has taken to calling me Dave." Jesse pulled back and the ghost of a smile played at his mouth. "He thinks it's a better fit than the name of an apostle."

His fingers laced through mine. "Visit with your sisters and brothers as much as you want but keep away from those you don't know. If anyone outside our kin asks about me, just say I'm away on business, looking to buy a farm."

Jesse leaned down to kiss me good-bye, and his eyes gleamed with excitement. He loved to flit from one place to another, and I wanted to share that part of his life. My stomach dropped, and I buried my head against his chest, though I willed myself not to cry. His last image of me tshouldn't be one of puffy eyes and a runny nose. Jesse was the first to pull away, flashing a grin so mischievous, it made me smile back in spite of myself.

"Jess, don't take any foolish chances, please."

"Always. And you'll be glad to know Frank says he'll bring Annie here after we get back. She can hardly wait to meet you."

I tilted my head. "Is she in Kansas City, too?"

"No. Her father has money enough to hire people to look for her. He's not the least bit happy she married the notorious Frank James."

Sympathy for my new sister-in-law flooded through me. My own mother had cut me from her life when I married Jesse and it pained me to realize we might never reconcile our differences. But at least my brothers and sisters had not abandoned me. Annie had no one but Frank.

"I think she and I will have much to talk about."

He arched a brow. "Don't all women like to gab? By the way, Frank uses the name Ben Woodson now. He changed Annie's name to Fannie, so don't let yourself slip when others are around."

While I waited for Jesse to return, I couldn't stop wondering about what he and Frank were up to. I hoped their new venture would finally put them on the right side of the law, although I certainly didn't want him to include the likes of the Younger brothers or Clell Miller, men from the Bushwhacker days, in any of his business affairs.

I kept myself busy as I'd always done, filled with pleasure at being mistress of my own home and able to decorate it just as I wanted. I arranged a bouquet of Black-eyed Susans I found growing near the road on a quaint table in the parlor. A colorful quilt from Zerelda fit perfectly folded over our bed. I measured the windows and walked to the mercantile to buy red-checked cotton fabric to sew curtains for the kitchen. When Jesse returned, he'd find a little house transformed into our own special home.

In the meantime, my family came to visit in dribs and drabs. Lucy proudly showed off her new baby girl. I cuddled the infant, studied her perfect features, and cooed every time she gurgled or moved a finger.

Lucy watched me with concern written on her face. "Some detectives came to our house a few days ago asking questions about Jesse and Frank. I'm worried for you, Zee. Are you certain he can keep you both from harm?"

"If anyone can do it, Jesse can. I trust him with my life and know he'll take good care of me." I couldn't keep the wisp of a shadow from my voice. "I only hope he takes equal care of himself."

"I've spent so much time praying marriage would be an anchor for Jesse. Do you think he'll ever abandon his wandering life and stay home with you for good?"

My fingers picked at small pieces of lint on the baby's blanket. "Truthfully, I'm not sure. Though his wandering wouldn't bother me so much if we could go together. Perhaps he needs convincing that I'd be helpful when he travels."

"Zee, don't go with him unless he gives up defying the law. It would be too dangerous."

"Or the best thing that ever happened. I've yet to see him do anything illegal when he's with me."

Lucy's eyes did not meet mine, so I hurried to change the subject. "In any event, we've talked about moving someday, maybe to Texas, near Susie and Alan. The trouble is both he and Frank worry about Zerelda. She has so much on her hands with the children and the farm. And Reuben's condition isn't getting any better."

Zerelda's husband had continued his slow but steady decline, and I realized this small sorrow provided another reason Jesse would be reluctant to leave Missouri for any length of time.

After Lucy left, her concerns magnified mine. I found myself looking out the window more frequently, twisting a towel between my hands at every sound. I'd had no word from Jesse except a scrawled note delivered by a nameless rider. The note said he planned to return near the end of September, and I comforted myself that at least he was alive. Then I remembered with a start how similar my thoughts were to those from before we were wed. Like Lucy, I had hoped marriage would settle him.

For the time being, I had no choice but to live my life normally as possible. It wasn't easy. The first time I played the role of Josie Howard, my cheeks sizzled with embarrassment. But soon the deception became second nature. One afternoon, I walked to the mercantile to restock the pantry, and noticed a small poster tacked on the wall. It offered a reward for information leading to the arrest of Jesse or Frank James. My stomach lurched, and I swallowed before going inside to see Mr. Arnell, the shop clerk.

"Good morning, Mrs. Howard, what can I do for you today?"

I handed him my list and watched as he measured out sugar, flour, and coffee to my satisfaction. A newspaper on the counter caught my eye, declaring the James gang had struck again. My hand shook when I paid Mr. Arnell and he put the change in my palm.

"And when will Mr. Howard be back?"

"Oh, I think within a short time," I answered, and hoped my words were true.

I stepped outside, pulled my straw hat down to shade my eyes, and hurried home in the warm September sun. With arms too full to do anything about it, the hem of my blue flowered dress dragged through the dust. Oh, well, laundry was the least of my worries.

Birds chirped merrily as I rounded the corner to see a buggy in front of the house. I stopped short, and wondered whether to go home or turn and walk away, when I noticed someone on the porch. A familiar figure leaned against the post with his arms crossed. Jesse! I kept my eyes fixed on him and hurtled down the road like a comet.

The packages tumbled onto the porch when he pulled me into his arms and pressed his lips to mine. My body tightened, helpless with relief and then desire, during the lingering kiss. Someone cleared his throat and I reluctantly pulled away to see Frank on the porch swing with his arm around a beautiful blue-eyed woman who had the palest yellow hair I'd ever seen.

Jesse bowed with a flourish. "Josie, I'd like you to meet Ben's new wife, Fannie Woodson."

She rose and extended her hand. "I'm so pleased to meet you, Josie. Ben and Dave"—her eyes twinkled when she used the assumed names—"described you so well, I would have recognized you anywhere."

Annie—or Fannie, as I reminded myself—stood only a bit taller than me, but in her deep blue traveling dress with a lovely veiled hat perched high on her head, I looked dowdy. I smoothed my well-worn calico and blushed at the dirty hem before I lifted my chin to smile at her. "I can see Ben made a good match. I'm very happy to welcome you into our family."

Impulsively, I embraced her, and she responded in kind. In that instant, I knew we would become fast friends as well as kin. How could we not? After all, we were both married to men hunted by countless others.

A neighbor walked near the house and stopped to stare. Jesse waved and then bent to retrieve the packages scattered on the porch. He took my arm and led me into the privacy of our home.

"Black-eyed Susans! They're my favorite flower." Annie touched the blossoms.

"I love them too. Their color always cheers me." I carried the supplies into the kitchen before taking a seat next to Jesse. He slipped an arm across my shoulders.

"We made some pretty good trades on this trip, sweetheart, and found a few lucrative deals. If things keep going the way they are, we won't need to rent a house much longer. I'll build you a fine new place that looks the way you want it to."

"I'm just relieved you're back home." My words rushed out before I could stop them. "I admit my nerves have been stretched. Just this morning, I saw a bounty poster at the mercantile asking for information on you and Frank."

"You know we only do what any Southern man worth his salt would. And it's not just us. Haven't you been reading the newspapers? We're among a group of men considered the last Southern heroes, still striking blows against Federal-held businesses to avenge the Confederacy. You should be proud, not afraid."

"I haven't picked up a newspaper since our honeymoon, and I'm not sure I want to. Anything can happen when you keep putting yourself in harm's way."

"I know how to get around in the dark and stay out of trouble. I'm like a coyote hunting at night. I like it best when the sky's black as ink and no one can see me watch them."

I stared at Jesse. Did he really believe he could become invisible to the rest of the world? Did Frank? I glanced at Annie whose brows had scrunched together. Did I sound disloyal? Was I stirring up her fears?

I stood abruptly. "After your travel, you must be parched. Wait here and let me bring you some cool water to quench your thirst."

Later, with Annie's help, I prepared dinner and we spent the evening cautiously avoiding mention of any topics except casual ones. I discovered Annie had planned to become a schoolteacher before she ran away to marry Frank. I wasn't surprised. She had a sweet, genuine personality that I instantly warmed to and knew she would make a natural teacher. I swallowed my disappointment when Frank said he had rented a house two miles away, deeming it unwise to be any closer to Jesse. It would have been nice to have Annie close enough so we could visit each day.

After they climbed back into the carriage and drove away, I thought of Susie in Texas and imagined living a normal life far from Missouri. If Jesse and I left, perhaps Frank and Annie would follow. We could be neighbors and raise our families together. If I laid my plans as carefully as William Quantrill had laid his, neither Annie or I would have to live in fear of an arrest or lynching.

Spirit soaring with the possibilities, I turned down the light in the front room and joined Jesse in bed.

21

I looked out the front window and wondered if Jesse would be home in time to eat the biscuits while they were still steaming. The days were getting shorter and the overcast November chill was a stark reminder of winter's approaching gloom. But the last few weeks had been happy ones. Jesse and Frank had stayed close to home and made no mention of travel. Could it mean they were tiring of their endless quest to punish the Union?

I turned back to the kitchen and a strong whiff of browning biscuits reached my nose. The smell made the room twirl and I held a hand over my mouth. I sank to the floor and gulped in deep breaths to keep from being sick. When I tried to get up, my legs were as unsteady as if I'd been spinning in a circle.

Unable to walk, I went to my knees and crawled to the bedroom. Struggling to keep my eyes open, I pulled myself into bed. My body burned with heat and my stomach churned. Influenza, I thought. I've got influenza! I remembered taking soup to the neighbors just last week after their diagnosis. The scent of dark smoke drifted into our room, adding to my stomach's rebellion. The smell made me turn my head into the pillow and long for the clean air of outdoors. Yet I couldn't rise to do anything about the burning biscuits.

The front door banged open, and I heard Jesse shout my name before the Dutch oven thudded onto the table. With no strength to call out, I waited for him. It didn't take long.

He appeared beside me like an apparition. "What happened, Zee?"

"I burned the biscuits. I'm sorry," I whispered.

"To hell with the biscuits. What's wrong?"

"I feel sick and dizzy whenever I try to get up."

He put a calloused palm on my forehead. "I'm going to open up the windows to get this smoke out. Then I'll find a doctor."

He tucked a quilt around me before he left. I fell into an uneasy sleep. When someone touched my shoulder, I jerked back into wakefulness.

"Josie, I've brought Dr. Schuster to see you."

Jesse stood next to a short stout man with a balding head and handlebar moustache.

"Hello, Mrs. Howard. Your husband tells me you're not feeling well. I'll need to examine you to find out why. Mr. Howard, could you give us privacy, sir?"

Jesse glanced at me then jammed his hands in his pockets and walked from the room. Dr. Schuster listened to my chest, looked in my mouth, and checked my body for fever. Finally, he straightened and crossed his arms. From the appraising look on his face, I feared the most dreadful news.

"Mrs. Howard, pardon me for being so frank, but when was the last time you had your monthly sickness?"

My eyes widened as I tried to calculate the weeks. "I'm not sure, but I think it's been a while."

He patted my hand. "Just as I thought. You don't have influenza. You're with child. I recommend you give yourself plenty of time to rest and keep your mind calm. You must eat properly even when you don't want to, or the babe will not flourish. I'll have a talk with your husband."

He smiled, picked up his bag, and left me. I was too stunned to say anything. A baby? Elation struggled with surprise as I fought back another wave of nausea. My mother had borne many children, and I didn't recall her ever speaking of feeling ill. Nor did any of my aunts or sisters mention such difficulties. I wondered how any doctor thought it possible to eat when one's stomach felt the way mine did. Yet I wanted to do as he told me, for I knew the risks of having a baby.

Three women of my acquaintance had died of infection and one of convulsions while expecting a child. While I prayed to avoid such dire circumstances, another worry lurked within my mind and I strained with all my might to hear anything that would tell me Jesse's reaction to what the doctor said.

But I heard nothing until the front door closed. A moment later, Jesse bounded to my bedside, his face beaming. He reached for my hand.

"We're going to have a baby! Imagine that. A child made up from the best of both of us."

I returned his smile.

"You're pleased? I was afraid such news might upset you."

"Of course, I'm pleased. I'd love to have a house filled with children."

"I'd like that, too. I'm sure I'll soon feel better. At least I hope so."

"Sweetheart, the doctor wants you to rest. Frank and I have been talking about a trip. Looks like now it's more important than ever for me to do what I need to do so I can provide the best things for you and our baby."

"But, Jesse—"

"Don't upset yourself, Zee. I'll have Lucy come stay with you while I'm gone."

In my weakened state, I could barely speak, let alone try to dissuade him from leaving me at a time when I needed him. Within a few days, he was gone.

Lucy arrived the morning after Jesse left. She clucked over me when I had trouble keeping down more than a mouthful of bread or a swallow of water and held my hair away from my face when it all came back up. Despite how truly awful I felt, her presence distracted me with talk about a woman's joy in having a child. I needed the reminder.

When the time came for Lucy to go home, my sister Nancy came, but she told me so many heart-rending stories of mothers buried with their babies that I wanted to clap my hands over my ears. I sagged with relief when Jesse came home, and Nancy said good-bye. Jesse's eyes twinkled when he steered her to the door.

He returned and sat on our bed. "The trip was a success. Frank and I made enough money to tide us over for quite a while."

My feeble state kept me from asking how he'd made the money, and then I realized the answer might not be one I wanted to hear, anyway. I clung to the notion that at least if he'd found success, he'd stay closer to home, and I'd have time to convince him not to leave again.

Jesse settled in the chair by my bed and pulled something from his pocket. "This is for you, Zee, for being the mother of my first child."

It was a lovely black onyx brooch with a woman's profile carved in white shell. I ran my fingers over it. The carving was so delicate, I could barely feel the artist's marks.

"How beautiful. Thank you."

"I bought a new horse for myself. Another long-legged bay, a real beauty. The man who bred her said she's the fastest horse in the state. This spring, I'll set her up in a race or two and see how many she can win. Yes, I do believe this is going to be a time we'll long remember."

Yet as the weeks passed, my strength did not return. Despite my happiness at the thought of a baby and Jesse's obvious pleasure over the idea of fatherhood, I couldn't leave my bed. Even by January, I still lay weak and listless. Jesse hired a girl to stay with me, as he and Frank had begun to go out in the evenings. When I questioned him over what they were doing, he paced the room.

"It's nothing, Zee. Nothing to worry about. More of our old friends have moved here, and we like to talk over old times, that's all."

I heard him and Frank speak of Cole and Bob Younger, Clell Miller, and Bob Stiles. My heart twisted. Nothing good would come of such associations. I wanted Jesse to stay away from them, but he made light of my fears, bringing on another wave of nausea. Even a sip of water made me feel ill.

Fear puckered his brow, when Jesse announced he would send me to his mother's farm. "Reuben's a doctor, even if he's slower than he used to be, and Ma knows everything about having babies. If they can't help you, I don't know who can."

I nodded miserably and drew a breath to speak. "I've been trying to focus on the time when my confinement is over. Perhaps we could take the baby and go back to Galveston. Ever since you showed me the ocean, I haven't been able to forget it. Living near such beauty might be a source of happiness for us."

Jesse shrugged noncommittally. "Zee, you know very well the Radicals and Northerners have made it impossible for me to make a living in any normal way. Everyone's out to get Jesse James. I don't plan to dangle from a rope or go to jail either. I want more for us. Maybe one day we can get together enough money to have our own farm or raise the best horses around. But a plan like that won't be easy. We've got a baby coming, and now isn't the time." He pulled out my valise. "I'm sending you to Kearney until you get well." His lips pressed together in a tight line that brooked no further discussion, even if I'd been strong enough to consider it.

Jesse shoved my clothes into the valise and helped me dress. He drove me to the train depot and held my arm solicitously as I went up the steps leading to the train.

Then he kissed my cheek and whispered to me. "Along with your clothes, I packed money and a pistol, just in case. I hope you don't find all your pretties in too much of a muddle."

I nodded. "Thank you."

To keep from tripping, I gathered up the skirt of a new yellow dress he'd bought me. I'd become so thin that none of my other clothes fit properly. I had no need for the flowing garments to accommodate the usual state of a woman with child. To calm my increasing dread, I tried to narrow my focus on Dr. Schuster's advice and calm the fears swirling through my mind.

When the train arrived in Kearney, a porter took my elbow and helped me to the depot platform. Reuben waited on a bench, with a rolled-up newspaper on his lap. When he saw me, his eyes widened in alarm. He picked up my bag and put a comforting arm around my waist. "Come along now, my dear. Let me take you home to Zerelda."

22

"We'll need to get some meat on your bones," Reuben said as we pulled up to the front door of the farm house. Zerelda will soon have you feeling better." I shivered as he lifted me from the wagon. "You weigh practically nothing, but Zerelda's cooking will fix you up."

I nodded vacantly and looked up at the gray clouds looming on the horizon. My breath puffed out in wisps of vapor. *Snow clouds.* With luck, it wouldn't be a bad storm. Reuben led me up the porch and into the house, yelling so Zerelda would know we'd arrived. He helped me to a chair and then left to see to the horse and wagon.

Zerelda appeared in the parlor doorway, hands on her hips. She clucked her tongue at me. "Come, Zee. Change into your nightclothes and get into bed. I'll bring you something that will help you feel better."

Too tired to reply, I did as Zerelda bade. By the time I'd settled under the covers, she brought me a cup of ginger tea served along with advice as only she could give it. "You'd better put aside all this nervousness and worry. I've seen women who make themselves so distraught they lose their baby."

Those weren't the words I wanted to hear. My eyes filled with tears, and she placed a cool hand on my arm.

"You must stay in bed and do as I say. Every few hours, I will bring you ginger tea and dry bread. If any notion that makes you uneasy enters your mind, open the Bible and read." She pointed to the book on a table near me. "I've marked Psalms for you. Psalms are good to quiet your thoughts."

I nodded and sipped the tea, its peppery taste warming me.

At first, after eating or drinking, I breathed in gulping breaths, to keep from being sick. But with rest and a few days of Zerelda's strict regimen, my strength and appetite began to return. I was able to keep down a bit of meat and potatoes, along with applesauce and corn that Zerelda had preserved for the winter. Soon Reuben had me leaving the bed for short walks, and for the first time in a long time, I began to feel like myself again.

Being in a lively household with Zerelda, Reuben, and their family cheered me. It reminded me of similar days from years ago, in the home where I grew up with brothers and sisters who fussed and laughed and chattered with me. I wished Mama had replied to the letter I'd sent to her soon after discovering I would have a baby, but this was no time to brood. Thankfully, Jesse's young half-siblings provided the perfect distraction.

I teased thirteen-year-old John and listened to ten-year-old Fannie gabble incessantly about her desire to become a nurse. Archie, at the age of eight, was still young enough to climb into my lap and tell me how he would capture a tadpole in spring so he could watch it grow legs and turn into a frog. The child's solemn expression kept me from smiling at his plan.

Even the Samuel house servants made me think of my youth. Charlotte's efficient ways brought memories of Mama's competent skills. Charlotte and Ambrose had been with the Samuels all their lives, choosing to stay even after Lincoln freed them. Charlotte's son, Perry, who had skin the color of cream in coffee, was two years younger than Archie. He and Archie played together as though they were the best of friends.

As my health and spirits improved, I took to my old habit of staring at the stars for a while each evening. My pensiveness must have prompted Zerelda to surprise me with a dinner she planned for late in January. She said both Jesse and Frank would attend and her eyes sparkled at my reaction.

When the day arrived, I took special pains to help Zerelda and Charlotte prepare a meal of venison, potatoes, and biscuits. After one look in the mirror, I shyly requested the luxury of a bath. Despite the cold weather, Zerelda asked Charlotte to heat water for me. Afterward, I put on my new dress and happily discovered I couldn't cinch my belt around the garment. I let the dress fall loose and gloried in the undeniable evidence that our baby thrived. Sitting in front of the hearth fire, I hummed and ruffled the damp strings of my hair while I talked to Archie.

Earlier that evening, Reuben drove John and Fannie to a party at a neighbor's farm. Although they could scarcely contain their excitement, Archie, who hadn't been invited, moped about with a long face. I tried to distract him with a story, yet half my attention strained for the sound of horse hooves.

Shortly after darkness fell, the front door flew open. Jesse and Frank sauntered in, followed by two of their old comrades, Clell Miller and Bill Fox. Zerelda raised her brows at the unexpected additions to her dinner table and their presence set my teeth on edge, yet I tried not to be frosty when Jesse leaned in for a kiss.

He took my hands and held them wide apart, staring at my belly. "You're blooming like a flower in spring."

With a broad smile, Zerelda nodded. "We've been keeping a close eye on her." She raked a dark glance across the faces in the room. "Well, everyone come sit while the food is hot."

I didn't recall the taste of anything I put in my mouth that evening. His presence reduced everything and everyone else to nothing more than buzzing gnats. He brushed his foot against mine under the table and grinned at me in a way that made my pulse race.

"Will you be ready for spring planting?" asked Frank.

"I think so," Zerelda said, though some are warning about the possibility of locust hatchlings coming out of the ground. In all my years, I never saw such a sight as what came to us last summer. I hope to God I never see such a thing again."

Jesse's attention turned to his mother. "I checked the field. It seems much better than a few months ago."

Zerelda buttered a piece of biscuit with vehemence. "Whatever happens won't keep us down, of that I'm sure."

The subject changed to merrier topics, and not even the presence of morose little Clell or tight-lipped Bill could take away my smile.

After dinner, Zerelda shooed me away from the kitchen. I pulled a shawl over my shoulders and walked outside into the cold evening for a private moment with Jesse. Stars twinkled from a sky black as ink, and moonlight sparkled on a thin blanket of snow that covered the ground. We sat on the top step and cold seeped through my skirt.

"I feel so much better now." I leaned against him. "I want to go back home with you."

"I knew Ma would soon have you on your feet." His smile disappeared. "I'm sorry, but I can't take you home just yet. We've got a meeting tonight at the old cabin on the other side of the woods, but I promise to buy your train fare within the week. It's time for us to be together again, Zee. I've missed you."

He pulled me tight against him, and I sighed. Jesse had spoken about the tiny cabin he used when his comrades were in the area. It was a few miles from Zerelda's farm, near a large pond. The men used it to avoid detectives or other lawmen who often rode past to spy on the farm.

"If you finish your meeting early enough, will you come back tonight?"

"No, it isn't safe. Too many eyes are watching. But we'll see each other again very soon."

I pressed myself into the warmth of his body until Frank, trailed by Clell and Bill, came outside.

"It's time we go, Dingus. We've been here too long."

Reluctantly, he pulled away from me and stood, grabbing my hands to help me to my feet.

"Good night. I'll see you soon, sweetheart."

He kissed me and touched my cheek before heading for the woods where they'd hidden their horses. The moon, although at three quarters, shone so brilliantly, I could see their shadows as they walked away. My lips moved in a silent prayer for them.

After they disappeared into the darkness, I shivered and went inside where Zerelda and Charlotte were clearing the table. Reuben put on his jacket to fetch John and Fannie home from their party. By the time the last plate had been stacked in the cupboard, the children came running through the front door.

Fannie went to where her young brother stood beside his mother.

"Look here, Archie, we brought you some peppermint candy."

The child's eyes rounded. He took the small gift and popped the confection into his mouth with a smile.

"No more of that now, young man," Zerelda commanded. "It's been a long day, and we all need to get to bed."

Charlotte, Ambrose, and Perry went to the pallets they used at night in the kitchen, shutting and bolting the door as was their custom. The rest of us went to the sleeping room we shared. John and Archie slept in a bed next to mine. I pulled a quilt up to Archie's chin and kissed him good night, then fell fast asleep as soon as my head touched the pillow.

A powerful crash shook the house. My eyes flew open.

Reuben leaped out of bed and shouted. "Get up! Get out of the house!"

I smelled smoke and saw curls of it drifting under the kitchen door. Reuben tried to open it, but the door wouldn't budge. He ran through the parlor to get outside. The rest of us followed in our night clothes and stocking feet. I grabbed a blanket and pulled Archie along with me.

On the side of the house, flames licked at the clapboards of the kitchen. Ambrose, Charlotte, and Perry stood there, the back door from the kitchen standing wide open.

Reuben shouted, "Tear off the boards!"

He and Ambrose worked frantically, prying boards from the structure, while Charlotte and Perry shivered. Over the sounds of splitting wood, I thought I heard gunfire coming from the woods, but smoke that billowed from the open kitchen door diverted my attention. Zerelda headed straight for it.

"Stay here," I told the children, and threw the blanket to Charlotte.

I followed Zerelda into the smoke, coughing as it burned my lungs. A light flickered from the center of the room where a small metal sphere lay, engulfed in flames. Despite my warning, the children followed us into the kitchen, their faces pale and mouths trembling. Reuben, Ambrose, and Charlotte chased after them, and we all stared at the strange object.

Archie pointed to it and spoke aloud what we all wondered.

"What is that, Papa?"

Reuben grabbed a tobacco stick, and used it to push the orb off the floor and into the fireplace. A moment of relief—and then the fireplace exploded.

An ear-ringing roar sent small pieces of hot metal flying in every direction. Reuben was struck. Another piece hit Ambrose. Zerelda screamed when a hunk of metal smashed through her right arm. Another burning fragment struck Archie below his waist. The child doubled over and fell. I gasped at a scene that seemed straight from the bowels of hell.

Rueben and Ambrose stamped out the flames before carrying Archie outside. I went to Zerelda, who groaned, blood pouring from her arm. The men rushed back in, and between the three of us we carried her from the kitchen to her bed.

She moaned. "Where's my child? Where's Archie?"

"I'm going to him now," Reuben told her.

A moment later, I heard Reuben howl into the night sky for help. I tied a rag around Zerelda's mangled arm, and Charlotte brought water to bathe away the blood.

Zerelda's eyes burned with pain and fear. "Zee, find out how my baby fares."

I nodded and left Charlotte—her dark eyes filled with sorrow—to care for Zerelda. In the yard, Ambrose had placed a kerosene lamp next to Reuben, who leaned over Archie's still form, ministering to his wound.

Neighbors had begun to appear with unbuttoned jackets thrown over nightclothes in their haste to arrive.

"What happened? I heard a terrible explosion," Dan Askew, the nearest neighbor, called.

Reuben's fingers were dark with blood. "Someone go for help," he cried out. "We need doctors right away. There are terrible injuries here."

I started to walk toward Archie, but Ambrose took my arm and pulled me away. A small stream of blood trickled down the side of his face.

"Miz Zerelda's arm is 'most tore off, and that poor little child took a hit to the gut. He ain't long for this earth. While tearing off those boards, we heard them cowards in the woods hollerin' and shootin' guns. Somebody came here and threw that fireball into the house on purpose." Ambrose wiped his face with his sleeve. "They meant to kill us in our sleep. Lord knows what they might try next. Somebody's got to get word to the boys."

My hand covered my mouth. More people arrived, running this way and that between Archie lying outside and then into the house. Three horses were tethered near the barn.

I nodded to Ambrose and slipped in the house to put on shoes, stuffing the pistol Jesse sent and an extra dress in a bag. I covered my sleeping gown with a wrap and slipped outside.

In the chaotic scene, no one noticed when I went to one of the horses and forked my legs over the saddle, just like a man. I dug my heels into its flanks and pointed the animal's head toward the cabin where I'd find Jesse, keeping my face so low over the horse's neck that his coarse mane whipped against my skin.

For the first time, I truly understood my husband's feelings. Anger and hate burned in my blood, too.

23

*B*ranches lashed at my face as I urged the horse forward through woods thick with branches and underbrush. I pulled the reins this way and that, trying to remember where the cabin stood. Finally, completely disoriented, I reined in and peered into the darkness. *Where is the cabin? Which way do I go?* When something rustled in the woods behind me, I reached for the pistol and turned my steed.

A man on horseback emerged into a patch of moonlight. His clothes were dark, his hat was pulled low, and the only thing I could really make out was the glint of the weapon pointed at me.

"What brings you this way, little lady?"

My fingers tightened on the pistol's grip. I said nothing.

"Seems there's quite a commotion going on at the James' place. I watched you ride out, so I know your husband's around here somewhere. On your way to fetch him, aren't you?"

"No," I spat the word.

"Come now. We both know better than that, Mrs. James. How 'bout you take me to Jesse? I've a mind to collect that reward money. Gonna enjoy seein' that southern piece of scum dangle. But I'm in no hurry. Got plenty of time for a bit of fun with his wife. It'd be an extra reward. A bonus I didn't count on." He smiled, lowered his gun slightly, and spurred his horse toward me.

The idea of the man's hands on my flesh made me want to retch. I lifted the gun and fired it straight into his chest. The man's eyes went wide as he slid from the saddle, hitting the ground with a thud. His animal snorted and bolted into the brush. I stared down at the unmoving form until my entire body began to shake. My teeth chattered, and my heart thudded in my throat. I turned the horse around, bent over it's neck, and sped away from what I'd just done.

"Jesse! Jesse! It's me!" I called into the night, trying to make sure I wouldn't be shot by one of his men. I finally found the clearing and saw Jesse and Frank crouched on the porch, weapons drawn. Two rifle barrels poked from openings in the cabin's walls.

I heard Jesse and Frank swear, and they holstered their guns. Jesse reached me first, pulling me from the horse, cursing softly under his breath. My hands were so stiff, Frank had to pry them from the reins. Jesse carried me inside to a chair by the hearth where a low fire blazed. Frank grabbed a blanket and threw it over my shoulders while Clell brought hot coffee.

My teeth chattered against the cup as Jesse murmured. "Just a small sip. Don't try to talk yet."

I pushed the cup away. "Someone came to the farm while we were asleep. They set fire to the kitchen and threw some sort of metal fireball inside. Reuben pushed it into the fireplace, and the whole thing exploded."

Jesse looked at Frank, their faces hard. When Jesse spoke, his voice made me shiver again.

"Was anyone hurt?"

"Reuben and Ambrose are wounded, burned. But they'll survive." I swallowed hard and stared into the lethal blue of Jesse's eyes. "Your mother's arm is torn up but … Archie …"

Jesse surged to his feet. An expression, unlike anything I'd ever seen before, sliced like a razor toward the others. "Get your weapons. We're riding to the farm now."

Clell grabbed his arm. "It's a trap. They'll be waiting to gun us down no sooner than we get there."

Frank's face was pale as death, and a vein throbbed in his neck. "Wait. Let's find out who did this first. Then I swear, we'll make them pay."

Jesse's lips were rimmed with white when I reached for his clenched fist. "Most of the close neighbors had come to help by the time I left. I'm sure if he's not there already, the sheriff will arrive soon."

My voice faltered as the image of Archie's colorless face and the bloody hole torn into his belly flashed into my mind.

"Drink," Jesse said, pointing to the cup. "It'll help." He squeezed my shoulder before leaving me to join the other men. They stood at a small table in the cabin's kitchen, methodically checking their weapons. The sound of sharp clicks mixed with whispers kept me silent, still trying to make sense of what had happened.

Finally, Jesse came back and hunkered down at my side.

"You've been through too much tonight. I want you to sleep here. Bill will stay with you, and then he'll see you back to the farm tomorrow. Ma's going to need you. I'll have some of the boys keep watch over the house. Once we know who's responsible for this, we'll make our plans."

My chin snapped up.

"Jesse, I took someone's horse to get here. I don't even know who it belongs to. And that's not all." My eyes closed while I drew in a breath. "A man tried to stop me in the woods. He knew who I was and wanted me to take him to you so he could collect the reward." I stared into Jesse's face, unable to tell him what else the man said. "I shot him with the gun you gave me. It's in my bag."

"Is he dead?"

"I think so … I don't know."

"I'll wager he's a part of this, either a Pinkerton or a bounty hunter. Why else would he be in the woods late at night watching? Bill will take care of everything. You rest now. And when you go back, tell Ma no one is to know you were there when any of this happened, or the sheriff will never let go of asking you questions."

"What if they've already told him or told the neighbors?"

Jesse shoved a second pistol into his waistband. "If there's one thing my family knows how to do, it's keep their mouths shut over things other people don't need to know."

I curled inside the blanket next to the fire with my hand protectively over my stomach. I didn't feel any cramps and could only hope the wild ride hadn't affected the baby. Then I remembered what I'd done and took deep breaths to keep from vomiting. I mouthed a prayer for forgiveness, and then, even frightened as I was, the fire's warmth lulled me into a troubled sleep.

When light peeking from behind a dark curtain finally woke me, I looked around and saw no one but Bill, who sat quietly at the table. He stepped outside while I changed and then stepped inside while I went out to relieve myself.

I walked past a horse and small buggy standing near the horse I'd taken from the farm. A third horse was tethered to a post. When I returned, Clell was tying the two animals behind the buggy.

"I've got your bag, ma'am," he said. "You're to take this rig back to the farm." He offered his hand and helped me climb onto the driver's seat.

"Where did it come from?"

"Oh, I 'quired 'em nearabouts."

"I see," my voice shook. I didn't ask any more questions, being in no position to fault him for anything he might do.

"I'll ride with you a ways then turn the nag you borrowed loose a mile or so from the farm. Somebody'll find him quick enough and take him back where he belongs."

"What about," I gulped, "the man I shot?"

"I tracked back from where you came and found him. He's dead all right. You shot true, and that's the best way to shoot when your life's on the line."

Another sin on my soul. Yet now wasn't the time to consider it. What I'd find at the farm filled me with dread enough.

Once we were close, Bill pulled the reins and stepped down from the buggy. He mounted his own horse and took the reins of the other.

"Keep your pistol handy and stay on the lookout."

I watched him ride off, took a breath, and then slapped the reins. The horse moved forward, buggy wheels crunching over frozen ground until ahead of me, in the dim light of morning, the farm appeared, eerily silent. The caustic scent of blackened and charred boards burned my nose, and bile rose in my throat.

Reuben sat on the front steps, hands covering his face.

I seated myself beside him and put an arm around his shoulders. He looked up finally, eyes red and face splotchy. "He's gone. My baby boy is gone."

My heart twisted. Sweet little Archie. He would not catch a tadpole in the spring after all. "I'm so sorry." We sat for a quiet moment before he spoke again.

"Zerelda's arm couldn't be saved. Dr. Allen amputated it just below the elbow early this morning. She's resting now, thanks to a dose of morphine."

"I'll go check on her." I gave his shoulders a squeeze and stood on shaky legs. Inside, I crept past Charlotte in the kitchen and on toward the sleeping room where someone had pulled a curtain halfway across the window. Zerelda lay in the darkened room with her eyes closed. Heavy bandages were wrapped around what remained of her arm. On a small cot next to her bed lay Archie's body, covered with a blanket as though he, too, was merely sleeping. Perry stood next to him, staring at his young friend with a trembling lip.

I rested a hand on his shoulder. "Your mama is in the kitchen. Run along and see if you can help her."

Perry took a final anguished look at Archie, and then left to do as I bid.

Zerelda stirred and moaned. Her eyelids fluttered open.

"What can I do for you, Aunt?" I asked.

She emerged from the fog of morphine enough to look up at me with bleary eyes. "It is too late to do anything but help get my child ready for the grave." Her words slurred and her voice rasped as though she'd strained it. "Were you able to find my boys?"

"Yes. Frank and Jesse are trying to discover what happened and will see you when they can." I smoothed her hair. "They're making plans. I know they won't let this go unanswered."

"We always have to get justice our own way, don't we? There certainly won't be any from the sheriff."

"Jesse says no one is to know about me being here last night. I'm not sure what difference it makes now, but that's what he wants."

She nodded. "He's right. The coroner and his jury are coming to the house tonight for the inquest. We don't need to give them anything more to pry into than necessary." She glanced at her bandaged arm. "Since I can't travel, they're coming to me. All they will hear is what they need to find the men who murdered my innocent baby." She choked back a sob. "Oh God oh God oh God ..."

I took her hand and prayed over her until the soft words calmed her into sleep.

Bundling myself against the cold night air, I drove the rig as far from the farm as I dared. By the time Ambrose came to let me know the inquest had ended, my hands were numb and my feet like blocks of ice. He tied his mule to the wagon and took the reins. On the ride home, he told me what happened.

At six o'clock, five men from the area had arrived, accompanied by a reporter and Mr. Albright, the coroner. They convened in the sleeping room, gathered around Zerelda and Archie, and spoke to each other in low tones.

Mr. Albright had stroked his beard before raising a hand for silence. "We are bound by law to investigate any violent or suspicious death. Our job today is to gather evidence on what happened here. If the jury finds a crime caused this child to die and this woman to be injured, then the matter will be turned over to the marshal for him to find the culprits and arrest them for what they've done. Do you have any questions?" The men looked at each other, but no one spoke. "Fine then. We'll get to our work."

The coroner pulled back the blanket, so the men could see Archie's wound. Then Reuben and Ambrose described what happened. When the men questioned Zerelda, she sat up in her bed, white-faced with pain and spoke in a voice that quivered with emotion. She pointed at Archie's body, and demanded the men who had murdered her child be found. Ambrose said by the faces of the jury, Zerelda's testimony had a powerful effect. Not even a heart of stone could fail to melt in the face of such passion.

After the questioning, the men examined the kitchen and went outside to view the damage done to the house. They walked the grounds and looked in the barn. By the time the jury went back inside, the moon had risen high in the sky. Mr. Albright told Reuben the matter would be turned over to the sheriff.

When I got back to the house, I gave Zerelda a dose of pain medicine and laid in a bed close to her in case she needed help. When her breathing came soft and regular, I closed my eyes. The image of Archie's dear face and sweet smile did not leave me.

The next morning, hammers pounded. Reuben and Ambrose were already repairing the damage outside. Inside, Charlotte and I filled a basin with water for the sad task of bathing Archie's small body. Despite the many wounds I'd seen in the past, his made me wince more than any had ever done. The child's pain must have been unendurable.

My tears fell as I worked. Zerelda looked at Archie and her mouth trembled as she directed us to dress him in a suit of Confederate gray.

News of the attack appeared in papers and spread fast throughout Clay County—then across the nation. People wanted to know what had happened, and they wanted to know why. Other news of the day disappeared, and reporters flocked to Clay County like flies buzzing around honey.

Zerelda's strong constitution and pure grit held her upright during Archie's funeral, despite the agony that throbbed in the stump of her arm. Our family, neighbors, and friends arrived to pay their respects. Reporters came too, their eyes darting through the mourners, no doubt hoping they'd find Jesse and Frank among them. John Newman Edwards shook my hand, his brows furrowed over intelligent eyes, to express his condolences.

"Rest assured, Mrs. James, I will write about this low blow against the South and demand justice."

My old friend Catherine, now newly married herself, came all the way from Harlem to Kearney, and kissed my cheek.

"Such a shocking tragedy. Zee, I'm so sorry for your loss. Will they ever find those responsible for this terrible deed?"

"The sheriff has gathered evidence, but we believe the Pinkertons are at fault. Those of us who stood with the South are given little in the way of fair treatment."

My words could have come straight from Jesse, but they described precisely how I felt.

It came as no surprise when the sheriff finally announced that Pinkerton detectives were indeed responsible for the raid, but when it came to light that they'd been helped by Zerelda's neighbor, Dan Askew, my fury matched Zerelda's.

Dan had allowed the detectives to use his home as an operating base in the hunt for Frank and Jesse, all the while pretending to be our friend.

Alan Pinkerton claimed the outcome of the raid was unintended. Some people sided with the detectives, but most were appalled and outraged against them. Yet regardless of anyone's opinion over where the blame laid, on one point everyone agreed. If Jesse and Frank caught up with the men involved first, there'd be hell to pay.

A week later, Zerelda seemed able enough to function without my help, and I bought a train ticket for home. The horrors I'd seen had drained me, and for my baby's sake, I needed the solace of rest. Not long after my return, a newspaper headline trumpeted a new death. Dan Askew had been found shot dead in his own backyard. The reporter quoted Zerelda, who'd been asked who she thought might have killed her neighbor. She responded in a fashion more cryptic than usual.

"Dan made a lot of enemies during the war. Any one of them could have come after him."

I shed no tears over Dan Askew and his treachery, and already knew what Jesse would say.

An eye for an eye.

24

By early summer, my belly stretched and swelled, although loose fitting garments disguised my condition. I'd spent an afternoon knitting a soft wool blanket for the baby, and when Jesse came home I showed it to him.. He nodded at my effort, flicked his glance toward the window, and then made an announcement.

"We're moving to Edgefield, Tennessee in a few days. I'll find a place for us near the Hite farm. Uncle George is looking forward to having us close enough to visit."

I dropped the blanket into my lap. "Why?"

"Frank's laying low, and I've got an itch to head south. Maybe when the Pinkertons find out we're not around anymore, Ma and Reuben can live in peace. Ever since they were attacked, one person or another is tramping through the fields to snoop. Ma says the children can't sleep at night without waking up a dozen times, scared about what could happen next."

"Well," I said carefully. "I don't think light travel would harm the baby. Perhaps Tennessee would be a good place to raise a child."

"It might at that." The fierce look left his face and he grinned at me. "Did you know some of the best horses in the country come from Tennessee and Kentucky? After we get settled, maybe I'll buy us a race horse or two."

"I'd like that. Having a champion would be a fine way to start the ranch you've talked about."

Jesse smoothed his hand over my hair. "My Zee, ever true. You're ready to go when I say and do what I want. Are you sure you won't mind moving away from your sisters and brothers?"

"I don't mind it at all as long as we're together. You're my family now, Jesse. Any time I want to see our kin, I can take the train to visit them."

I packed the trunk, and Jesse helped me box the few household items we owned. He took me to my younger brother, Thomas, before pointing the wagon with our belongings toward Tennessee. Jesse had refused to let me ride next to him on the bouncing wagon seat, fearing it might harm the baby. I counted the days until Thomas drove me to the train station.

When I finally arrived at the Nashville depot, Jesse waited for me with one booted foot on a bench, puffing a cigar. My breath caught in my chest after he tossed the stogie to the ground and took me into his arms.

"Hello, sweetheart." Despite the gazes of amused onlookers, he kissed me.

"Let's get you home. I imagine you could use some rest."

"You've found a place for us to stay?"

"A nice little house on Boscobel Street. I think you'll like it."

He drove us from Nashville to Edgefield, near the Cumberland River. The small town reminded me of Harlem by the muddy Missouri, and the raw scent of river water made me feel as though I'd come home.

Jesse stopped the buggy when he reached a small white house in a row of similar homes on a quiet road. A large hackberry tree shaded the front porch. I knew the tree's ripe fruit would attract birds of all types, and even though they'd leave behind a mess, I didn't mind. One of my favorite morning sounds came from twittering birds.

A young woman and her small daughter waved at us from the porch next door. I lifted my hand in return. Jesse waved too, but rather than speaking to them, he took my arm and hurried me into the house.

Our new home had a parlor with a side table and settee, a kitchen with a sturdy pine table and two chairs, and a sleeping room with a bed and a dresser.

"You can buy whatever else you'd like from the mercantile in town. I rented the house under the same names we used before and told the landlord I'm working as a wheat speculator. That way when I need to travel, no one will be surprised."

Alarmed, I turned to look at him. "You aren't planning to leave soon, are you?"

"Don't worry about any of that now. Take a good long nap, then we'll go to town later, so I can show you where things are."

It didn't escape me that he'd avoided my question. "But I'm not tired. You know it won't be much longer until the baby comes. Will you be here with me?"

"Of course, I will. As a matter of fact, I've already found a doctor for you. His name is Dr. Vertrees, and you'll meet him soon."

I sat on the settee and pulled off my gloves. "During

the entire trip, I daydreamed about you finding a job in Tennessee. Farming or ranching, either one would be fine with me."

"Perhaps, someday. Remember that the war took away more than our liberty. It turned me into a hunted man. A job working for someone else is risky. They'd ask too many questions, and next thing you know, I could be sitting in a jail cell. Besides," he looked at me, "I'm not ready to forget what the Federals did to us." His brows drew together. "Think of Archie and Ma. The one thing I can still do is pick the pocketbook of any business owned by Radicals or Federals. In that way, we can devil them and be repaid, at least in part, for everything we've lost."

I put my hand on his arm. "I know there's a lot to avenge. I can't forget what happened any more than you. Remember I was there to witness it. Things have been done to make our lives difficult, and I understand how you feel, but I want you here so our child will know his father."

Jesse pulled away from me and paced to the window. "All right then, I'm giving you the truth. Next week, I must go meet up with Frank, but the less you know of any other details, the better off you'll be. If I name a destination, any wind blowing from that direction will make you sick with worry. As for the baby, I promise nothing will keep me away. I have no intention of missing the birth of my child."

"So, I'll be alone here?"

"Not alone. Dr. Vertrees has a son named John. He's a steady man, not much younger than us, and willing to stay with you whenever I have to leave. I don't want you to be by yourself, not in your condition."

I swallowed hard and he put his arms around me. With the sticky heat of summer, I knew my rounded belly and puffy ankles did not make an attractive picture. I buried my face in his shirt, and a woman's worries made my voice sound smaller than I wanted.

"I'm sorry I look so terrible."

"Terrible? Is that what you think? I tell you, Zee, you have never looked more beautiful. You're carrying our child. Nothing is more important than that, and I intend to make sure both you and our baby have everything you deserve, no matter what it takes."

My gaze dropped to the floor. "Will you be away long?"

He tilted up my chin, and laughed. "You know I'm smart enough to get back home soon as I can."

His words were true, yet in superstitious fear, I wished he hadn't said so. It tempted fate.

The next morning, Jesse introduced me to John Vertrees, a dark-haired, brown-eyed man who made me smile because he reminded me of my brother David. Before leaving, Jesse hired a house girl named Patsy to help during the day while John took on a husband's chores, hammering a few pictures on the wall and fetching items from the mercantile that were too heavy for me to carry. Settling into our new home kept me busy enough to stave off most of my worries while I waited. And within two weeks, Jesse returned.

Despite my increasing bulk, his presence made me lighter on my feet, and I thanked John for his kindness in helping me during Jesse's absence.

Jesse had a more extravagant method to show gratitude. He pulled a thick wad of bills from his wallet and carelessly counted out one hundred fifty dollars. Then he handed it to the astonished young man.

"You've done well by me, John. Take this for your trouble, and remember, I may need your services again soon.

I don't want Mrs. Howard without a man's protection when I travel."

Jesse's good humor and bulging pockets told me his trip had been successful. Profit meant he'd be in no hurry to leave, and I felt torn between relief and dread over his determination to carry out plans for which he refused to share details, despite the many questions I asked.

I'd reached the point where my size and propriety meant I could no longer walk into town. During my confinement, Jesse avoided our neighbors more than usual, but occasionally he would visit his uncle George, who taught him to play faro, a card game held in barrooms throughout the city.

When he had good luck, he'd show me his winnings and crow. "Look at this stack of greenbacks, Zee. Sometimes twisting the tail of a tiger pays off."

A keen interest in horses drew him to the track time after time. His activities seemed harmless enough to me, because they meant he'd return home each night. We'd begun to live what I saw as a more normal life. A married couple in a cozy house surrounded by a community that did not question his identity. Yet there were times when I saw him sigh. I knew he missed the people and places back home.

When I saw Jesse writing a letter to John Newman Edwards, apprehension rippled through me. He penned a passionate condemnation of Alan Pinkerton and what had happened at the farm, including the punishment he predicted would come to Mr. Pinkerton either in this world or the next. Jesse's hatred for the man still burned hot. I didn't fault him for his feelings and hoped the letter's mere publication would be enough to relieve his torment.

Late summer's stifling warmth gave me more discomfort than usual. At midday, heat rose in visible waves from a field near our home. On the final day of August, I sat with my feet elevated, fanning myself and sipping a cool cup of water. I was dreaming of autumn days that would soon bring relief when a sudden sharp pain made me gasp aloud. I dropped the cup as warm water gushed from between my legs, running down the chair and onto the floor.

Jesse came from the kitchen, his forehead grooved with concern.

"What is it?"

"I think the baby is ready to come. Can you help me to bed and then go for Dr. Vertrees?"

Jesse's face paled and his eyes widened. He helped me to stand, and I paused to look at liquid puddling on the chair and floor.

"Let me clean this mess first."

"Let the devil take care of it. You're going to bed. John's out in the barn now. I'll have him fetch his father."

I gasped again as a vise-like pain doubled me over. Jesse carried me to our bed and laid me on sheets that smelled like sunshine.

"Please, help me get on my gown."

He loosened the ties on my blouse and skirt then helped me pull off the wet garments. My nightgown slid over me, and I sank against the pillows when another pain hit.

"I'll be right back," Jesse said before he raced from the room. My belly cramped again, yet between the spasms, my mind and body rallied with an alertness and energy that had escaped me for weeks. I took a series of deep breaths and prayed.

When Jesse returned, he took my hand.

"How are you doing, sweetheart?"

"It's not so bad at the moment, but I know it'll get worse. Once the doctor arrives, you may want to go for a walk. Sometimes babies take a while to come."

Another strong pain bore down, stopping me from speaking further. I squeezed Jesse's hand so hard he winced. He dipped a cloth in the pitcher near our bed and patted my forehead, until someone knocked at the door. Jesse shot an agonized glance at me and then brought Dr. Vertrees to my bedside.

"All right, Mr. Howard, it's time for you to leave us to our work. A birthing is no place for a father."

Jesse's face said he wanted nothing more than to do just what the doctor had told him, but he gallantly asked. "Do you want me to stay?"

"No. I'm fine. Someone will come get you after the baby is here."

"I'll be in the yard," he told me.

Dr. Vertrees opened his bag and studied me. "You did the right thing. No husband should witness this. He might fear ever coming near you again."

I blushed at his frank words but conceded he was probably right. Men had little stomach for pain or suffering. No wonder it was in God's plan that it be women who all but tore themselves in two creating new life.

A searing pain pummeled me, and I gasped.

"Some doctors use chloroform to dull the pain, but I believe it puts the baby at risk. However, if you need it, I will do as you wish," he said.

"I don't want to risk my baby's life."

"Then let's try this. It may help you through the contractions."

Dr. Vertrees tied a rope from the bedpost for me to clutch whenever the worst pains gripped me. I soon forgot about Jesse as wave after wave of deep cramping racked my body. I sweated and groaned and pushed for what seemed like hours, until the sheets were drenched in perspiration.

Finally, Dr. Vertrees ordered me to a final push until the baby, wet and bloody, slid from my body. He cut the cord and held up the infant, slapping it once then twice. I sighed in relief when I heard a cry. He wiped the small red infant with a damp cloth, in the same way he had ministered to me during my labor.

"Mrs. Howard, you have a fine boy. He looks strong."

The doctor gave me the baby, and my son squalled, loud and indignant. I had never heard such a beautiful sound.

"I'll have your house woman come in right away to clean you up. Then I'll speak with your husband before sending him in to see you. You've done a hard job. The best thing you can do now is rest."

I nodded but didn't take my eyes off the baby in my arms. His face was blotched and squashed together from his perilous journey. Tiny blue eyes looked into mine, and for the second time in my life, I fell in love.

Once Patsy cleared away the soiled sheets and clothing, I lay in semi-darkness, alone with my child.

Jesse tread warily into the room and peered at the bundle in my arms. "Dr. Vertrees says we have a son."

"Yes. Look at him." I pushed aside the blanket to allow a good view of the baby's face. "This is your boy. Isn't he handsome?"

Jesse's lips parted, and he leaned closer, touching his finger to the baby's cheek. "He's perfect. And I've decided what to name him."

"Yes?" I waited.

"Jesse Edwards James."

My husband had given himself a namesake and honored his friend John Edwards at the same time. My lips curved into a tired smile.

"Yes. I think that will suit him perfectly."

"That will be his name, but only you and I and the family will ever know it. He can't be the son of Dave Howard and have the name Jesse James. For the time being, he must be called something else."

"Of course," I murmured. His reasoning made sense, although it knotted my stomach.

"I like the name Tim. We'll call him that—like a nickname."

But even this small cloud couldn't dim my happiness. I put the baby to my breast. He turned and rooted, as though he didn't know what to do. I guided him and after a few tries, he finally understood and began to nurse.

Jesse settled into the chair beside me and yawned. "You did good today, my dear. No one could have done it better."

I cuddled the baby, and Jesse's soft words soothed me. My body ached from the ordeal it had endured, yet that didn't prevent my eyelids from getting heavy. The baby turned his head and fussed. I guided him back into position again and smiled.

We had become a family of three.

25

*L*ittle Tim sat on the kitchen floor with a wooden spoon in his plump and dimpled hand. He pounded it on a chair leg as though he'd become a miniature drummer boy. My lips curved up, remembering his mouth rimmed with the chocolate cake I'd baked for his first birthday. At Jesse's insistence, we'd celebrated the occasion a week early.

My husband had commissioned a wooden rocking horse, painted the same red-brown color of the bay horses he loved, complete with black mane, tail, and stockings. The mane and tail were long and fashioned from real horse hair. Tim's eyes were wide with enchantment when he saw it, and, when he was held secure in the saddle by his father, he giggled out loud with every rock and sway.

Jesse even surprised me with a small box containing a pair of luminous cream-colored pearl drop earrings. When I looked at him with brows raised, he grinned. "That's for giving me my first son."

Yet in the days that followed, I suspected the gift meant more than that. Jesse had already been away earlier in the summer, and lately his movements were more sharp and hard. His restless spirit stirred again. He'd scribbled more letters and sent them to John Edwards, to defend himself from accusations he'd participated in recent robberies, some of which had included cold-blooded murder.

Tim and I were often in bed long before Jesse came home from meetings with old comrades. When I asked who they were, he teased that I didn't need to worry for he wasn't spending time at Madame Zilphia's. I didn't smile, for I suspected the quiet I'd come to enjoy in the months after Tim's birth would soon come to an end.

Then we received a letter from Annie that stirred the embers of Jesse's anger. Hired detectives had swooped in to search her father's home in Kansas City for signs of Frank or Jesse, upsetting the household and embarrassing her family. Jesse fired off yet another letter to the newspaper and vented his fury to me.

"I can't sit here and twiddle my thumbs while our kin are harassed. Now Annie's family is a target, same as my mother has been."

"How will you strike back? What can you do?"

"There's a man who killed a good friend of mine during the war. He's got a lot of money in a bank that's ripe for picking."

"Jesse, the war is over and you have a son now. It's time to turn your attention to your family instead of endangering yourself and our baby."

He only laughed and picked Tim up off the floor. Jesse boosted the baby high over his head and Tim crowed with delight.

"Come with me, son. Let's take a ride on your horse. Perhaps we should name her Kate, after the finest mare I ever owned."

Jesse set Tim back on his feet and took his hand. With his father's help, Tim toddled to the porch, where the elegant wooden horse waited. Jesse put Tim in the saddle and rocked the horse, laughing along with his son's squeals.

I shook my head and picked up the jacket Jesse had flung on a chair. A piece of paper fell from the breast pocket to the floor. I picked it up to tuck it back in his pocket, but hesitated. A good wife would never dream of reading her husband's private correspondence, but when a husband refused to discuss his activities with his wife? The rocking horse moved on the wooden slats of the porch, and Tim squealed again. I chewed my lip and opened the paper. A single word appeared in Jesse's careless scrawl.

Northfield.

The word meant nothing to me, and I quickly returned the note to the coat's pocket before he could see what I'd done.

Within days, Jesse left and John Vertrees again came by each morning and every night as was his habit. He spoke little, but his hard-working nature, whether fetching supplies from the mercantile or hammering a board on the porch, put me in mind of Papa's generous spirit.

Jesse had discouraged me from making friends with our neighbors, but in view of his frequent absences, I gave myself the luxury of visits next door with Tom and Sally Carson.

They were close to our age, with a three-year old daughter named Janie. Even though I knew Jesse wouldn't approve, I chatted with Sally every day. We talked about children and recipes and commiserated with each other over a cup of coffee when the rain kept us from hanging laundry outside.

She talked rapidly and affected silly mannerisms, but she meant well, despite her vaporing. One morning, it occurred to me I should take Tim next door to play.

Before I made it to the porch, Tom Carson appeared at the door, flustered and pale.

"Will you please come over? Janie is very sick and Sally is beside herself with worry. I'm going for the doctor."

I wiped my hands on my apron and put Patsy in charge of Tim before I ran to the small house next to ours. I pushed open the door without knocking and went straight to the bedroom. Sally knelt by the cot of her daughter.

Without even touching Janie, I could see the child blazed with fever.

"I'll get some water and a cloth to sponge her."

"Oh, Josie, what will I do if I lose my baby?"

"Don't even think such things. Janie will pull through this. She's a strong girl, and with the doctor's help, I know she'll be fine."

Sally continued to moan and weep, her hands covering her face. I took the cloth and dipped it in water then sponged Janie's forehead and arms until Dr. Vertrees arrived. He examined the child and asked Sally questions, which she answered between hiccupping sobs.

Finally, the doctor sighed and spoke to me. "I believe she has a summer fever. Give her a spoonful of this every few hours to help her sleep and try to keep her cool until the fever breaks. I'll be back in the morning to see how she's doing."

The doctor's comments prompted Sally to cry even harder. When Tom came into the room, I had to shout over her near-hysteria. "Sally is distraught. Go to my house and tell Patsy I'll stay here tonight to help with Janie. Ask her to please watch Tim for me. Oh, and let Mr. Vertrees know where I am, too."

Sally did not leave the room all night, though she dozed on and off in the chair next to Janie's bed. Thank the Lord her wailing subsided! In the quiet, I wiped Janie's skin with a damp cloth and watched to be sure her breath came without labor. The task reminded me of sitting by another bedside many years ago.

By early morning, Janie opened her eyes and asked for a drink of water. When Dr. Vertrees arrived, she was sitting up supported by pillows. She'd asked for a piece of skillet toast, but I told Sally we needed to wait.

"She will be fine," the doctor said. "Give her broth at first, then let her eat whatever she wants." With this news, Sally smiled, and the haunted look left her red and swollen eyes. She hugged me before I trudged back home, weary and grateful Janie had recovered, but even more thankful my own boy had so far remained healthy and strong. The world wasn't always kind to children. I remembered the babies my mother had buried, and I thought of Zerelda and little Archie. I shuddered to think what I'd do if anything so tragic happened to a child of mine.

The first week of September arrived with the sun so bright and air so fresh, I abandoned my plan to beat dirt from the braided rug and took Tim by the hand for a walk. Birds chirped at us, and an eagle soared over the river. He toddled along beside me with an intent expression, as he concentrated on the task of moving one foot in front of the other. After we'd walked for a few minutes, he let his legs go soft and sank into the dirt.

"Is my little man tired?"

He gave me a toothy grin.

"All right then. Come here and we'll go home."

I lifted him to my hip and started back to the house. By the time we reached the porch, I saw Sally waving at us. She held Janie's hand and had a bundle wrapped in a red-and-white checked napkin tucked under her arm.

"This is for you," she told me.

I took the warm bundle and smelled the fragrant aroma of fresh baked bread.

"Thank you for your help, Josie. I don't know how I could have managed without you."

"We're friends, aren't we? You'd do the same for me." I held the bread up to my nose. "This smells wonderful. There's no need for you to bring a gift, but I'll take it all the same. Let's go inside and sit down. Tim and Janie can play on the porch while we visit. Patsy will keep an eye on them."

I poured us each a cup of coffee, and Sally began to chat in her artless way. The aroma from my cup soothed me as I listened to her prattle on and on. Then she lowered her voice as though she had a secret to tell.

"Did you see the newspaper today? There was an attempted bank robbery in Minnesota. A place called … what was it again? Oh, yes, Northfield. Tom is quite fascinated by the whole affair and told me all about it."

Northfield in Minnesota? Could they be so far away?

With a long familiar rush of adrenaline, my heart pounded, though I spoke in a studiedly measured tone.

"Really? What happened?"

"The paper says it was the James and Younger gang that did it. A bank clerk got killed and two of the robbers were shot dead in the street. All of that, and the bandits didn't even get one penny from the bank."

I swallowed past a lump in my throat. "Did the paper give names of the men who were killed?"

"Umm, let's see. I think Tom said it was Clell Miller and Will Chadwell, but I'm not sure since I was busy braiding Janie's hair and didn't read it myself. Anyway, the whole town got shot up with bullets flying everywhere. The rest of the gang escaped, and now there must be a hundred men out looking for the ones who got away. Everyone says this will put an end to the gang's robberies and that they'll all be strung up in no time. Isn't it exciting news?" She paused to take a breath and stared at me. "Josie? Are you all right?"

Sickness spread from the pit of my stomach. My ears buzzed, and I saw gray spots. I had to grip the table to keep from falling over in a faint.

"I'm fine. I must have eaten something to upset my stomach. You must excuse me while I go to the bedroom and lie down. Thank you for the delicious bread."

I fled from Sally's concerned face, then kneeled and retched into the chamber pot. Sitting up, I wiped my mouth. No one knew better than I how often newspaper stories were contrived. I needed the truth of what had happened. But there was no one I could contact. No one with whom I could talk out my fears. No one to reassure me. All I knew was that Jesse could be wounded or running for his life. I steeled myself to face the fact he might even be dead.

In the weeks that followed, I read every newspaper I could find, looking for stories about the robbery. I'd become frantic enough to think even skewed accounts were better than nothing at all. Headline after headline appeared. One story said the robbers who escaped had been seriously wounded. Another speculated the

Northfield bank had been targeted because one of the bandits had a spite against Adelbert Ames—ex-governor of Mississippi and a Radical—and also a major depositor. A reporter interviewed Zerelda about the manhunt. She declared her sons' innocence. and brought up injustices she and her family had endured from authorities in the past. A shudder rippled down my spine. I needed no reminder.

Soon, a headline claimed Cole, Bob, and Jim Younger had been wounded and captured near Madelia, Mississippi. Charlie Pitts, who was with them at the time, wasn't so lucky. He'd been shot dead. Now the pursuers had their sights on only two suspects: Frank and Jesse James. I picked at my thumb nail and trembled over what might come next. If only I could contact Annie. But with detectives thick in Missouri, I feared the possibility of correspondence being intercepted.

No one led such a charmed life that would allow them to escape detection forever. Something was bound to happen sometime, and I wondered what I'd do when I came face to face with widowhood or a husband condemned to many years in jail. The more I considered the prospect, the more difficult it became for me to rise from bed each morning. My son's face became my source of strength, and the single buoy that kept my head above the swirling darkness of despair that threatened to pull me under.

On a bleak and frosty early October morning, John Vertrees came to me with his hat in hand. He stomped off mud caking his boots, before he gave me a piece of paper.

"Good morning, Mrs. Howard. A rider brought a telegram for you."

I took it, my hand shaking so hard the message nearly slipped away. "Thank you, Mr. Vertrees."

He eyed me with concern but put on his hat and went back to the barn. I shut the door and tore open the message.

Josie,

   I am well. Business delaying return. Love to you and Tim.

   Ever yours,

   Dave

My knees lost their starch and I sank into a chair. Those few words were all it took for my battered heart to soar. He was alive. And I knew he'd find a way to get back home.

26

By early December, Jesse arrived on the saddest-looking old horse I'd ever seen. His clothes were looser than when he'd left, and he favored his right leg, wincing when he walked. Yet what I noticed most was the hollow look in his eyes. He refused to answer my questions about what had happened, other than to tell me he and Frank had survived a disaster of monstrous proportions.

Frightened, I tried to bring back the man I remembered, cooking his favorite foods and fussing at him to eat. We put on jackets and took Tim for long walks in the crisp, fresh air. I read funny stories to him from the newspaper. Still, he remained distant until the morning he made an announcement.

"It's time for us to move. This place is too small, and I don't like the neighbors being so familiar. Tom Carson is always asking me about my business, and Sally keeps telling me I ought to stay home and tend to my family."

"But, Jesse, it's natural for them to wonder. You've been gone for a long time."

"I've had more than I can take of people watching me. It's time we move somewhere new."

"But Tim was born in this house."

"And he can grow up somewhere else. Children move with their families all the time. It makes them stronger."

I wondered if many moved as often as we did, but bit my tongue to keep from saying it, fearful of deepening the darkness of his mood. Instead, I started packing our trunk. Within days, Jesse hired a wagon and men to move our belongings from Boscobel Street. He insisted we leave during the night and tell no one we were going. I stared at my hands and wondered what Sally would think when she woke up in the morning to discover we were gone.

Jesse shifted us from one place to another around Nashville, blinking as he selected and then rejected each house. His pulse beat madly at his throat as he searched for a place that suited him. I grew so weary of living like a gypsy that I no longer bothered to unpack boxes. I took out the few things we needed to get by each day and made a point of not talking with the neighbors so Jesse wouldn't be upset. I no longer cared whether I ran a brush through my hair or had wrinkles in my dress.

Finally, when Jesse said he'd found a place that pleased him, I stared, wondering if he meant it, and then I wondered even more what another move might bring. "Are you sure?"

"It's a nice place near Hyde's Ferry Road outside Nashville. It'll do for us."

"When do we leave?"

"Tomorrow. And there's one other thing." He straightened his jacket. "Frank and Annie will be living right next door."

"What?" I swallowed to keep from bursting into tears of happiness.

"I've been waiting to surprise you. Frank and I thought you and Annie would be good company for each other."

"That's the best news I've had in months," I told him. "It'll be so wonderful to live near our own kin again."

He smiled, and my heart lifted higher. On the day Ben and Fannie Woodson welcomed Dave and Josie Howard as their new neighbors, Annie and I clung to each other and smiled through teary eyes.

Jesse shook Frank's hand and seemed lighter in spirit, as though a heavy load had been lifted from his back. I supposed he must have been as lonely for Frank as I'd been to have the people I loved near me.

Together again, Frank and Jesse spent time going out in the evening to play faro, and during the day, they visited the horse track. Jesse bought another bay mare named Red Fox and entered her in a race. One day, Annie and I went to the track to watch the mare run. We both placed small bets, sure she would win.

The scent of horses, manure, and sweat surrounded us as we squeezed to the front of a large crowd of spectators. Flags waved in the breeze and people elbowed each other to find the best spot to stand. Annie and I stood alone, as our husbands were busy giving last-minute instructions to the rider Jesse had hired.

We watched as six beautiful long-legged horses were ridden onto the track. They lined up, prancing with eagerness, until a shotgun fired to start the race. I jumped at the sound, and the steeds galloped hard, their hooves flinging dirt everywhere. Several of the animals fell behind right away, but Red Fox ran neck and neck with another horse at the head of the pack. I grabbed Annie's arm and squealed when, just before the finish line, Red Fox edged ahead to win by a nose. We jumped up and down, hugged each other, and laughed. With the money we won, we treated our husbands to a grand celebratory dinner.

A few weeks later we were eating supper when Jesse suddenly pushed away his plate. "I can't believe it. Frank wants to start farming." He shook his head at me as though dumbfounded. "He must have inherited Ma's love of putting a plow to the ground. I can't understand how such a common job that takes so long to pay off could possibly appeal to him."

I shrugged. "Yet I've never seen Frank happier. Annie says he's started to read Shakespeare again, as he used to do when they first met. I understand Charles Eastman offered him a job."

Charles and Polly Eastman lived on a farm nearby. Frank had become friendly with them, walking over in the evening to sit on their front porch and talk. They were generous people, sharing produce from their garden and apples from an enormous orchard behind their house. Polly had invited Annie and I to help her put up apple butter in the fall.

Like Frank, I'd grown content with our new life. I didn't think I could be happier, until the day came when I learned we would have another baby. I confided my secret to Annie before saying a word to my husband.

She took my hands and laughed. "What a strange coincidence. I was going to tell you Frank and I are expecting a baby, too. Our children can grow up together and be the best of friends."

I hugged her, and a tear slid from my eye. "I'm so happy for you, Annie. You've waited a long time. I suppose this is the sort of thing we can count on when our husbands stay home, rather than a kiss and a wave. Gone away again."

Annie blushed at my meaning. I'd come from a large household and wanted for Tim the same happiness I found in having many brothers and sisters.

As the months passed, our bellies swelled. We counted weeks on our fingers and concluded we both should have our babies early in 1878. Unlike my first experience, I now knew what to expect and could help Annie with her questions. We giggled over the idea of our children coming on the same day and hoped they would be as close as Frank and Jesse had always been.

With this pregnancy, my belly grew much faster than it had before. I went to Dr. Montgomery, and he tutted about a second baby showing earlier than the first. But when my stomach blossomed larger than Annie's, I thought it strange. I didn't remember being so big even by the time Tim was born.

Jesse showed me nothing but his kind and gentle side, eyes sparkling over the thought of another child. Now more than two and a half years old, Tim placed his small hands on my stomach, and I told him he would soon have a fine surprise. "We're getting you a baby brother or sister."

He listened to me, eyes wide and serious. "Alice?"

I smiled at him, knowing he referred to *Alice's Adventures in Wonderland*. I'd started reading the story to him at night. "Maybe an Alice. Or you might get a brother."

I had to admit to myself that I liked the idea of a little girl. My mother had passed away in Kansas City the previous summer, during the height of the hunt for Jesse after Northfield. I hadn't been able to risk going to Harlem and a pain in my chest swelled to know we'd never mended our relationship. A daughter of my own would give me a second chance to nurture the bond between a mother and daughter.

Winter soon brought a heavy chill that didn't leave. Every time I opened the door, my breath appeared in frosty clouds. Annie and I contented ourselves by sitting together before a roaring fire, knitting small caps and blankets to keep our babies warm, while Frank and Jesse amused themselves at faro games.

My increasing bulk prompted Dr. Montgomery to advise that I rest as much as possible, so Annie came over to pass the time with me. My stomach had stretched to such proportions, it tingled. I couldn't rise from a chair without help. The doctor thought my baby could come at any time, yet on February 6, it was Annie, not me, who doubled over with pain.

I sent word for Charles Eastman to find Frank and fetch Dr. Montgomery. Polly Eastman came to stay with us and watch Tim. She and I helped Annie into a cot next to our bed as pains gripped her.

"How can I stand this? I feel I'm being ripped in half."

"I know it hurts, but this is the torment a woman must endure to have a child," I said. "Think of how much you love Tim and know this pain will bring a sweet baby of your own."

She nodded, and perspiration dotted her forehead despite the cold air outside. By the time Dr. Montgomery arrived with his new partner, Dr. Gould, her pains were coming harder. Annie thrashed her head from side to side and cried out, but her labor progressed much faster than mine had.

She pushed her baby into the world just before Frank arrived home, rushing into the room to meet his new son. His face glowed when he kissed Annie, and tears rolled down his cheeks. I ducked my head and hurried from the room, overcome at being privy to such an intimate scene.

Dr. Montgomery soon came out and spoke to me, his face grave. "Mrs. Howard, I must order you to rest. You have grown to a size that worries me." He took my hands and looked at them. "Do you see how swollen your fingers are? There are signs your delivery may be complicated. When your time comes, I believe it will be wise to have Dr. Gould with me to assist."

Annie had protested vehemently to my offer that she stay with us. She insisted on going home, so Frank carried her there, followed by Polly with the baby. I went to my room and lay down. I knew I'd been pushing myself harder than I should, and the stress brought on by helping with Annie's delivery had exhausted me.

Jesse came into our room and took my hand. "The doctor is worried. He talked of doing something to force the baby's birth if he doesn't come soon."

The thought made me shiver. "I don't think that will be necessary. We must be patient. The baby will come when he's ready."

But I did follow the doctor's orders to stay in bed. Polly and another neighbor, Louise Brandell, helped Annie with the baby and took Tim with them during the day so I could rest.

Within two weeks, Annie was strong enough to leave her bed. She brought the baby, who Frank had named Robert, to me so I could coo over his perfect features. Robert fussed and kicked his small legs. Annie watched me holding him and her face seemed more pensive than usual.

"I'm worried about him, Zee. The doctor says he's not getting enough milk from me."

"It's always hard at first. In the beginning, I struggled with feeding Tim, too. Sometimes it takes longer than we'd like for everything to work out."

She sighed and ran a finger over Robert's perfect cheek. "I hope you're right." We soothed each other with talk of babies until time for Annie to go. She wrapped Robert in a thick white blanket that I'd knitted for him and waved to me. Just as she reached the door, I cried out.

"Wait! My pains have started." I took a panting breath." Jesse's in the barn. I think you'd better have him go for the doctor."

Her mouth gaped. She put the baby's blanket over his face, and raced out the door. Another pain hit just before Jesse bounded into the room, rubbing his hands on his pants.

"Is it very bad yet?"

"The pain is coming, but it seems different than before." I floundered, helpless to explain the strange waves of contractions that rippled over my body.

"Annie's getting Polly. I'll go for the doctor as soon as they get here."

Within minutes, Annie and Polly trotted into the room, puffing from the effort. Jesse kissed me, his face tight with anxiety, before he left. Annie wiped my forehead and spoke with a gentle voice whenever the worst pains hit. After what seemed like hours of misery, Dr. Montgomery and Dr. Gould came into the room with Jesse. They shooed him away, and he backed out the door, eyes clouded, the armpits of his shirt damp.

Dr. Montgomery prodded at my stomach, while I bit my lip to keep from screaming. "I can't seem to push the baby out. Please, I'm so tired."

"Hold on, Mrs. Howard. The baby might be breech. I need to see if we need to turn him or if forceps will be necessary."

Dr. Montgomery probed my body while Annie held my hand. A part of my mind quaked at the idea of forceps, compelling me to summon every bit of strength I possessed. On the next cramp, I pushed and pushed, and the baby finally slid out.

Dr. Montgomery held up the child. "It's a boy, but he's small."

Annie took the baby to clean him. I waited for the welcome respite I remembered after Tim's birth, but the pain didn't stop. Waves of cramping came again. I bit my lip until I tasted blood.

"Something is wrong." Dr. Montgomery said as he bent to examine me. After a moment, he looked up at Dr. Gould and then at me. "There's a reason you're still having contractions. Another baby is coming."

Between my agony and the shock of his statement, I couldn't respond. He talked quietly, telling me when to push and when to rest. Finally, my body expelled the second baby and, like a blessing, the paroxysms left me.

"It's another boy."

The pain subsided, and I moved my head to see the babies while Dr. Montgomery tended to me. One lay bundled at my side. Dr. Gould examined the other.

Dr. Montgomery smiled down at me. "You did a fine job, Mrs. Howard. I'll bring your husband in to see what miracle has been wrought here." He laid one infant in my right arm while Annie put the other in my left. They were small—much smaller than Tim had been.

Jesse crept into the room as though he'd arrived on sacred

ground. His dazed expression brought a weary smile to my face. "Twins. I can't believe it."

I looked at the tiny, perfectly formed faces. One slept peacefully while the other squinted in a way so like my papa that I laughed out loud.

Jesse shook his head. "I'm nearly speechless. How did you manage such a thing?"

"They came from us both, and God must have intended it to be so. You always told me you wanted many children. I guess we're getting a good start."

Dr. Gould stood over me, observing the infants. He frowned, and called to Dr. Montgomery. "These babies don't look as pink as they should."

"Bring them over here," Dr. Montgomery said. Dr. Gould whisked them from my arms. Jesse stared, and I twisted my head to watch. A shiver shook me.

Dr. Gould spoke softly, but not so quietly that I couldn't hear him say, "Their breathing is feeble."

"What's wrong?" My voice rose until it broke, and Jesse put his hand on my arm to steady me.

Dr. Gould spoke from where he and Dr. Montgomery labored, ever more frantically, over the babies. "You must understand how it is with twins. They compete to grow."

Tears streamed down my cheeks. The doctors bent over the bed where my babies lay. They massaged tiny naked bodies with so much vigor, the collars of their shirts grew damp. Annie and Mrs. Eastman sponged my skin, but their pale faces and soft words were lost as I strained to hear what the doctors said to each other.

It seemed a very long while before Dr. Montgomery came to me, his eyes grim. He took my hand. By that time, I had no more tears left to shed.

27

The room smelled of sickness and blood and sorrow. The doctors said I could hold the babies for as long as I wished. Nestling them in my arms, I studied their tiny eyes, noses not even the size of a small button, and rosebud mouths, trying to memorize each feature. They looked as though they were asleep, and so similar to Tim when he was born, I wondered if the doctors were mistaken. Surely at any moment I would see some movement and they both would open their eyes and begin to breathe again.

Dr. Montgomery patted my arm and spoke of God's will. Dr. Gould described the extra difficulties with multiple-birth babies. Annie held my hand and cried as though it had been her own little one taken away. Jesse stared at the floor with hooded eyes like he'd encountered a battle he had no idea how to fight.

Tears weren't enough to allay a sorrow as deep as this. I remembered my parents, burying three babies not long after they were born, and felt a new respect for the stoic way they had returned to daily life. Then there were the other times when the voices of children born to family or friends were stilled by the gray hand of death. I'd been among those who brought food and spoke words of comfort to grieving parents. For them, life would never be the same again. Why must such a terrible price be paid by innocents?

When the doctors pressed me, I kissed each of my babies good-bye. Dr. Gould handed me a glass of water, into which he'd mixed a strong dose of laudanum to bring the peace of sleep.

Before I drank it, I clutched Jesse's hand. "They must have names before we bury them." I thought for a moment. "Montgomery and Gould. For the doctors who tried so hard to save them."

"Yes, sweetheart. Whatever you want is fine with me."

The next day, our babies were buried. I insisted on a single pine box no bigger than my footstool, for I couldn't bear the thought of them being under the ground alone. Jesse, Frank, and Annie went to the cemetery. I stayed at home, too weak and sick at heart to ask permission from the doctors to leave my bed.

Polly Eastman brought food and offered to keep Tim until my strength returned.

"Thank you," I told her. "I won't forget your kindness."

Neighbors stopped by to comfort me. I spoke only enough to make the correct reply and accept their awkward condolences. It didn't matter what anyone said. My babies were gone and I sensed the tendrils of darkness hovering around my bed like living things. Wild animals that waited to devour me.

When Polly brought Tim to see me, I couldn't rouse myself enough to respond with more than a silent, detached hug, but Jesse wrapped his arms around his son.

"I'll take him outside to the barn."

I nodded and turned my head away.

Over the next few days, my comfort lay in the few drops of laudanum that brought a dreamless sleep. It shielded my mind like a heavy curtain blotted out light. Jesse helped me to sit in a chair by the bed for a while each day and I stared out the window. It didn't help to see the sun, for the pull of something dark and sinister threatened to swallow me.

A week later, Annie came to see me. She held Robert, who she'd bundled against the cold of an early March day. "I'm so sorry to bother you, Zee, but I'm frantic and need your advice." Her lip trembled, and her cheeks were pale.

Seeing her baby made me wince. I longed for the comfort brought by laudanum, but roused myself enough to say, "What is it?"

"I've tried and tried with Robert. He wails from hunger, yet I cannot do much to help him. Frank refuses to hire a wet nurse. He thinks it could bring danger into our home. Dr. Montgomery says he's seen cases where boiled cow's milk can be given to an infant. Do you know how this is done?"

I pulled the tatters of my wits about me to think. "Some people use a rag dipped in milk for the baby to suck. Others use a spoon to trickle liquid into the infant's mouth. I've heard of rubber nipples attached to a bottle, but I've never seen one."

Robert began a weak, mewling cry.

Annie looked as though she might cry too. "He's so hungry, yet I can't help him."

I heard the baby, but had to close my eyes against the sight of a living child. It seemed too much to bear. I wanted Annie to take Robert away from me, so I could erase the sound of his cries with more laudanum. The pitiful wailing continued and got louder, more frantic. Then something happened in my battered body—an unmistakable tingling pressure in my breasts.

My eyes opened. "Give him to me."

Annie stared. "What?"

"Give him to me. I can feed him."

I untied the bodice of my gown and took the baby from Annie. The infant turned his head toward me, rooted, then latched. At first hesitant, then more eager, he suckled. The cramping pull from my womb was almost painful, but the baby ate as though he'd been long starved. I looked down at him and touched his soft cheek, my tears falling in silent drops. I cried for Robert and for my own babies. I cried for Jesse and for Tim and for myself. Yet as others had done before me, I had to move on with life.

Annie continued to bring Robert to me over the next many months. He grew rosy and plump, and each time I nursed him, I fancied my own babies were smiling from within Robert's precious face.

As I occupied myself with him, my body healed. Despite all that had happened, I couldn't help but notice that the dreaded restlessness had returned to my husband. Frank and Annie had started to attend the Methodist church every Sunday and became friends with other parishioners, while Jessie brooded over a chasm growing wider between him and his brother.

When Frank stopped by one evening and asked Jesse if he'd like to go sit on the front porch with the Eastmans, Jesse shook his head. "What pleasure do you get from talking about crops and spouting Shakespeare? I can't think of anything more boring."

"I like talking with Charles. It makes me feel like I'm part of this town. Like I belong here."

"You know better than to get friendly with people who aren't our kin. What if they discover who you are? No one can be trusted."

"Well, I say you're wrong," Frank glowered, shook his head, and walked out.

Jesse went to the table and slammed his hand on it. The dishes rattled.

"I'm going out to feed the horses," he called over his shoulder.

The lines around his mouth worried me. I knew Jesse still mourned for our babies. He'd told me he couldn't get their faces from his mind. Even when he lifted Tim in front of him on the saddle and cantered his horse along the path near the house, I could see a shadow of grief following him.

On a sunny afternoon, I hung clothes on the line. while Tim napped. When I dragged the empty basket to the house, I found Jesse on the porch. He handed me one hundred dollars. "For the rent and the doctor."

I stared at the money. "Where did this come from?"

"I sold Red Fox."

My mouth gaped, and I dropped the bills. Jesse knelt to gather them before the breeze could.

"But why? You loved that horse."

"We needed the money. You might as well hear it now. I'll be leaving for a while, and I had to have some cash. I've got to get away from here. And"—he slapped at a persistent summer fly—"I'm asking Frank to go with me."

"He won't go, Jesse. He's happy here."

"He's my brother. He'll do it."

Tears filled my eyes at the look on his face when he walked away. Jesse left the next morning—alone.

When Jesse returned, dark hair bristled over his lip and chin, but he wore his hat cocked to the side. His whiskers scratched my face when he kissed me and then he gave a bear-growling hug to Tim. He handed our son a peppermint stick and sent him off to play.

We sat at the kitchen table, and Jesse took my hand. His fingers were ragged and rough, as though he'd been baling hay without wearing gloves.

When he spoke, his blue eyes hardened. "I sent a letter asking John Edwards to meet with me. He didn't even bother to answer it. Ever since publishing his book, he seems to have forgotten all about what I'm still trying to do for the South."

"Jesse, your brother is making a fine life here in Tennessee. Why can't we do the same? Instead of fighting old battles, you could work the farm as he is and forget about the past."

"Forget it?" Jesse's face reddened. "How can I ever forget the past? How can you forget it?"

"I have to forget or I'll go mad." I squeezed his hand. "Remember, nothing from the past can break us as long as we're together."

He leaned over and pressed his lips to mine. "At least you haven't deserted me." A half smile played at his lips. "I'm afraid I've become what I am, and there's no going back now." He sighed and rose from his chair. "Could you fix me something to eat while I take care of my horse?"

Over the years, I'd seen Jesse filled with many emotions: playfulness, passion, even anger. But I'd never seen him quite so empty.

I tucked Tim into bed and fixed Jesse a simple dinner of cold chicken, corn, and tomatoes. When he returned from the barn, listless and silent, I rubbed the tight knots in his back until he'd cleaned every morsel from his plate.

"It's too warm in here," I said. "Let's sit together on the porch."

He followed me outside, and we settled into the wooden rocking chairs. Evening had softened the day's heat. Night creatures chirped, and an owl hooted from behind the barn. I rocked back and forth while the cool breeze fanned my face. Jesse sat still as a stone, his countenance naked with despair

After a while, I stood and reached for his hand. "Dearest, come with me." I knew he needed the comfort only a wife could give. I led him to our bed and blew out the lamp.

When the first light of day peeped through the window, I got up to put the iron skillet on the fire. By the time ham sizzled and popped, Jesse appeared. He put his arms around me, and I noticed a glimmer of light had returned to his eyes.

"You understand like no one else, Zee. I don't know what I'd do without you. Thanks for giving me more than I deserve." He kissed me and patted my back. "Buck's out at the barn. I have a few things to talk over with him, but I'll be back soon for some of that ham."

He went out the door whistling. If I squinted my eyes, he looked almost as young as he had on the day he asked me to marry him.

I dressed Tim and cut up some ham and a biscuit for him to eat. Then I fixed a plate for Jesse and cleaned up the kitchen mess. Just as I wiped out the skillet, Jesse came through the door, rubbing the back of his neck.

"I have the perfect opportunity to make some quick money, but Buck says he won't go. He's grown fat and lazy here in Nashville. The will to take a chance seems to have gone plum out of him. I talked until I ran out of things to say, but he won't budge an inch. He likes things just the way they are."

I patted stray crumbs from Tim's mouth. "Did that change your mind about leaving?"

He looked at me and rolled his eyes. "When did I ever let any other man influence me? I'm master of my own fate. We need money, and if things go as well as I think, I can get enough to buy the land we want and build our own house. Doesn't that sound good to you?"

I wanted to tell him I'd rather rent a small place right in the middle of town than have him leave again. I wanted to tell him he'd been promising that we'd have the money for our own house for years. I wanted to … but I didn't.

Within days of our conversation, Jesse left. Frank watched him go, his shoulders hunched with Annie's arm tucked around his. She looked up at him and smiled her gratitude. I rubbed an ache in my lower back and put Tim down for a nap.

A few weeks later, I discovered I was once again with child.

hankfully, Jesse wasn't gone long. As the months passed and my belly swelled, Frank and Jesse decided to move us from Hyde's Ferry Road to a small farm owned by an old bachelor, Felix Smith. Jesse wanted the continued assurance of a place for Tim and me near Frank's family, while he made plans for what would come next.

My first view of the whitewashed farmhouse made me smile. The two-story residence was even larger than the boarding house from my childhood. We took the second floor, while Frank and Annie lived on the main. Mr. Smith resided in a small addition on the side but would share meals with us as part of our board.

"This is the most charming place I've ever seen," I said.

"I knew you'd like it. The house has plenty of room, and the land is good. I've decided to try my hand at something new because I want you to be happy, Zee," he nuzzled his face against my cheek. "Frank says there's potential to grow a good crop. With the baby coming, I'd like to stay closer to home."

I gulped, and my heart summersaulted. "Oh, Jesse. Nothing would make me happier. I know this is a different life, but I'm grateful you're willing to try. I've always thought I'd make a good farmer's wife." I tweaked his ear. "Perhaps we can get a milk cow, too. How wonderful if we could provide for our own needs and not be beholden to anyone else."

"Beholden to no one," Jesse said with a kiss planted on the tip of my nose. "That sounds like a good life."

Jesse rose early each day and went to the field, tinkering with the plow and arguing with Frank over whether tobacco or hemp would bring more profit. Once they shook hands on planting both, Jesse harnessed the mule and coaxed neat seams into the ground. On Saturdays, he drove into town and talked with other farmers to hear their suggestions. When he came home, he had a bounce to his walk and I suspected he enjoyed the conversation far more than he did the long days of working under the sun.

At the end of a day thick with heat and humidity, Jesse woke in the middle of the night with a pounding headache. His body burned, and so much sweat poured from him, I fetched a towel and sent for the doctor. When the doctor came, he studied Jesse's symptoms and turned to me.

"He's got malaria."

My hand flew to my belly until the doctor assured me the sickness wasn't contagious. He left a bottle of quinine and told me to keep Jesse in bed.

I sponged his arms and legs to keep down the fever that reddened his skin. Jesse tossed and turned, but I didn't stop until he grabbed my hand.

"Here you are, stuck with taking care of me again. I'm sorry, Zee."

I dipped the cloth and ran it down his arm. "I don't imagine you got sick on purpose. If you take your medicine and do what the doctor says, you'll be up again soon."

"This won't help us in growing our crops, will it?"

"Don't worry yourself. Frank hired some men to help. The crops will be planted on time," I said.

He fretted with the sheet that covered him. "You know money is scarce. One of the things about farming I hate most is that it takes spending a lot of cash and waiting months before there's any return. And that's if the weather's mild, bugs and blight stay away, and the crop grows the way it should."

"Don't worry about it, dearest. You must keep your mind easy and rest."

But several weeks passed before Jesse could leave his bed. Even then, his energy remained sapped, and along with it, his will for the hard work of farming. After investing what it took to plant our crop, we had almost nothing left, and the time for my confinement drew closer. The worry over how we'd pay the doctor's bills kept both of us up at night.

Jesse grew increasingly morose over his powerlessness and our empty pockets. He told me he planned to leave again.

"But I need you here when the baby comes. I'm afraid what happened before might happen again."

His eyes shadowed before he pulled me to him. "I won't be gone long. Frank and Annie will take care of you until I get back. I've an idea for something to bring in quick money."

I toyed with the collar of his shirt. "I pray each time you leave that nothing will happen to you, but I can't help wondering. What if God is looking at the things that have happened and passing judgment on us?"

His eyes widened. "I can understand why you might believe such a thing of me. I know what I've done. But why, pray tell, do you think God would sit in judgment of you? You've done nothing except defend your family. Could it be you've become unhappy married to a man who can't do anything well except be an outlaw?" He swallowed, and his eyes did not meet mine.

I cupped his face and turned it toward me. "Jesse, I'd never think such a thing. You've always been good to me and the best father to Tim. You've done everything you can for us. Yet I keep thinking of what happened to our babies."

Jesse wrapped his arms around me. "I tell you no just God would punish you in such a way. Do you think God was punishing Ma when the Pinkertons killed Archie? Do you think our babies were taken away because God wanted to teach me a lesson? I remind you of your own words to me not so many years ago. God doesn't punish people for doing what they have to do."

A tear slipped down my cheek, and I rested my head against his chest. "When our babies died, Dr. Montgomery spoke of God's will." I gulped and went on. "Please rethink going away. At least consider a different life as your brother has done and pray over the right thing to do."

His arms dropped to his sides and he stepped back. "I haven't been much on prayer for the past few years, and even if I was, I can't think about that now." He turned and walked toward the door. With his hand on the knob, he turned back. "Plans have already been laid, Zee. It's too late to change them."

Now would be the time for me to insist. To demand he do what I asked of him. I took a deep breath to speak, when the baby in my womb kicked hard. My hand flew to my belly. We had no money. My confinement was near, and I dared not let emotion compromise my baby's welfare. I had no choice but to wait.

Over the next few weeks, Jesse rode away then returned many times. With each trip, he gained more of his old strength, sitting tall on his horse the way he used to. By early July, I had begun my confinement, and when Dr. Goodman, who attended me, said our baby appeared to be growing in a normal way, I breathed out a sigh of relief. My legs and feet weren't swollen, and my belly didn't grow as large. The doctor seemed satisfied there would be no complications.

When Jesse returned that evening, I told him what the doctor said. He glanced at me then jerked his gaze away. I chose not to ask what he was thinking, fearful of inflaming emotions that could risk the health of my baby.

But on July 17, 1879, Dr. Goodman delivered a plump and rosy girl. I wept at the sight of her, at hearing her loud cry, at running a finger over her ruddy pink skin. Jesse stood beside me as the doctor announced her arrival and handed her to me. This time, Jesse had remained in the room, sitting with fingers steepled and a grim look on his face during my labor. When he saw the baby at my breast, his features finally relaxed, and his eyes sparkled with unshed tears.

Soon, Annie and Frank appeared with Tim and Robert to admire the new baby. Robert stared.

Annie prodded my son. "Who is that, Tim?"

"Sissy," he responded.

I smiled and nodded. "That's right. She's your baby sister."

"Now we need to let the new mama and baby rest." Annie smoothed Tim's errant cowlick. "Let's go downstairs and I'll fix dinner."

Tim happily scampered away with Annie and Frank, as Jesse stroked our daughter's tiny hand.

"I have an idea what to name her," I said.

"Well, I suppose it's fair for a mother to name her daughter. What do you suggest?"

"I thought we'd christen her Mary Susan, after my mother and your sister."

"Ah," he said, letting the baby wrap her fingers around his pinkie, "I think that is perfect."

Jesse seemed easier now that his pockets were filled with money. He paid off the debt we owed at the mercantile, gave cash to the doctor, and paid Felix Smith for back rent.

One week after Mary's birth, Jesse presented me with a Smith and Wesson pocket pistol. It had a mother-of-pearl grip inscribed with my initials.

"That's for giving me a daughter almost as pretty as her mama."

"I've never seen anything like it. Thank you, Jesse."

"I know how you feel about my old pistol, but I thought you'd like this one. Of course, you won't be able to shoot for a while, but when you're up again, I'll show you how to use it."

Later, I gave Annie some money to buy pretty little dresses and bonnets for Mary at the mercantile. Dressed in bows and frills, my daughter looked like the blue-eyed china doll I'd once seen in a store window. Showering her with the gifts our twins would never have eased my pain a little and helped fill the hole they left in my heart. It was a happy time, yet most of my smiles were due to Jesse staying close to home. Perhaps Mary's birth had given him peace, too.

One late afternoon, Mary nestled in my arms as I stroked her soft hair. Jesse walked into the kitchen. His eyes were downcast, and he stared at a paper in his hand.

My heart jumped at the look on his face. "What's wrong?"

"It's a telegram from home." He lifted his chin to look at me and swallowed.

I held my breath.

"There's no easy way to say it, Zee. It's your sister. Lucy. She ... a sudden fever settled on her, and she's gone."

My eyes closed and another hole ripped open in my heart. "Oh, no."

"I'm afraid it's true. Your brother Thomas sent the telegram. I can't believe it either. Lucy was so good to us both." He shook his head and knelt beside me. "It might not be a good idea for you to travel, but if you want to go home, I'll find a way."

"You know I can't leave with the baby so young." I shook my head, and tears dropped on Mary's head like soft rain. "What could I do for Lucy now anyway? I'll write a letter to Boling and pray for her soul."

Later that night, in bed, Jesse held me until I fell asleep. I dreamed Lucy came to see me. We hugged, and she kissed my cheek before her spirit—for I know she'd come to comfort me—faded away. When my eyes opened, my cheeks were wet, but I knew she was at peace.

And so was I.

While I regained my strength, Jesse began to wander from home again.

"I'm finished with the idea of farming," he told me. "It's not in my blood. I'm going back to take what we need from those who can spare it until we've got enough money to buy the ranch we want."

His words chilled me, and I noticed he didn't mention Frank. Over the past months, they'd become more distant with each other. Frank avoided Jesse, and the only recent moment of levity they shared came on the day Annie found a newspaper story that declared the famous outlaw Jesse James had been shot dead. The brothers clapped each other on the back, succumbing to spasms of laughter. I couldn't even smile over their amusement. The story made me shudder.

With Frank in pursuit of his passion for farming, Jesse's world narrowed. Most of his old companions had been killed or remanded to jail, so he sought out new friends, and found men such as Dick Liddil and Bill Ryan. Bill lived in Missouri, but he often stayed in our barn when he came to Nashville. Bill made me uneasy from the moment I met him, and I felt as though his eyes bored into my back every time I walked past him.

His presence made me anxious and drove a wedge between Jesse and me. I tried not to let it show, but sometimes my tone was sharpened. One evening, after a long day of tending to the two children and watching Jesse come in and out making mysterious plans for his next trip, my voice betrayed me.

"So how many will we have for dinner tonight?"

Jesse acted as though he barely heard me. "I don't know. Depends on who shows up."

I narrowed my eyes at him. "But I need to know how much food to make."

He turned to look at me, a scowl on his face. "Use your judgment, Zee, and don't peck at me."

Stung, I marched to the kitchen and put a kettle on to boil. Something gnawed my husband, though I had no idea what. He was so secretive, and I feared the influence his new friends had over him. I sliced potatoes into chunks and mulled over our situation.

A few moments later, Jesse came to stand behind me, circling his arms around my waist. "I'm sorry, sweetheart. There are a lot of things happening. You know money's tight again. I've got to do something to make quick cash."

I stiffened, and he nuzzled my neck. "Please, sweetheart, you know how much I need you."

I put down the knife and the sound of his smoky voice turned me like a flower to the sun. "Please don't leave, Jesse. I'm worried. I don't trust these new men."

"Try to understand my position. Now that Frank refuses to go with me, I had to find others to help. You understand that, don't you?"

"I try to, but this life is wearing me thin. When will this marauding ever stop? When will we be free of it?"

"Maybe sooner than you think. I sent a letter about some property in Nevada, and I'm getting more information about acreage I heard of in Nebraska. Either would work out well for raising horses. Once I find out how much money I'll need, we can make our plans."

I said nothing and picked up another potato to slice.

The next morning, Jesse rode out, not returning this time until the middle of September. I could tell by his beaming face that the trip had gone well. He kissed Tim and the baby before putting his arms around me.

"I have something for you," he pulled out a small velvet bag. "This is my thanks for being such an understanding wife." He opened the bag and withdrew a diamond ring. Then he took my hand and pushed it on my finger next to the thin gold band I hadn't removed since the day we were wed.

"It's beautiful," I said as the ring sparkled from the fire's light. Even though I knew his guilt had prompted the gesture, I still loved it.

"You deserve this and more. I tell you, my dear, it won't be much longer until all our dreams come true."

But by the time the year ended, Jesse was gone more than not. It seemed like he'd been driven into a frenzy of activity, though he spoke little of it to me. When at home, his eyes seldom left the window and he wore his guns until he went to bed at night. Jesse kept the pocket pistol he'd given me loaded and hidden in the bottom of a trunk near our bed.

Only his love of horses did not change. Jesse bought a new sorrel stallion named Jim Malone. He and Dick Liddil raced the animal at the track. Occasionally, Frank left Annie to join them. The horse won an impressive nine times, and Jesse boasted that none could beat him. Yet he soon grew disenchanted and sold Jim Malone, vowing to find an even faster horse.

By early 1881, I wondered how much longer he could keep such a pace and how much longer I could deal with it. Only my children gave me something to think of other than the devils chasing Jesse's soul. Even the children had grown restless. Tim, now more than five years old, had taken to staring out the window when other children played near our house. "Mama, can I go outside and play with them?"

"I'm sorry, but Papa feels it best that you stay in the house with me."

Tim's eyes were wide. "Doesn't Papa like other children?"

"It's not that, dear. He worries about you and doesn't want anything to happen. Come along. I've been thinking about making some candy. Would you like to help?"

He looked longingly out the window but turned away to join me. My boy tried so hard to be good. It broke my heart that he couldn't be like the other children. Jesse had become fiercely protective, and jittery that any slip of the tongue would bring dire consequences. He'd even forbidden me from talking to the neighbors except on occasions when such rudeness became impossible. I thanked God to have Annie and little Robert nearby, or my world would have grown even smaller than when I lived at the boarding house. Some invisible force drove my husband, and I despaired of discovering what it could be—or of how to fix a wound I couldn't even see.

On a cool late March evening, a rider galloped to our house just after I'd put the children to bed. Jesse pulled out his revolver and peered through the window. A moment later, he sighed and holstered the weapon. "It's Dick," he told me and opened the door.

Dick Liddil rushed in, puffing, and carrying the odor of dust and layered sweat. "I just heard Bill Ryan's been arrested. He was drunk on his ass at a bar in White's Creek. They found him with money and weapons in his pockets, and he started to brag in that Irish brogue of his about being an outlaw and fighting the government. You know how thick-headed he can be when he's in his cups. The man can't be trusted. I'll wager he'll soon squawk to high heaven about everything he knows."

Jesse's face grew pale, and his body stiffened. The flames from the fireplace made his eyes glisten like a fox's.

"Frank's visiting at the next farm. I'll ride over to get him," Jesse said. "We need to clear out of here before Ryan talks, or there'll be a noose for each of us." He turned to me and repeated the words I'd heard so many times.

"Start packing at once. We need to be gone before the sun comes up."

29

t took Jesse and Frank mere minutes to plan our exodus. Because they said it would be too obvious, they decided Annie and I couldn't travel together.

"I'm putting Annie and Robert on the train to Kansas City," Frank said. "Her father will let them stay until I can get back."

Jesse had already told me that the children and I would take the train to Donnie Pence in Nelson County, Kentucky until he came for us. Jesse trusted Donnie, a former guerilla comrade, completely. They'd grown up together in Clay County, and I remembered his bushy walrus moustache from the few occasions I'd seen him since. After the war, he'd ridden with Jesse in the early years, until a bullet helped convince him to settle in Kentucky.

Dick Liddil rented two large buckboard wagons and horses to pull them. When the sun dropped low enough to peek over the horizon, we scrambled to load the items we could take. With Mary on my hip, I gave Tim a small bag of clothes to carry, while the men loaded trunks, the dismantled pieces of our beds, and even a small stove.

Annie carried her bags to the wagon, looking as though she might burst into tears at any moment. The men arranged items with practiced skill. I looked at the clear evening sky and gave thanks for the absence of heavy clouds that might bring rain.

Jesse, Frank, and Dick planned to linger near Nashville until they discovered what information Bill gave authorities and whether what he said would connect John Howard and Ben Woodson to the outlaws everyone sought.

Our wagons would of necessity travel in different directions, so before we parted, I hugged my sister-in-law. Tears trailed down her cheeks.

"Good-bye, Annie. I hope we'll see each other again soon."

She held me close and swallowed a sob. "I'll pray hard we make it through this."

"As will I. Take good care of yourself and my little Robert." I kissed the cheek of the now three-year-old boy, remembering the months I had nursed him for Annie. "Good-bye, my little sweetheart. May God bless you."

There were shadows under Frank's eyes too, when he kissed me good-bye. He'd been so content in his role of farmer. I knew he would miss the life he'd created for himself, and I sensed his sorrow at becoming a wanderer yet again.

Jesse took his brother's hand to shake it, but Frank grabbed Jesse's shoulders in a tight hug. It lasted a moment before Jesse broke free and rubbed his sleeve across his eyes.

"Damned dust," he muttered to me.

Frank drove the buckboard away, his horse tied behind it so he could turn the reins over to Annie when they were closer to the depot. Jesse watched them with an attentive gaze. Then he turned and slapped the reins, and the horse carried us away. Dick rode alongside, slouch hat pulled low. Jesse's mare, tied to our buckboard, followed behind.

"I'll have you on the train first thing for Kentucky," Jesse said. "You'll need to travel from a different depot than Annie so a nosy reporter doesn't put two and two together. Donnie will be waiting. He's a loyal man and will look out for you and the children."

"How long until you come for us?"

"I'm not sure. It may take a little while but keep watch. I'll be there soon as I can."

A breeze blew against my face while the children dozed. Stars blinked through the maze of treetops, and I considered the quiet strength of the tall oaks and pines along the road. They had to sink their roots deep to flourish through strong winds and stormy weather. If someone tried to transplant them, they'd soon wither and die.

"What are you thinking, Zee?" Jesse asked in a soft voice.

"Only wondering where we'll go next. Have you decided yet?"

"I'm considering a stay in Kansas City. We've been away a long time. I think we both need to be among our kin again."

"Is that wise?"

"I won't take us anywhere that isn't safe." He pulled back on the horse's reins. "We're close enough to the depot for me to leave you now." Jesse handed me twenty dollars in greenbacks. "This is the last of our cash. I don't think the tickets will run you much. After you buy them, use what's left for any expense you have until I get to Kentucky. Be frugal as you can."

"But what if you need money?"

"I can take care of myself. Don't worry about me."

The children stirred and stretched. Jesse leaned down to kiss them and Mary clung to her papa.

"Be a good girl, Mary. Tim, you must stand in for me. Look out for your mama and sister."

"I will, Papa," came his small voice, speaking as stoutly as he could manage.

Finally, Jesse took me in his arms. He kissed me hard and whispered, "I love you."

"I love you, too. Please be careful and come back to us soon."

He touched his hat and smiled. "You know I will." He pulled an envelope from the pocket of his coat. "I need you to mail this when you reach Kentucky."

I nodded and tucked the envelope into my bag. "I'll take care of it for you."

Jesse untied his horse and swung into the saddle. Dick Liddil pushed ahead on the road, and I swatted the reins across the horse's back. When I turned to give Jesse a final wave, he was gone.

The creak and roll of wagon wheels and the horse's clip clops silenced any other sounds. We didn't have far to go. By the time the sun peeked around clouds and lightened the horizon with color like a ripe peach, we'd arrived at the depot. I pulled the horse to a stop and tied him to a post. An engine hissed in readiness to leave, waking Tim and Mary.

"Tim, you stay here with your sister while I get our tickets for the train."

"Yes, Mama," he replied, dangling a toy horse in front of Mary's face.

She giggled and reached for it.

At the ticket window, a man with spectacles and long gray whiskers raised his head from the papers on his desk. "May I help you, ma'am?"

"I'm traveling to Nelson County, Kentucky, with my two children. We need tickets. I also have a wagonload of goods to ship."

"Let's see. For you, the children's fares, and your cargo, the charge will be twenty-five dollars."

My eyes widened. "What? How can our passage be so much?"

"I'm sorry, ma'am, but it's twenty dollars for your fare and five dollars for a shipment to Kentucky."

"Let me think about it for a moment, please. I'll be right back."

I turned from him and pondered what to do. How could I travel with two young children and not so much as a penny to spare? What if something happened to delay our arrival and I couldn't feed them even a scrap of bread or send a telegram for help? I stared at the wagon where my children played together, and an idea came. I gulped and went back inside the depot.

"Sir, I have a fine horse and a wagon filled with household goods. I'm a widow trying to get my children back to our family and can't afford to take everything with me. Do you know anyone who might like to buy the wagon and horse and all the goods except for my trunk?" The lie came so easily that my cheeks burned. I forced myself not to look away.

But the man at the window misunderstood my embarrassment and regarded me with kind eyes. "Well, ma'am, I suppose we can always use another buggy and horse to rent. And come to think of it, there are often folks passing through who need to buy a few items they forgot to bring along. How would it be if I gave you forty-five dollars for everything? Would that help you out?"

"Oh, yes, thank you. You're most generous."

"That's all right, ma'am. I'm sorry for your loss. I'd like to think if my wife was left alone, somebody would help her out, too."

The clerk counted out the money, less the cost of our tickets and payment to ship the trunk. I put the cash in my purse and smiled at him. "Thank you again, sir. Can you tell me when the train leaves?"

He pulled out a pocket watch. "It's scheduled to go in thirty minutes. It should be a nice ride for you unless some bandits decide they like the looks of our train." He laughed at his own joke until he saw the color drain from my face. "Oh, don't worry, ma'am. Our train hasn't been held up in a long time. You got nothing to fear."

I nodded and swallowed hard. As I walked back to the children, I had to press my lips together to keep them from trembling. I'd just lied to a gentleman who did me a kindness and sold him a horse and wagon that belonged to someone else. I supposed what Jesse had said was true. A person could do just about anything with their back pressed against the wall.

Tim looked at me with his father's eyes. "Mama, can we have something to eat?"

"I have a sandwich to split between you. It will have to do for now."

They reached for the small offering from the sack I'd brought from home. Tim took slow and purposeful bites while Mary stuffed her cheeks so full, she looked like a chipmunk. I wasn't hungry.

A loud whistle caught my attention. Mary covered her

ears while we watched passengers climb the steps to board the train. I took the children's hands. We walked to the car, and I pointed out my trunk to the porter. Reaching our seats, Tim and Mary settled across from me. Fearing some quirk of fate might cause me to be hauled from the train and sent to the sheriff, I closed my eyes and prayed we'd soon be underway.

But no one chased me. When the train chuffed from the station, I breathed a sigh of relief. Tim and Mary peered out the window to see a herd of cattle. They pointed and giggled until the rocking motion lulled them to silence, then to sleep.

I pulled from my bag the envelope Jesse had given me. He'd addressed it to D.T. Bligh, of the Pinkerton agency. The name sounded familiar, and I searched my memory until it came to me. Bligh was one of the detectives who'd been after Jesse and told everyone in Kearney he hoped he'd live long enough to see Jesse James at least once. I stared at the envelope, and noticed the flap wasn't quite sealed. I knew I shouldn't, but at that point, nothing could stop me from opening it to see what Jesse had written.

The plain white paper showed a simple message in Jesse's scrawl.

Mr. Bligh, you have seen me. Now you can go ahead and die. From your friend—Jesse James

I shook my head. His hatred for the Pinkertons still rankled him, even though Alan Pinkerton had given up on the idea of finding Jesse James. Jesse took a strange delight in toying with his enemies and did things calculated to fan bright flames even higher. It was as though he lived for the challenge of outwitting anyone who hunted him.

I rested my head against the cool window and stared at

the scenery flashing past. The day's deeds had soured my stomach. I closed my eyes. *What has happened to us, Jesse? What has happened to me?* My thoughts circled back to the money in my bag, and I deliberately tucked what I'd done in a corner of my heart where rested all the things for which I hoped God would someday be merciful enough to forgive me.

But something else in my thoughts could not be so easily banished. Each minute, the train took me farther away from two small babies lying in the cold damp ground of Tennessee.

30

When our train arrived in Kentucky, I stood and stretched my neck. Both of the children were still sound asleep, exhausted from the rapid scramble from home and late-night ride.

I called to them softly. "Tim, Mary, it's time to wake up. We need to go."

Tim rubbed his eyes. Mary yawned, and I smoothed her rumpled hair.

"Come along now, children."

They left their seats and stumbled after me. The porter offered his arm as I stepped to the planked depot station platform.

"Sir, where might I find my trunk?"

"Three cars back, ma'am. That's where the cargo is unloaded. I hope you and the children enjoyed your trip." He tipped his cap to me.

"Yes, we did. Thank you."

Mary, never one to waken without effort, moved so stiffly I had to pick her up and carry her. She nestled her head against my shoulder while Tim trotted at my side.

I searched through many boxes and crates piled in a haphazard heap before finding my battered old trunk among them. Knowing better than to lift it myself, I looked around for help. I'd decided to pay someone to carry the trunk, when a deep voice growled.

"Hello there, ma'am!"

I turned and saw Donnie Pence, walrus moustache bushy as ever. He walked toward me with an ear-to-ear grin, moving like a man who spent a great deal of time on his feet. Relieved to see a familiar face, I dimpled when he took my hand.

"How are you doing, my dear? These little cherubs must be your young-uns. I've heard all about them from their pa."

"Yes. This is Tim and Mary."

Mary hid behind my skirt and peeked at him with round eyes. Donnie bent over and stuck out his hand for Tim to shake like a big boy would. "How de-do," Donnie said as Tim's small hand disappeared into Donnie's ham-sized fist.

"Well now, where might your bags be?"

I pointed at the trunk and Donnie hoisted it over his shoulder as though it contained nothing more than feathers.

"Follow me," he said.

The children and I traipsed behind him, dodging other passengers, until I remembered Jesse's letter. "Could you give me one moment to post this, please?"

"You go ahead and do what you must. I'll stay here with the small fry."

I mailed the letter and returned to see Donnie sitting on the trunk deep in conversation with the children. Tim listened with rapt attention, and even Mary had become bold enough to sit on his knee.

"I see you've charmed my children."

He chuckled and put Mary back on her feet. "I was just telling them about the litter of puppies my hound dog had yesterday. Told them they could go to the barn and take a look when we get home."

I could tell by their shining faces that the idea pleased them very much. Donnie lifted the trunk again and we resumed our trek behind him. It surprised me to notice nearly every passerby greeted Donnie with a smile and a wave.

"Good day, Sheriff."

"How do you do, Sheriff Pence?"

"Hello, Sheriff."

With my perspective narrowed to my own circumstances, I'd completely forgotten that Donnie had long ago put his past behind him and had been voted sheriff of the county. He'd served honorably for the past ten years and, according to Jesse, who still visited him from time to time, had become one of the most beloved citizens in the community. That a lawman and my husband would be on such good terms seemed strange to me, yet he, Jesse, and Frank had grown up together in Missouri, fought side-by-side in the war, and even ridden through a few private battles once the war ended. Their ties remained unbroken.

On the drive home, we kept our conversation to nothing more significant than the weather and crops and happier times, for Tim and Mary were both wide awake and listening to every word we said.

I adjusted my hat and smiled. "So you're a farmer in addition to being sheriff? How do you find time for it all?"

"Sheriffing is simple enough. We hardly ever have a crime, short of a stolen chicken once in a while. Farming is harder. But it helps when you can hire a few men who know what they're doing."

When we passed the neatly plowed fields of Donnie's farm, his chest expanded with pride. He drove us toward a clapboard two-story farmhouse and shouted for his wife. "Belle, they're here."

A short, plump dark-haired woman came out on the porch, wiping her hands on a towel. She smiled cordially. "Hello, Mrs. ... Howard. It's good to meet you at last."

That she paused a moment before saying my name, spoke volumes. Someone told her what to call me.

I nodded. "How do you do? I'm pleased to meet you and so grateful for your hospitality."

"Come with me. I have a room fixed up for the three of you. Donnie will bring in your trunk." She led us to a room with a full bed and a smaller cot that Tim and Mary would share. Mrs. Pence's eyes followed my children hungrily. "They're very sweet. I pray someday Donnie and I may be so blessed. Is it all right if I get them something to eat?"

"Oh, that would be wonderful. They haven't had much since yesterday. We had to leave so fast."

She slanted a sympathetic glance toward me before turning back to the children. "I have a nice lunch for you in the kitchen if you're hungry."

Ever cautious, Tim first looked at me. "May we go, Mama?"

"Yes, Tim. You and Mary go with Mrs. Pence. Remember your manners."

All shyness gone at the promise of food, Tim and Mary followed her. I took off my hat and sat on a chair near the bed. The thought of a good night's sleep made me run my hand longingly over the faded patchwork quilt thrown across the sheets.

I jumped when Donnie thumped my trunk near the door.

"Thank you. I'm not sure where we would have gone if not here with you."

"Always happy to help my friends." He shook his head. "I keep trying to convince Jesse to quit his old ways. Sooner or later he's going to get caught, you know. That boy sure is a lot different from his brother. Buck would like to settle down, but Jesse's always had a restlessness about him. From what I know, his pa did too, which is why he's in a grave out in California instead of at home with his family. Jesse was too young to be a part of the things he did during the war. It marked him for good. Of course, old Mrs. Samuel doesn't help matters much, either. She practically spoon-fed her boys defiance from the time they was old enough to listen."

I sighed. No one knew Jesse's nature better than I. "I hope our presence won't bring you any trouble. After all, you are the sheriff."

He stroked his moustache for a moment before he spoke. "You know, there's a lot of things that happened to us during the war. Things that made men who rode together become closer than brothers. Like the day I rode with Quantrill's gang and some bluecoat shot my horse dead. That old plug fell over, and I got pinned under him with a regiment of Federals coming my way, whooping and hollering. There were a few of us left standing, and most everybody high-tailed it for cover—except Frank. He came back and pulled me from under my horse. Then he and Jesse helped me get away. They saved my life. You don't soon forget something like that."

"I understand war makes a strong bond. But what about your wife? Will this bother her?"

"Belle understands. She's a Kentucky gal, born and raised. You needn't have any fear over her feelings."

Perhaps his home was, indeed, the safest place for us. Who would think to question the motives of their beloved sheriff?

After dinner, I went to bed and fell into a dreamless sleep. In the morning, I awoke with a throat that scratched and my skin felt hot.

Belle put her hand on my forehead. "I'd better send for the doctor. We can't be too careful with fever, you know."

By mid-afternoon, she returned with a tall, gray-haired man.

"Mrs. Howard, this is Dr. Spencer." Belle smiled. "I'll leave you for now. I promised the children I'd take them out to see the new puppies."

The doctor bent over me. "Now, Mrs. Howard, let me see what's ailing you."

The doctor completed his examination and diagnosed me with exhaustion and a cold that had settled in my head. I took a spoonful of a bitter-tasting concoction and he told me I should rest. Then he set a bottle of medicine by my bedside, patted my hand, and left. I followed his orders, always fearful of the onset of a blue spell.

But within a few days, I felt myself again, and rose from my bed, more anxious than ever for Jesse to come. The children had been well-entertained during my recovery. Donnie let them follow him about on the farm while Belle baked so many sweet treats, I hoped we wouldn't need to call the doctor for a return visit.

It took another week before Jesse, Frank, and Dick Liddil rode in late one evening. I breathed a prayer of thanks. Newspaper stories of the ongoing manhunt for

Jesse James, made me despair over whether they'd ever make it back. Even Donnie had looked pensive over their prospects. Yet once again, Jesse returned to me, though not without effort.

The three men were thin, covered with sweat-dampened travel dirt, and ravenous. Belle and I put together a quick meal of cold meat and bread. Since the children were already asleep upstairs, we were free to speak as we wished.

"Zee, I'm sending you on the train to Kansas City with the children. When you arrive, I'll have somebody take you to your sister Nancy's house until I meet you there."

"But you just came back. Can't we travel together?"

He sighed. "You know better than that. There are too many men looking for me, but there's no law against a woman taking her children to visit their aunt. I expect in about a week or so, I'll follow you. By that time, I'll have figured out where we go next."

I didn't want to question him in front of so many listening ears, but had to ask, "What if we try Texas or Mexico? Maybe no one will hunt for you there."

"I'm not letting any man chase me away from where I want to be. Besides, I'd feel better if you're near both my family and yours. That way there'll be someone to look out for you if anything happens to me." He reached into his pocket and pulled out a handful of money. After peeling off one hundred dollars from the roll, he pressed it into my hand.

When we went upstairs, I couldn't help but whisper, "Where did that amount of money come from?"

Metallic as a coiled spring, his voice chilled the room. "I've been busy. Doing what I do best."

31

O n May 1, 1881, the children and I arrived in Kansas City. Clarence Hite, Jesse's cousin, took us to Nancy's house. Nannie fussed over the children and clucked her tongue at me. Her husband Charles peeked over a newspaper in front of his face and acknowledged us with a smile that didn't reach his eyes.

When Jesse arrived a few days later, I scrambled into his arms. He told me he'd rented a small house in Kansas City for us, not far from my brother Thomas. Although we still would live under assumed names, after four years, I would once again be near family, and the thought soothed my soul, save for one lingering doubt.

"Will it be dangerous for us to live in the heart of Kansas City?"

"The best place in the world to hide is right out in the open." He picked up my bag to load it. "That way folks don't suspect you're up to anything."

Jesse did take a few new precautions. He grew a thick beard and let his usually neatly cropped hair grow to over his collar. A potion he bought from the mercantile turned his hair and beard from sandy blond to a dark brown, and he used a cane when he strolled about the city, walking with a feigned limp. Jesse guffawed when he told me of stopping in to say howdy to the sheriff, just to prove he could do it. My uneasiness over his behavior grew.

On a sunny afternoon, he pushed away his empty plate and leaned back in his chair. "I have a meeting tomorrow night. Don't wait on me for supper."

I gathered up the dirty dishes and put them in the dry sink. "Who are you meeting?"

"Just Frank and a few of the boys."

My brow arched. "I thought Frank was busy working for his father-in-law."

"That doesn't mean he's abandoned the idea to make some quick money."

"It'll upset Annie if he rides with you again. She has her heart set on him working a regular job."

Jesse chuckled. "I haven't said he will and I haven't said he won't. It's all just talk now."

I poured hot water into the sink and scrubbed a pan until my wrist hurt. If only he'd forget about secret meetings and quick money. And then, as though providence had answered my prayers, Jesse awakened the next morning with a swollen jaw. His tooth throbbed with pain, so he canceled the meeting. The affliction kept him in bed for days, and he only slept with a heavy dose of laudanum.

But when news came that President James Garfield had been wounded by an assassin's bullet, Jesse rose from his bed. The story captivated him, along with the rest of the country. He read every article he could find about a man named Charles Guiteau who shot the president before he could step on the train to leave for a summer vacation.

"By heaven," Jesse told me, "even I have better protection than the president of this country does."

Much to my distress, the event energized him, and his health improved enough to reconvene his meeting. By mid-July, he had packed up to leave.

"Don't worry, Zee. I wouldn't go if I didn't think it would all work out. I promise no one will be hurt."

When he hugged me, I felt the jab of a pistol-shaped lump under his jacket and shuddered.

Only a few days later, the newspapers heralded a bold train robbery in Winston. The story pushed aside President Garfield's battle for life, as reporters gleefully announced the James gang had struck again. Apparently furious at the brazen act, Governor Thomas Crittenden gathered railroad executives to meet on the subject. Newspaper stories spread the outcome of their discussion like wildfire. The governor had offered ten thousand dollars each for the capture or killing of Frank and Jesse James. Ten thousand dollars! I went white with fear. For such an enormous sum, anyone could be tempted toward betrayal. A stranger, an enemy—a friend. Jesse had done many things wrong, but he was my husband, and I couldn't stop loving him even if I wanted to.

When Jesse made his way home, I begged him to take us far away. But as he always had, Jesse made light of my fears. Indeed, he appeared more stimulated than I'd seen him since the days right after the war ended.

"My name's in the papers again," he said to me. "Just where it ought to be."

I wondered how quickly a fire burning so bright could be extinguished.

In September, Jesse left with Dick Liddil riding beside him. I wasn't surprised when the papers reported another train robbery, this time near Blue Cut. Governor Crittenden stormed all the way to Kansas City, determined to take down the James gang, along with anyone who dared offer them help. Bill Ryan's trial would soon start and bring with it even more notoriety. I tried to talk to Jesse about the risks of his choices and how much I feared what might lay ahead. But Jesse refused to be swayed.

Yet for some inexplicable reason, in November, he changed his mind. "You were right. It's time to pack up. We're moving to St. Joe."

Bone-weary, I went through the motions of packing and loading a wagon. Since our marriage, I'd lost count of the number of times we'd run from one place to another. I looked at my son's face and almost cried.

Tim had been happy in Kansas City, living near cousins with whom he could play. When I told him we were moving, he looked at me with heartrending questions in his eyes. "But, Mama, why must we go?"

"Papa has business in St. Joseph. I'm sorry, sweetheart."

It tore my heart in two that Tim and Mary must live the lives of vagabonds, wandering from one place to the next, through no fault of their own. I remembered how I'd once spurned the conventional security of my parents' home. Now I longed to set down roots. St. Joseph wasn't the answer. We needed to find somewhere far away where we could live in peace. I stopped packing and went to Jesse.

"The children are getting older and these constant moves hurt them. They hurt me, too. We need to find a place where we can stay put and have a normal life. I don't think St. Joseph is right for us."

"You know very well how important it is to stay on the move. I know what I'm doing." At the look on my face, his brusque tone softened. "I'll tell you something, Zee. I know I can't keep up the same pace forever. The only answer is to settle down someplace where we can be happy—when I have enough money to do it."

I wanted more than anything to believe him. Yet I remembered how many times before he'd made promises that had failed to materialize. "This can't go on, Jesse." Tears burned behind my eyes. "I know something terrible will happen if you don't stop what you're doing now and consider your family."

"But I do consider my family." A brow rose over one eye. "You're never far from my thoughts. And you'll soon see how much better life is going to be for us when everything you've asked for comes to pass."

Soon. That's what he always said. My nerves were at a breaking point, and I feared uttering the caustic words on the tip of my tongue. Now even Frank had taken his family far away, moving east without speaking a single word of his plans to Jesse. When Jesse found out, he bristled with shock and anger. "Buck's run out on me! Never thought that day would come." His hands clenched into white-knuckled fists, and he turned away from me, unwilling to look me in the eye.

In fact, most of Jesse's old comrades were gone. Even Dick Liddil didn't come around the way he used to. I had hoped such changes would persuade Jesse to consider the hope of new possibilities, but instead, he became more wary and began to fill his broken circle with new men.

One of them was named Charlie Ford. I'd met him a few times and found his presence tolerable. He was a tall man, and young, with a jutting jaw that reminded me decidedly of a neighbor's bulldog. Jesse liked him, and treated him with the same teasing affection he'd always given Frank.

Charlie helped us move to a tiny rental house in St. Joseph.

"It won't be long until I find a better place," Jesse said. But then he added something I didn't expect. "I'm moving Charlie in with us."

"What? You mean until he can find a house of his own?"

"No, I mean for him to stay. I'd like an extra gun. It will make my mind easier knowing he's around to help keep an eye on things. I know how you think, sweetheart, and I'm telling you there's no need to worry. Charlie's a good friend. I trust him."

"But this house is too small for all of us."

"We'll move to a bigger house soon as I can find one."

His reassurance, meant to placate me, made my shoulders slump in growing despair.

The gray, damp chill of November didn't help. I shivered at the weather and viewed the upcoming Thanksgiving holiday with a grim eye, expecting a pitifully poor celebration for us. Jesse had warned me we were out of money. Until he could replenish our funds, we would have to buy from the mercantile using credit. I chafed at the way the clerk looked at me when I made a purchase, but with the children to think of, there was nothing I could do.

Inside the tight quarters of the house, we nearly tripped over each other. It grated on me to see Charlie everywhere I looked, following Jesse like a shadow. Despite my misgivings about him, Charlie spoke polite words to me, yet they were oddly reminiscent of someone who didn't really mean what he said. He kidded with Tim, the same way Jesse did, and told my son to call him 'Cousin Charlie'.

One day, Jesse brought home news I'd been waiting to hear. "I've found the perfect place for us. It stands high on a hill, taller than any other house in St. Joe. I can see anybody who comes near. And no one will be able to see me."

For once, I didn't mind getting ready to leave. The new house wasn't much more than a stone's throw from where we were staying, so the move would be easier than many others had been. The only thing that bothered me was that it would take place on Christmas Eve.

As we packed, Tim tugged at his papa's pant leg. "But how will St. Nicholas find us?"

"It will be an adventure," Jesse told him. "Saint Nicholas is the one who showed me the house and said how much you'd love it. When it snows, you'll have a fine hill to slide upon. If you're good and help your mama, he'll bring you some nice surprises on Christmas morning."

I wondered how Jesse planned to accomplish such a feat. We already owed the mercantile for food. I knew we wouldn't be granted further credit to purchase toys.

When we arrived at the new house, my worries diminished enough for me to smile. It had been recently whitewashed, and green shutters at each window made the place look cheerful and familiar. We hauled in boxes of household goods and clothes. Jesse and Charlie carried a few pieces of furniture inside, but the house already held most of what we needed. I unpacked my iron skillet, the large pot, and our plates.

Jesse and Charlie talked to each other in whispers while I worked. Then they called a hasty good-bye in my direction and left. I paused from putting away dishes to notice the children's drooping eyelids. I'd lost track of time.

"You both need to go to sleep. Come along now."

"That's right, Mary. St. Nicholas won't come unless we're asleep," Tim announced, in a voice full of brotherly authority.

I tucked them both in bed and rubbed my forehead. I didn't want to think about Christmas morning. The thought of seeing hurt and disappointment in their eyes made my own sting with unshed tears. There had to be something I could do. Perhaps if I fixed a fine breakfast of flapjacks, they'd at least have something special to eat. I couldn't remember if I had maple syrup and went to my knees, sorting through a box filled with food.

Then the front door opened, and a cold wind swirled inside, startling me upright. Jesse carried in a small evergreen tree, and the scent of pine filled the room. Following him, Charlie held a box.

"Here's a tree with a few pretties to put under it for the children," Jesse told me. Charlie put down the box, and Jesse reached inside. "How about this? A painted sled for Tim. He can use it to slide down the hill, or I can pull him behind my horse. And don't you think Mary will like her?" He showed me a cloth doll dressed in blue indigo and wearing a bonnet.

Tears of relief and exhaustion filled my eyes. I clasped my hands together over my heart. "Oh, thank you. I was so afraid they'd wake up to nothing. That would have broken my heart."

"Well, we can't have anything like that. Here." He pulled a small bottle of my favorite lavender scent from his pocket. "For you, sweetheart."

Jesse had even gotten hold of a few ripe oranges, although heaven alone knew how. I couldn't let my mind wander to the sorrow of where any of it had come from. I focused instead on the joy I would see in my children's eyes.

The tears spilled over. I hugged my husband and whispered, "But I have nothing to give you."

"Don't you know you're all I need? Now and always."

I smiled through my tears. Charlie blushed and slipped out the front door.

32

*I*n January, Dick Liddil put an end to any speculation on his whereabouts and surrendered to authorities. Not long after, we heard Clarence Hite had been arrested. I knew Jesse would be shaken by the news and work himself into either frenzy or fury. Yet surprisingly, he remained remarkably calm, strolling about town and waving at others he met on the street as though nothing had happened. He even made jokes with me.

"You'll never guess what I did," he said one day.

I turned from the dry sink, wiping my hands, to look at him. His eyes glinted mischievously when I replied. "I can't imagine. Do tell."

"I went to the train depot and saw they'd posted a sign looking for help."

My eyes narrowed. "You didn't."

"Yes, I did. I told the clerk I wanted to apply for the job because I've got plenty of experience with the railroad business." He couldn't hold a poker face any longer and slapped his knee with a loud guffaw.

I could only shake my head at his impudence.

After adding a column of figures early in March, Jesse showed me an advertisement in the newspaper.

His voice lifted with excitement. "Look at this, Zee. Nearly one hundred sixty acres of good ranch land for sale up in Lincoln, Nebraska. I'm going to take a look at it."

"Really, Jesse? That sounds wonderful. Why don't the children and I go with you?"

"Sweetheart, there's no point in you coming. I don't even know yet if it will suit me. This time, I'll just take Charlie along and get his opinion since he knows a lot about ranching. If I decide to make an offer, I'll take you and the children to see it."

I turned away with a heavy sigh. "When will you leave?"

"In a few days. On the way back, I plan to see Ma and John. You know my brother is doing poorly. I told her I'd visit him when I could."

As Jesse packed to go, Tim stuck to him like a cocklebur. He was growing old enough to miss his father's presence at home.

"Papa, do you think I could have a dog of my own? Then he could be my best friend. I always wanted a best friend."

Jesse looked over Tim's head at me. I didn't try to hide the tears brimming in my eyes.

"Well, young man, that sounds like a fair enough request. If you promise to take care of a dog and not give another burden to your mama, I might be able to arrange something."

Tim's face lit up and my heart soared. "Yes, sir. I promise to take care of the dog all by myself. Mama won't have to do anything."

Jesse seemed to consider the matter for a moment then spoke the answer I knew he'd give our son. "I'll keep my eyes open on this trip. And if I can find a dog who's looking for a little boy to be his best friend, then I'll be sure to bring him home to you."

"Oh, thank you, Papa! Can you please go and start looking now?" Jesse and Charlie laughed together as they put on their jackets.

"Yes, I can, son. I'll be back in a week or so, after we stop in to see your grandma and tie up some loose ends." He turned to me. "I prefer you keep the doors shut and stay inside as much as you can. I don't expect trouble, but we can't be too careful. Your pistol is loaded and in the trunk. Don't be afraid to use it if you need to."

I kept the little pocket pistol hidden. I hadn't even fired the gun once since the time Jesse gave it to me. At the thought of using it, I dug my nails into my palms. "You know I'll do whatever I must."

My words were sluggish and took more effort than usual. With Jesse eager to leave again, only Tim and Mary kept me from the temptation of my bed. When I tallied the miles we'd run, a resigned lethargy settled into the marrow of my bones and hovered, dark and persuasive.

Tim stood at the window and traced a finger across the glass when his father rode away. I had to coax him from his post for dinner. "Tim, it will be a while before Papa comes home. You must eat." He followed my request but dragged his feet all the way to the table.

Not many days after Jesse and Charlie left, I wiped off the table while Tim and Mary played with marbles. Mary scattered them on the floor, and then chased them as they rolled. Tim didn't scold her, even when she slipped a marble into the pocket of her calico dress and giggled. Then I heard a knock at the door.

I stood frozen and the children looked up at me, wondering what to do. We had few acquaintances in St. Joseph, and none of them were close enough to come visiting. I peeked out the window in the same way Jesse always did. On the porch stood a tall, dark-haired man with whom I was not familiar. Torn between ignoring the knock, as Jesse had told me to do, and fearing the man might be carrying important tidings, I lifted my chin and straightened my shoulders.

"Children, go into the bedroom," I told them. Both had long been trained in the value of listening and obeying without question. Tim took Mary's hand and led her from the parlor.

"Who is it?" I called without opening the door.

"This is Sam Boswell. I'm looking for Mr. Howard. I've got some information for him."

I took a deep breath, now wishing I had the comfort of a pistol in my hand and opened the door a sliver.

The man smiled and held out a piece of paper. "Good evening, ma'am. Mr. Howard and I spoke at the drugstore last week, and he said he has interest in buying some land in Nebraska. I have a cousin who's looking to sell his property. Could you please give his name and address to Mr. Howard?"

A weight lifted from my shoulders, and I opened the door wider. "Yes, I will. Thank you, sir."

I took the paper and closed the door, shaking my head and wondering what my life had come to that even a simple visitor made me quiver like a trapped rabbit. When I turned around, I saw Tim coming from the bedroom. He had my pistol in his hand. With a sharp intake of breath, I rushed to his side. My fingers shook as I took the weapon away from him. "No, Tim. You must never handle a gun. Not until you're older."

"But Papa said you should use it if someone comes around."

"That man meant us no harm, Tim," I said, my heart still thumping wildly.

"When Papa goes to the door, he always takes his gun."

"Listen to what I say. No guns until you're older and Papa teaches you how to use them. When you're big enough, you can go hunting with him. Now why don't you and Mary go back to playing with the marbles?"

With a child's innocence, Tim considered my words and then went to get his sister. I told myself such incidents would not happen once we moved to Nebraska. We would have nothing to fear there. No reason to have a pistol in hand every time someone knocked at the door. I hoped Jesse would buy the land whether I saw it first or not. I wanted no more of running and hiding. No more fear of detectives or betrayals. I wanted a place where our children could go to school, have playmates, and feel safe. I knew the time had come for me to tell him I couldn't run any longer.

Blood hammered at my temples. I needed to keep busy, needed to keep my mind on providing for the children. I went to the pantry and found our flour and salt bags were nearly empty, so I bundled the children into their jackets, and much as I wanted to abide by Jesse's warning, headed to the mercantile.

The clerk, Mr. Sutter, stood behind the counter. He stared at me with cold eyes. "Please remind Mr. Howard your bill must be paid in full by the end of the month."

My face flamed with heat, and a well-dressed woman standing near enough to hear what he said stared down her nose at me. I nodded and, in a voice I could barely hear myself, asked for flour and a few fresh eggs. I kept my eyes focused on the children until he set the packages on the counter and picked them up with as much dignity as I could muster before I hurried out the door.

Despite the brisk March wind, my cheeks didn't cool until I'd reached home. I counted on my fingers the number of days Jesse had been gone and wondered when he'd return and how soon we could reach the safety of Nebraska.

A week later, Jesse came through the front door and I ran to meet him, filled with nervous courage and ready to express my feelings no matter the cost. Instead, I stopped just short of his arms and stared. Charlie and a man I didn't know, followed Jesse into the house.

Charlie grinned and presented the stranger to me. "Mrs. Howard, this is my brother, Bob."

Bob was shorter and thinner than Charlie, with light brown hair and deep-set eyes. He smiled and extended a hand. For the sake of courtesy, I took it but did not smile in return. His palm felt damp and soft. I pulled my hand away and hid it in the folds of my skirt. When I turned to Jesse, my eyes narrowed.

He downplayed my displeasure. "Sweetheart, Bob will be with us for a few weeks. I'll be needing his help soon."

Anger swiftly replaced disappointment. "Children, please go to the bedroom and play."

At my abrupt tone, Tim took his sister's hand and left with a curious backward glance as I turned back to Jesse.

"May I speak with you in the kitchen?"

He raised a brow and glanced at Charlie "You boys see to the horses."

Bob shrugged at Charlie, then pursed his mouth together as they headed for the door. Jesse followed me to the kitchen. I kept my voice low. "Why have you brought someone else into our home?"

"I told you, I need his help. In case you've forgotten, there aren't many left to lend a hand when I need one."

"I haven't forgotten. And I haven't forgotten the reasons they're gone. Most of them are dead or in jail. Jesse, I want more for us than this. We must get away from Missouri like Frank and Annie have. We need to give our children a normal life. I believe your association with these men is dangerous to all of us."

Jesse opened his mouth to speak, then pressed his lips together in a tight line as though he'd thought better of it. Finally, he sighed and took my hands. "You're overwrought. You must listen to me. I want the same things you do. I liked the land I saw in Nebraska, and plan to buy it. There's a nice farmhouse with lots of room for us and the children. Think of it. No more nosy neighbors poking about in our business. This is a perfect opportunity, but you know how things are. My pockets are empty, and I must have money before we can do anything. I love you but remember that I make the decisions for our family. The Federals still owe us a debt. Just one more job, then I promise we'll go."

"I'm begging you for the sake of our children. We must leave this place and these people. I don't care what kind of work you do as long as it's not what you've done in the past."

Jesse put his hand on his chest. "You can count on me this time, Zee. By all that's holy, I swear it. No more after this. We'll leave and never look back. Now let's drop the subject." He halted our conversation by calling out, "Tim, Mary!"

At the sound of their father's voice, the children rushed from the sleeping room to his arms. Jesse kissed Mary's cheek and Tim grabbed his father's jacket lapel. "Papa, did you find anything when you were gone?"

"Anything? What do you mean by that?"

"Did you find a dog? One who was looking for a little boy?"

"Let me think." Jesse made a show of furrowing his brows and then shook his head. "No, I'm afraid I didn't find a dog."

Tim's face fell, and he looked ready to cry.

Then Jesse tickled under Tim's arms until Tim couldn't help giggling. "No, I didn't find a dog. But I did find something else at my aunt Sallie's house. Come with me."

Curiosity won out over disappointment. Tim followed his father to the door. On the front porch sat a box with a small white-and-brown puppy peeking over the top, whimpering for someone to lift him out.

"Oh, Papa!"

Tim had no other words. He scooped the small bundle of fur into his arms, while the puppy squirmed and licked with wild enthusiasm. Tim laughed harder than I'd ever heard him before and the puppy chimed in, yapping with excitement.

"Go and make up a nice bed for your little friend and give him some water. A puppy needs to learn manners, so you'll have to teach him. Remember what I told you. He's your job."

"Yes. Thank you, Papa. I will take care of him always."

Tim glanced at his sister. "Come with me, Mary. You can help."

Mary followed Tim with a hand stretched out, trying as best she could to get her fingers on the new addition to our family. A small measure of my determination wilted.

"Thank you. That means so much to Tim. He's had to miss out on too many things."

"He's a good boy and deserves something special. And taking care of that puppy will help teach him responsibility. Someday he'll be man of the house, you know."

"Not for a good long while, I hope. Please, Jesse, remember your promise." My voice sounded pathetically pleading, even to my own ears.

Jesse kissed me and smoothed my hair before he left the kitchen. For him, the issue was settled. I should have been pleased to hear about the farm in Nebraska, but my mind burned with shame and terror over what might yet happen.

I went to the parlor and noticed my Bible sitting on the table. I picked it up, flipping through the dog-eared pages. Long ago, Jesse told me he'd asked the Mount Olivet Church to drop his name from their rolls because he wasn't worthy for it to be there. I knew my husband had broken many of the ten commandments. I'd broken some, too. But the time had come to call a truce and seek forgiveness. I closed the Bible and sighed.

Gazing through the window, I watched Jesse walk toward the horse shed with the Ford brothers. He clapped Charlie on the shoulder and laughed as though he hadn't a care in the world. And even though the sun shone so intensely not one of them needed to wear a coat, a shiver rippled down my spine.

33

*T*im named his new puppy Buster. The animal soon followed him around like a small furry shadow. Tim kept bits of food hidden in his pocket and gave them to Buster every time the pup lifted his paws and begged. I'd never before owned a dog and found myself drawn to the tiny creature even though he chewed on any item he came near. When I scolded him, Buster licked my hand, and the sweet scent of puppy breath soothed my annoyance. But the best part of having a puppy was the sound of Tim's laughter. No longer did he stare out the window, and that alone made Buster worth any number of ruined shoes.

The atmosphere between the Ford brothers and myself wasn't so settled. During each meal and whenever I had to be near Charlie or Bob, I kept my head down and spoke little, feeling a palpable tension between us. Jesse attempted to gloss over my frostiness and filled the silence with more banter than usual. But despite what he wanted, I found it impossible to hide my feelings. Having the Ford brothers in my home was far worse than the discomfort of a blackberry seed stuck between my front teeth.

For the first time in my life, I gnawed at my fingernails until they were ragged.

Charlie studied Jesse and seemed to hang on his every word, but Bob averted his eyes, and bayed a nervous chuckle that grated on my tightly wound nerves. I tried to make Jesse understand my feelings, but again he dismissed my worries with a laugh.

"You sound like Ma. When she met Charlie and Bob, her face looked like a pair of Federals had just stepped into her house. She told me I ought to give them both the boot."

"And why would you not heed us if both your mother and I have the same opinion?"

He slipped his arm around me. "I know how to judge men. Charlie is true as can be, though I'll admit Bob has a sneaky side. I intend to keep a close eye on both of them. Haven't I always been careful before?" He waited for my nod which I gave him just as he expected. "Well, there's no reason to doubt me now. Just keep in mind what we both want—our own ranch, far away from here."

But I couldn't still the voice within me. "I know your soul, Jesse, and you know mine. Over the years, so many things have happened. I beg you not to add to that list. I don't want anyone else hurt."

"As you say," he quipped with a shrug, impatience evident in his face as he walked away.

Jesse's once-ramrod straight posture had curved. Whether from time in the saddle or the cumulative effect of so many injuries, I didn't know. Years had roughened him into someone hard and as unyielding as granite. I wanted to believe he meant what he said about settling down, but reminded myself how many times I'd heard the same words from him. Long ago I'd been so sure of my decisions. Why was I so uncertain now?

A letter from my sister Nannie that I'd thrown on the table waited for me. I sank into a chair to read it.

Josie,

Duty compels me to send you this message. I've had long words with Charles, and he has agreed. With things as they are, we believe it best if you and the children come here to stay. There is no sense in risking your life, or theirs. You needn't worry over your financial distress. Charles and I are quite comfortable and able to provide what you need.

With affection,

Nancy

Her offer, colored with the slightest tint of disdain, shook me and forced me to study my situation as if seeing it for the first time. Jesse fed on his association with men like the Ford brothers and the notoriety and fast money he made from outlawry. Like a thunderbolt the truth shook me. My husband careened toward ambitions only the dark hand of death would stop. The revelation sent my heart thudding and made me toss and turn in my bed all night.

In the morning, I sat on the porch with Tim and Mary. Tim held Buster while Mary tried to smooth the wriggling pup's fur with her own hairbrush. I watched them and wondered what I could do to change the course of our lives.

If I took the children and fled to Nannie, accepting whatever charity she chose to give me, Tim and Mary would never see their father again. Nor would I. Jesse would lose the only anchor he had, along with any hope of salvation. My heart pounded into a drumbeat of purpose. I took a deep breath of early spring air and made a decision.

I would do what I'd never done before. I would tell Jesse he had to choose. He could pick me and the children or continue to live the life of an outlaw. The thought of such a confrontation made my stomach roil, but if my husband preferred the Fords and fast money over his wife and children, then I no longer had reason to stay.

Butterfly wings fluttered in my stomach. I tried to soothe myself with the notion of Jesse sending Charlie and Bob away. We'd take the children and leave for Nebraska, Texas, or even Mexico. With new names, we could start over in a place where no one spoke of their past or asked questions of their neighbors.

My thoughts bobbed in my brain like a cork vest struggling to keep a drowning woman from slipping underwater. I looked across the yard to where Jesse leaned against the barn, his face animated, hands moving rapidly as he spoke to the Fords.

With a course of action in place, my chin lifted. The challenge would lie in finding a way to speak with Jesse without Charlie and Bob listening nearby. I couldn't shame him in front of his comrades, and the Fords seldom let Jesse out of their sight, huddling and speaking in low tones that stopped whenever the children or I came near. The three of them had made a habit of leaving the house after dinner and often didn't return until long after I'd fallen asleep. If I woke in the morning to find the Fords sleeping on the floor next to my own bed, it wouldn't have surprised me one bit.

I smoothed dust from my skirt. In the morning, right after breakfast, I would tell Jesse I had to speak with him alone. Then I would draw the line, and it would be up to him to decide which way he would go.

If only I hadn't decided to wait.

I rose early to put an iron skillet on the stove and heat the bacon lard until it sizzled, then sliced potatoes and dropped them into the hot grease. When bacon lard began to sizzle, I sliced potatoes and dropped them into the hot grease. The fat hissed and spattered as my mind ran over what I would say to Jesse, practicing each word as my papa had done before Sunday morning service.

From the parlor, I heard the sound of boots on the floor, a chuckle, and muffled conversation. Good. The scent of frying potatoes had roused them all. I stirred the pan and dreamed of what life might be like on the Nebraska prairie or near the beach in Galveston.

Tim wandered into the kitchen, followed, as always, by Mary. She carried her baby doll in one hand and rubbed her eyes with a small fist.

Tim sniffed the air. "Good morning, Mama."

"Good morning, my darlings. Are you very hungry?"

Tim sniffed again. "Yes, my stomach is growling like Buster does."

The puppy twined around his legs, nose up to capture the scent of food.

"I hungry, too, Mama," Mary added in her sweet, little voice.

"It's almost ready. Tim, will you be my best helper and get the coffee mill out for me? Put it on the table, and then get some plates. Mary, please help your brother."

Mary dutifully went to Tim's side. Buster followed Tim, his tail curved up and wagging so fast it was a blur. Mary laughed.

A tune I hadn't thought of in a long while popped into my head. I began to sing the words in a soft voice. "Oh, Susannah, oh, don't you cry for me, for I come from Alabama with a banjo on my knee."

"I like that song, Mama. It feels happy," Tim said with a sleepy smile.

"Yes, it is a happy tune. I used to sing it a long time ago." The men's feet scuffled across the wooden planks of the parlor, and I called out to them, "Breakfast will be ready soon."

Voices murmured, and I heard Jesse chuckle. Then someone dragged a chair across the floor.

I picked up a dishcloth, folded it, and lifted the hot skillet off the stove. Bowl. I needed a bowl.

"Tim, will you—"

A deafening boom made the walls shake. I dropped the skillet back onto the stove and glanced at the children. A gunshot. Someone had fired a gun in my house!

"Tim, stay here with Mary."

Mouth drier than an August day, I raced to the parlor and then gasped. Jesse lay on the floor, face up, next to an overturned chair, his eyes wide open. A dark sticky pool of blood under his head grew larger with each second. The scent of gunpowder filled the room as Charlie and Bob stood at the open door with wide eyes, breathing heavily, as if they'd just run a race.

I dropped to my knees next to my husband and shouted at the Fords, "What have you done?" I turned long enough to see Bob run out the door, but Charlie looked down at me with a strange expression on his face.

"A pistol went off accidentally."

I lifted my head long enough to spit out the words, "Accidentally? It went off on purpose. You coward!"

Charlie's face grew pale, and he bolted from the house after his brother. I lifted Jesse's head onto my lap. Using the cloth still clutched in my hand, I tried to wipe blood that flowed from the back of his head. He made no sound, even though his lips moved. His eyes were open, but as I watched, the light in them faded until they became glassy and cold as marble.

Tim and Mary ran toward me, Buster at their heels. At the sight of their father's body on the floor, Tim hiccoughed out the question of a child. "What happened to my papa?"

But I couldn't answer them. Instead, the room filled with a high-pitched wail that emanated from the depths of my soul. I keened and wept and rocked with Jesse's body clutched to my chest until my throat grew raw. Then I closed my eyes.

Finally, I turned to see my children, wide-eyed and staring at the bloody scene, crying in great gulping sobs. Tim clutched the puppy and Mary held her baby doll as if those were the only things in the world that mattered. Their grief and fear brought me to my senses. I put a hand on Jesse's cheek in a feather's touch, kissed his lips, then placed his head gently back on the floor.

When I stood, the room spun around me. To steady myself, I touched the wall, then jerked away my hand from the spatters of my husband's blood. "Tim, you must help me. Take your sister and go to the sleeping room. I'll be there in a moment."

His little shoulders shaking, he led Mary away. The puppy, tail tucked between its legs, followed them. I kneeled again and pulled my skirts away from the blood puddling on the floor to focus my mind on checking Jesse's pockets. He had nothing more than a few dollars and the lucky penny he'd carried for so long. I slid both down the bodice of my dress, then I went to the children.

Tim and Mary were still crying, arms wrapped around each other. Buster sat on the floor at their feet, whimpering. Numbly, I pulled my children close, and tears trailed down my cheeks, wetting their still sleep-ruffled hair. We stayed that way until our weeping ended and my body grew numb.

I heard footsteps pounding through the parlor. A pause, an exclamation, and then the bedroom door swung open. Two men stood in the doorway and stared in. The bearded, gray-haired man spoke first. "I'm Mr. Heddens, the coroner, and this is Marshal Craig. Who are you, ma'am?"

I opened my mouth to speak, but nothing came out. I swallowed and tried again. "Mrs. Howard."

"We got word of a shooting and came right over. Can you tell us what happened here today, Mrs. Howard?"

"My husband has been shot."

"Who shot him?"

"There were two boys staying with us. They did it."

The marshal's eyes narrowed. "Why would they do such a thing?"

"I don't know. Oh, my God, I don't know!"

Hearing the words spoken aloud made the unthinkable real. The numbness evaporated, and I choked out a desperate sob. The children clung to me and wept anew.

"I'm sorry, Mrs. Howard, but you must compose yourself and tell me what happened." Mr. Heddens crossed his arms.

Before I regained enough control to speak, another man, this one with a badge pinned to his jacket, came into the room. He whispered to the marshal before he turned his gaze to me.

Marshal Craig pointed at the children. "My deputy will take your kids outside. I need to speak to you alone."

I rose, but my knees wobbled so that I couldn't stand. I steadied myself and sat on the bed. My whole body shook, as I stared down at my hands, still covered with Jesse's blood.

Marshal Craig stepped closer and stood over me. "I am the lawfully sworn marshal of this county, and you are obliged to be completely truthful with me." Despite his gruff tone, he took my blood-stained fingers into his hands. "The boys you spoke of, the ones living here with you, are Charlie and Bob Ford, aren't they? They're out in the yard right now, surrendering, and they've told us everything about your husband." He dropped my hand. "Your name isn't Mrs. Howard, is it? And the man lying dead on the parlor floor isn't Mr. Howard." Eyes hard, he stared at me. "Your husband is the outlaw Jesse James. And you, ma'am, are his wife."

I thought of Jesse dead in the next room and wanted to scream and weep and rend my clothes like Job. My hopes for the future were gone, disappeared like a wisp of smoke in open air. I couldn't pretend a minute more. Taking a deep breath, I stood and straightened my spine. My eyes met Marshal Craig's squarely.

"Yes, sir," I said, my voice as even as I could make it. "I am Mrs. Jesse James."

34

I peeked out the window. Despite an approaching wall of dark clouds, people were still gathered outside our house, as they'd done all day since the shots were fired. Even after the undertaker removed Jesse's body in a shining horse-drawn wagon of death, it wasn't enough to satisfy public curiosity. A few faces in the crowd were familiar to me, but most were strangers, standing in groups to whisper and point. They reminded me of dark buzzards circling a carcass, waiting to feed.

Small footsteps pattered behind me, and I turned to see Tim. His cheeks were still damp with tears, but he had the same determined look I'd often seen on his father's face.

"Are the people who hurt my papa out there?"

"No, dear. The men who hurt Papa are in jail now," I said, caressing his hair.

"What will happen to them?"

"I don't know, son. That will be up to the law."

I thanked heaven for the kindness of our neighbor, Mrs. Terrel, who would spare the children the next ordeal. An inquest had been scheduled for three o'clock, only hours after Jesse's death, and Mrs. Terrel, our next-door neighbor who'd brought us an apple-cinnamon pie after we moved in, sat in the kitchen. She offered to watch the children for me, and I accepted her gesture with gratitude.

I'd discarded my blood-stained dress in a heap and scrubbed my hands until they were raw. Yet the bleak aura of death still clung to me. The sheriff insisted his deputy drive me to the courthouse. There were so many people surrounding my home that he feared for my safety.

Thunder rumbled, and a gust of wind fluttered the white sheer curtains at my window just as the deputy arrived.

I walked outside and drops of rain splattered on my hat. Men scribbling on pads of paper shouted questions. Jesse would have pegged them at once as reporters. I ignored them and hurried into the buggy as rain sliced down in earnest, hammering on the roof. We lurched forward and the horse's hooves splashed through muddy puddles while I stared at the downpour. When we reached the courthouse, the deputy helped me down and shouldered people away as we climbed the courthouse steps.

The courtroom was packed. Someone pointed at a chair and bade me sit. Still in shock by the morning's events, I followed his direction without a word while everyone in the room stared at me. I'd just taken my seat when a deputy brought in Charlie and Bob. They strutted down the aisle, Charlie with his shoulders back and Bob thrusting his chest out like a peacock. My vision blurred with tears. We had sheltered and fed those two men. My husband had treated them as friends, and his trust had cost him his life. Neither Charlie nor Bob were man enough to meet my eyes.

Coroner Heddens had me stand and raise my trembling

hand, swearing to tell the truth. Then he walked across the floor, tenting his fingers. "What is your name, ma'am?"

"Mrs. Jesse James."

"Some folks think Jesse James was killed a few years back. They aren't sure who the man is at the undertaker's. We need to be certain he's properly identified." Mr. Heddens cleared his throat and proceeded to ask questions about me, my marriage, and the places we had lived. He inquired about my husband's wounds, the missing tip of his finger, and the names we'd used in the past. The questions seemed to go on endlessly until the final one.

"Who is the man lying at the undertaker's right now?"

"Jesse James," I said, and put a hand on my throbbing forehead. "I'm dizzy. May I please step down now?"

He coughed and rustled papers on the table before coming to take my arm and help me to a chair where other court officials sat. One of them fanned my face, and another brought a glass of cool water for me to sip.

Once the men were satisfied I wouldn't collapse, the coroner called Bob Ford to the witness stand. Someone had given Bob a new set of clothes. His fine gray coat and green-striped trousers added to his smirk of self-satisfaction. I had little stomach to see Bob's traitorous face, but need compelled me to hear the loathsome story for myself.

Bob reported his name and age and acquaintance with my husband.

Then the coroner went to the heart of the murder. "So you are the one who shot the man who called himself John Davis Howard?"

"Sir, I shot Jesse James, for that was his true name. I did it when he took off his guns and climbed on a chair to straighten a picture that hung on the wall."

"When did you decide to do this deed, Mr. Ford?"

"After meeting with Governor Crittenden. He told me if I helped capture or kill Jesse James, I'd be given a large reward."

"And what was your answer to the governor?"

"I told him I thought I could do it," Bob said. "He promised a pardon for Dick Liddil, my brother, and me if we fixed it so Jesse James could never rob or kill anyone again."

My mouth dropped open. Bob Ford just admitted to a cold-blooded murder planned with the approval of Missouri's governor. Nausea cramped my stomach, and I covered my mouth with a handkerchief.

"Please, may I leave?" I whispered to the court official sitting next to me.

"You may go," he said, "but you must return in the morning."

I nodded and left the courtroom, my legs quaking. Bob and Charlie Ford had posed as Jesse's friends in nothing more than a ruse to commit murder.

Outside, the sun peeked between clouds and sparkled on rain puddles. I walked to the buggy where the deputy waited. "Please take me to the telegraph office. There's something I must do."

Even though reporters were sending the news everywhere, I had to personally give the message to Zerelda.

Jesse has been murdered. Come to St. Joseph at once.

The deputy drove me to Mrs. Terrel's house, and when I went inside, she put her hand on my shoulder.

"Your children are fine. They cried for a while, but I persuaded them to eat a bit of bread and soup."

"That's so kind. Thank you for your help. We have so few friends here."

"Please sit down and let me get you something to eat or drink. You are pale as a sheet."

"No, thank you. I have no appetite. But there is something you can do that would be a great help." Tears brimmed again. "If it's possible, may we stay here tonight? My house is a place of such sorrow, I can't bear the thought of going back, and I fear what will happen if the children return so soon to the horrors they witnessed."

"Of course, you may stay, my dear. I'll do anything I can to help."

I smiled wanly and sat down. A prayer rose to my mouth then faded. This time, no matter how many appeals I lifted, Jesse would never return.

Tim and Mary clung to me throughout the night, and they cried the next morning when it came time for me to go back to the courthouse. I couldn't leave my children behind again and took them with me into the waiting buggy.

In front of the courthouse, a crowd milled about on the lawn, but a black bonnet stood half a head taller than anyone else. Zerelda had arrived.

The lines of her face were etched with sorrow. When she saw us, she hugged Tim and Mary. Then she put her arm around me and sobbed. "I have just come from the undertaker's, where my poor boy is lying on a cold slab. Those miserable traitors have taken him away from us!"

Her grief erased my numb acceptance and brought forth anew the horror and sorrow I'd been trying to suppress. The children broke into tears again at this new display of grief. After a few moments, I composed myself enough to take

Zerelda's arm and climb the steep courthouse steps. Tim, my little man, took Mary's hand and followed us.

When Zerelda walked inside, the men whispered to each other. Coroner Heddens hooked his thumbs in his pockets and raised a brow. He had a few words with the judge and then he called Jesse's mother to the stand. Zerelda went to the witness chair and sat down. She raised her stump of an arm, swearing to tell the truth, and answered the coroner's questions between pauses to dab tears from her eyes.

"Mrs. Samuel, you say that you have been to the undertaker. Did you recognize the body of your son?"

"Yes, sir," she told him.

"There is no doubt at all in your mind about whether the body you saw is that of your son, Jesse James?"

"I wish to God there was."

"And who is that lady who walked in by your side?"

"That is my son's wife and his poor little children. Oh, dear God." Tears streamed down Zerelda's face as her gaze raked the courtroom. At once, her cheeks went from pale to crimson. She quivered with emotion and waved what remained of her arm like a vengeful sword. "Dick Liddil! You helped to bring this about. Coward! Traitor! See what you have done. God will have his vengeance!"

Dick cowered in his seat, speaking over the buzz of spectators, "I didn't do it. It was Bob Ford."

But Zerelda had worked herself into a fury, sputtering epithets at the top of her lungs until three court officers pulled her from the room while the coroner smacked his palms on the table in an attempt to regain control.

The children and I hurried outside to Zerelda. I murmured soothing words and rubbed her back until the tightness disappeared, and then we climbed into the waiting buggy. Neither of us had energy enough to speak on the ride home, and when we arrived, I blew out a breath of relief. The crowd had disappeared. From the outside, our home looked the same as it always had. But in the parlor, splotches of blood stained the wall, and the dark puddle on the floor had seeped into wooden planks. Pictures were knocked askew, and a chair still lay sideways on the floor.

Zerelda looked around the room and a steady stream of fiery words came from her mouth. "Traitors. Cowards. Snakes!"

I left her to say and do what she must and took the children into the sleeping room. My mouth dropped open in disbelief. Drawers were open and boxes had been riffled through as though a tornado had swirled about.

I called to Zerelda. "Someone has been here. Most of Jesse's guns are gone. My rings and a few pieces of jewelry are missing, too."

"So the vultures have come to pick clean our bones. Find a box. We must pack what's left before they come back and take everything."

We filled a large wooden crate with what was left of our possessions. It was a pitifully small amount to represent the eight years Jesse and I had been married.

Tim brought out his bag of marbles and bent to pick up something from the floor. It was a pair of blue spectacles that Charlie Ford sometimes put on to disguise himself. "Grandma, look. Cousin Charlie used to wear these."

She snatched the glasses from his hand. "Charlie Ford is not your cousin. Don't ever call him such a name again. He was the traitor who killed your papa."

Tim came to me with tears welled in his eyes.

"It's all right," I said. "Your grandmother is very upset. You must try to understand."

He sniffed, but his face told me somethng else troubled him. "Mama, a man pointed at me today. I heard him say, 'That's young Jesse James.' Why did he call me that?"

I sighed and went to my knees to hold him. "It's your real name. Since people who wanted to harm Papa were trying to find him, we couldn't use our own names."

"My real name is Jesse James?"

"Yes, it is. When you're older, I hope you can understand why it had to be this way."

Tim nodded, but the mist of confusion did not clear from his eyes.

The next morning, news of Jesse's death appeared everywhere. Headlines blared the story of Jesse James being murdered in his own home by his friends. A photographer had taken a picture of Jesse's body lying on a long board while onlookers posed next to him. The sight sickened me and led to a new fear.

I went to Zerelda. "What if they don't give us his body?"

She stood at her full six-foot height. "They wouldn't dare do such a thing. We are his kin and have the right to his remains. No one better try to keep him from us. We're going right now to the marshal and let him know we want his body released without further delay."

Zerelda's breath huffed in outrage by the time we arrived at the marshal's office. Sorrow and bewilderment kept me from adding a word when she shouted in righteous wrath.

"I demand my son's body now!"

The marshal held up a hand to silence her. "Mrs. Samuel, I just received a telegram from Governor Crittenden. He says the body is to be turned over to the family."

But Zerelda wasn't satisfied. "And while we're here, I demand protection for my family." Her eyes shot daggers at him. "Scavengers have already rooted through the house. When we try to leave for Kearney, someone may tamper with what little is left or even attempt to steal my son's body the same way they have his belongings."

"In regard to what happened at the house, any stolen property has been confiscated. We'll see what we can do, Mrs. Samuel, to prevent any problems when you travel to Kearney."

Zerelda shot him another scalding glance before we left to make our way to the undertaker's office. Once we were there, Undertaker Sidefaden gave me a paper filled with figures for preparing Jesse's body and purchasing a coffin. For the second time that day, my mouth dropped open.

"The cost is two hundred sixty dollars? I can't afford to pay a sum like that."

The tall, thin man shook his head in practiced solemnity. "There's no need for you to worry about it, Mrs. James. The Kansas City police commissioner and Sheriff Timberlake from Clay County have paid the bill in full—with their compliments."

35

*J*esse's final journey would take him home to Kearney, to where he'd grown up, and our departure from St. Joseph could not come soon enough for me. We would take the train first thing in the morning, thanks to tickets bought for us by my sister Nancy. But first we must spend one more night in the place where my husband had breathed his last.

We left the undertaker and my stomach lurched with each bump of the carriage at the thought of where we were going. When our driver slowed the clopping horse, I inhaled a sharp breath. People had gathered around the house again, as though waiting for the next act of a stage play. The driver helped us down, and I lifted Mary to my hip. She hid her face against my shoulder as Zerelda took Tim's hand and plowed into the melee. The crowd surged toward us, and shouts carried over the sound of tramping feet.

"If you tell your story, I'll see you are well paid."

"Your husband must have left you a fortune. I have stock certificates to sell. You can make a pile of money for your children."

"Mrs. James, if you're arrested for your husband's deeds, I can represent you for only five hundred dollars."

Zerelda shoved through to make a path for us much as Moses must have parted the Red Sea. When we pushed our way inside, she slammed the door and muttered.

"They're nothing but vultures."

But I had more pressing worries. "I don't know what we'll do next. I have nothing more than the few dollars Jesse had in his pockets."

Zerelda tilted her head. "My circumstances are as dire as yours."

I looked at her in disbelief. "What do you mean?"

"Did he not tell you? With so much trouble at the farm and Reuben more feeble every day, Jesse gave me money whenever he could. Now I don't know how I'll keep the farm going."

An ache throbbed at my temple. "Papa would say God will provide."

Zerelda sat down and rubbed her arm. "Sometimes God can use some help. It might be good for both of us if you and the children move to the farm."

My gaze did not meet hers. "That's a very kind offer. Let me think on it for a few days, please. The marshal said he would keep the house under guard. I'll sell whatever we have left. Then I'll make a decision."

Zerelda sighed and closed her eyes.

Nancy had the mercantile deliver a mourning dress and bonnet to me. The next day, when I put on the snug crepe dress and pulled the bonnet's veil over my face, an unexpected sense of composure sustained me.

My brother Robert met us at Undertaker Sidenfaden's office where a new crowd had gathered on word of our departure. We watched as four men labored to pull the heavy polished casket from the cooling room. My head bowed under the shield of my widow's veil and I boarded the train with a sense of relief, knowing we'd soon be away from the curious stares.

The train's steady clacking lulled me to sleep. But when I opened my eyes in Kearney, my heart sank. An even larger crowd of people had gathered at the depot. More faces than I could count.

We stood in silence as Jesse's casket was unloaded and carried into the Kearney Hotel. By order of the sheriff, a man pulled open the coffin's top. Zerelda looked at her son and railed against the world with sobs and shouts.

The undertaker had dressed him in a white shirt and striped ascot, his dark beard neatly trimmed. He looked as though he'd fallen asleep with only one blemish marking his left temple. I held my children close as they looked upon their father's face for the final time. Then I lifted my veil long enough to kiss his firm, cold lips.

The hotel clerk escorted us outside, where a carriage waited. A reporter armed with paper and pencil rushed toward us. "Do you have a statement?"

Zerelda's voice thundered over the murmurs of the crowd. "I can tell you this—I'm proud of my boys. Proud to be the mother of Jesse James. I thank God Frank is far away where he cannot be shot in the back by a traitor!"

I couldn't bear the sight of people gawking at Jesse, so Robert took over to receive those lined up to file past. He didn't return to the farm until late in the evening, his shoulders drooping with weariness.

"There must have been hundreds of people. The sheriff told me even passing trains delayed their journey so the passengers and crew could march by. After so many years, I guess everyone wanted to see Jesse James."

I shuddered. "Thank you for sparing us such an ordeal."

The next morning, we drove to Mount Olivet Baptist Church, which was filled to bursting. Many more people milled around outside. The front row sat empty, reserved for Jesse's family. Walking past other mourners toward the coffin in front of the altar blurred my vision. I sat between my children, and they each pressed themselves against me.

Reverend Martin spoke on the certainty of death and our duty to prepare ourselves for it. He thundered about sin and punishment. Each word pounded into my brain even as Zerelda swayed back and forth moaning, "Oh God, oh God," in such dramatic fashion I wanted to clap my hand over her mouth.

When the sermon finally ended, Reverend Martin cast a stern eye before speaking his final words.

"Before the coffin leaves for its resting place, I bring a request from the family. As John Samuel is sick and very low on account of the shock caused by the death of his brother and as the grave is very near the house, only close friends and family are invited."

Zerelda had arranged for Jesse's burial to take place on the farm, not far from her bedroom window. With my own future uncertain, I had no other suggestion. After all, what did it matter now? No decision to the contrary would bring back my husband.

As I stood next to the deep hole that would be Jesse's final resting place, what seemed like a countless number of people surrounded the farm. They'd ignored Reverend Martin's words to come and watch. The enormity of my loss hit me again. I put a hand on the box and kissed it, tears streaming down my face, and couldn't help crying aloud. "They took away any chance you had, and I don't know how I shall bear it."

Zerelda sobbed and shouted over me, "My son helped those traitors, but when he turned his back, they murdered him for money. God's vengeance will come!"

She continued her wails as I watched the coffin that contained the body of the man I'd loved for most of my life lowered into the ground. Pain sharp as a surgeon's knife pierced through me. What would I do? A vital part of my soul had been cut away. People always say the pain of those who have loved and lost is numbed over time. That someday, the heavy yoke of sorrow lifts and days are filled with new light. I didn't know whether to believe such a thing or not, for the oppressiveness of my thoughts kept hope far from my heart. I looked at Zerelda, her feet planted solidly on fertile soil.

She would survive this blow in the same way she'd gotten through every other pain and adversity. I loved Zerelda but realized we could never live in the same house. Her mercurial ways were too discordant for someone like me. After the burial, I would swallow what remained of my pride and accept the offer made by my sister. She and her husband lived a comfortable life, and I could stay there until I found some way to make ends meet.

Tim sniffed and rubbed a sleeve over his nose. I looked down at his blond head. Even though the truth had been revealed to my son, he would always be Tim to me. His shock at discovering the identity of his father had shaken the timbers of his foundation. Life would be different for my boy now, and for Mary, too. Jesse wasn't alone in paying a high price for the life he led.

36

On the morning of the auction, dozens of people stood outside our house in St. Joseph, trampling over the grass until it disappeared beneath their feet. The auctioneer smiled and waved, making a great show of describing the pitifully few things left to sell. One by one, he held each piece of my life high for the crowd to see.

"Here's the coffee mill the children played with right before Jesse James was shot."

"This is a coal scuttle Jesse used the day before he died."

"How about this high chair, folks? Jesse's little girl sat in it."

I flinched over every word, but Tim stood manfully next to me. He had begged to come, and his pleading had melted my resolve to spare him. That he would witness the sale pained me, yet he didn't speak a word.

The auctioneer pushed back his derby hat and grinned. He presesnted the coffee mill first, prompting half-hearted bids from several men.

The mill sold for two dollars.

Other things went as cheaply. It became clear that most

of the spectators were there only to stare at the goods once belonging to Jesse James. Few offered a bid.

I wrapped my fingers around Jesse's lucky penny in my pocket and turned away from the greedy faces.

"Come with me, Tim. Let's go to the house for a while."

We walked to the porch and I pushed open the door.

Two men were on their knees in the parlor, busily cutting blood-stained splinters from the floor.

I gasped and goose flesh pimpled my arms. "*Get out of here!*" I didn't care if every single person in the whole wide world heard me shout. Tim stood open-mouthed as the men snatched up their grisly trophies before they scrambled past us and out the door. I hugged my son and took a few deep breaths to compose myself before I could face returning to the auction. We went outside in time for the final item. Tim squeezed my hand with all his might.

The auctioneer lifted his puppy, Buster.

"This little cur dog was brought as a present for Jesse Junior by the famous outlaw only a few days before he died. Ladies and gentlemen, what am I bid for this one-of-a-kind treasure?"

Buster whimpered. Ladies whispered to each other behind their fans.

The auctioneer said, "Who will give me two bits?"

A man's hand went up, then another man countered. A third man joined in, and the three competed against each other, the bids going higher. The cat and mouse game went on until one of the men shook his head and dropped out. Then another declined to go any higher.

The auctioneer mopped his brow and crowed breathlessly.

"Sold! For fifteen dollars!"

It was the highest price paid for anything in the auction,

and the only one I wished I could have kept for my boy. The auctioneer handed Buster to the winning bidder, a man in a fine dark suit with a gap-toothed grin. He held up the puppy, and the crowd applauded. My son's narrow shoulders slumped, and he buried his face in my skirt. I pulled him close to me as he cried out his heartbreak in front of total strangers.

I had nothing left but my children.

In all, the auction's proceeds amounted to $117.65. It was far from what we would need.

On a cloudy day a few weeks later, I twisted my handkerchief, waiting in my sister's parlor for news. The trial of Bob and Charlie Ford had pushed every other matter from my mind. I couldn't bear to attend the hearing, so Nancy's husband, Charles, had gone on my behalf. He returned home with brows drawn and hands fisted. I twined my fingers together, dreading what I'd hear.

"It's over. Bob confessed to his deed, and Charlie admitted to helping him. People were standing elbow to elbow in the courtroom so they could hear the sentence. The judge declared the Fords were both to be hanged next month for murder. He had to pound his gavel to silence the spectators."

My knees went weak, and I dropped into a chair. "Thank God. I feared they wouldn't have to pay for their crime."

Charles looked down for a moment and then cleared his throat. "I'm afraid Governor Crittenden sent an order right away, pardoning them. Charlie and Bob are free to collect their reward."

My hand went to my chest. "They admit to the crime of murder and are pardoned and rewarded? What kind of justice is that?"

"I'm sorry, Zee. When the sentence was announced, the Fords were smiling as though they hadn't a care in the world. If it's any consolation, there were many in the crowd who shouted that they were traitors."

I shook my head and dabbed my eyes with a handkerchief. I found no consolation in any of it. None at all.

The children and I lived with Nancy and Charles for several months. I tried to keep from intruding in their lives, but my brother-in-law's forced politeness soon told me he'd grown weary of strangers knocking on the door in an effort to see me. We moved to the home of my brother Thomas, where I could at least help by cooking and sewing.

I shook my head at so many people who believed Jesse had hidden away a secret fortune. In the last few months of his life, he'd scrambled for money. How foolish to think he would fail to retrieve a treasure if there was one to be had. Yet people contrived to see me for countless wild schemes.

One man sneaked through a window at night. Another sent a letter asking me to invest in a gold mine. But most were hungry for the details of my husband's life. A promoter asked me to tell my story on a lecture tour, and my circumstances were dire enough for me to agree. At the last minute, my head spun at the thought of standing in front of an audience to speak, so the promoter engaged an actor to disclose pieces of our lives while the children and I sat on stage. My face burned with shame the entire time we were on display, and I was thankful when the promoter abandoned the entire idea.

Later, a man named Frank Triplett offered Zerelda and me royalties if we agreed to let him interview us for a book. Zerelda convinced me to accept his proposal in hopes we could tell Jesse's story from our point of view.

"And," Zerelda said to clinch her argument, "God alone knows we both need to bring in some money."

I regretted my decision at the very first meeting. When Mr. Triplett refused to let us see what he'd written before the book came out, I feared the worst. Frank, upon hearing of the project, sent a tersely worded note to Zerelda and another to me. Since he and Annie still lived as fugitives, he accused us of putting them in new jeopardy. We promptly withdrew our support of the book, but the damage had already been done.

Upon publication, Frank Triplett sent me a copy. I read it and squirmed with every word. It described the life of Frank and Jesse in flowery terms that reminded me of the worst dime novels I'd ever read. At a time when I wanted nothing more than to fade from the public's eye, the book increased by ten-fold the efforts of people trying to contact me.

But what hurt most, I read in the book's final section. Frank Triplett implied that I had failed Jesse by not influencing him, as Annie had done for Frank, to be a better man. It brought back a question I'd wrestled with for many months. In many ways, Jesse had failed me. But had I failed him as well?

The book project drove a wedge between Frank and me that we would never fully repair, and I mused that selling a few of my husband's secrets for money hadn't been much different from what Charlie and Bob Ford had done.

A deep sense of weariness settled over me. I refused to leave the house without a widow's veil, and allowed no photographs be taken of me. Even after society declared my mourning ended, I did not abandon wearing black. It would be part of my penance, a punishment for what I'd done and for what I'd left undone.

The blue spells that had plagued me in the past came more often and lasted longer. I lived in fear of strangers befriending me with intent to harm my children, and limited visitors to my kin and my pastor.

But I wasn't the only one who struggled in the years following Jesse's death. Zerelda sold pebbles from her famous son's grave to the many curiosity seekers who visited the farm. She gloried in standing tall and raising her stump for emphasis as she told stories of her children, her life, and most of all, of Jesse and Frank.

Frank continued in hiding until Jesse's old friend, John Newman Edwards, negotiated terms of his surrender to Governor Crittenden. The event made headlines across the country when Frank and the governor shook hands. He would stand trial on three separate charges and each time be pronounced "not guilty". Frank and Annie would need to wander no longer.

He and Annie moved away to live a life of peace, if not prosperity. My happiness for them had a bittersweet hue. When I sent a note of congratulations to Frank, he did not reply.

As I'd always hoped, young Jesse—for he'd insisted that I call him his real name—and Mary went to school each day. Every Sunday, they attended the Methodist Church.

At the age of eleven, my dear son found a job, and over my objection, he left school and went to work. He'd become the man of the family, as his father had bid him, and he smiled with pride when he handed me his earnings.

With the money we were able to save and the help of some unlikely friends, we bought a small cottage in Kansas City. It soothed me to sit on the porch and take satisfaction in knowing that after so much time, we finally had a place to call our own.

Over the years, thoughts of loved ones who were gone came to me often. I prayed for Papa, Mama, Lucy, my babies far away in Tennessee, and of course Jesse. When the stains on my soul over what had passed became too dark to bear, I spoke with my pastor, while tears spilled from my eyes. He read to me 2 Corinthians 5:17:

> *Therefore, if any man be in Christ, he is a new creature: old things are passed away; behold, all things are become new.*

"You must seek forgiveness from God," he told me, "for things which are over and done, but you must also forgive yourself. Focus only on what lies ahead."

I listened to his words with an unsettled mind. From years of habit, I couldn't help thinking about Jesse—the rebel, the crusader, the bandit, the husband, the father. Strong-willed and stubborn. A terrifying specter to those he despised, but loving and loyal to his wife, his children, and his family. Was Frank Triplett right? Could it have been within my power to change him?

Jesse loved me as he loved no one else. Of that, I had no doubt. If I'd forced him to choose, he would have tried. He might even have succeeded, but I would never know for sure. I realized my only salvation—and Jesse's—would come from raising our children to be true and diligent and wise. Love would not fail.

On pleasant evenings when stars twinkle overhead, I often sit outside and listen to the chirp of crickets and the call of night birds. When the moon is bright, I fancy that I can see a charming rogue among the flickering shadows, someone who wooed me in days before hate and revenge twisted his heart. A smile lifts the corners of lips I remember so well.

My husband, Jesse James. The young man who once gave me a penny for a promise.

Afterword

There were no fortunes hidden away to support Jesse's family. After his death, Zee and her children lived in poverty, and stayed with various relatives willing to take them in. Young Jesse quit school at the age of eleven to help support his mother and sister. In a strange twist of fate, he obtained employment as a copy boy at the law office of Thomas Theodore Crittenden, Junior; the son of Governor Crittenden, the man who made a deal with Bob Ford that led to the murder of Jesse James. Between the boy's earnings, and financial assistance contributed by Crittenden, John Newman Edwards, and other friends, the family bought a cottage located at 3402 Tracy Avenue in Kansas City, Missouri. For the first time, they had a permanent home.

Zee shunned the public eye and devoted her life to raising her children. She attended the Methodist Church each week until her health declined, and lived long enough to see her son marry Stella Frances McGown.

With Zee's health failing, Stella—by now expecting a baby—along with Zee's daughter, Mary, nursed Zee through her final illness. On November 13, 1900, she died at the age of fifty-five. Only a month later, Zee and Jesse's first grandchild would be born. The young couple named their infant for Zee's favorite sister Lucy, a favor Zee had requested before her death.

A few months later, the family arranged to have Jesse's body moved from his mother's farm to lie next to his devoted wife at the Mount Olivet Cemetery in Kearney, Missouri. Yet there remained one more promise—unfulfilled until October 31, 2004.

One hundred and one years after her death, one of Zee's final wishes was granted. Young Jesse's great-grandson, Judge James R. Ross, obtained a court order to have Gould and Montgomery, the twin boys born to Zee and Jesse in Nashville, exhumed from their gravesite in Humphries County, Tennessee. The babies were buried next to their parents on November 22, 2004, finally together again at the Mount Olivet Cemetery.

Jesse's mother, Zerelda Cole James Simms Samuel, has been described as one of the most formidable women of the Civil War era, giving anyone who opposed her reason to keep a sharp watch over their shoulder. After Jesse's death, Zerelda remained at the farm in Kearney where her infamous sons were born and stayed there for the rest of her life. To support herself, she gave tours of the farm and sold pebbles from Jesse's grave to visitors. Many claimed she gathered new stones from a nearby creek bed to replenish the grave on a regular basis. Strong-willed and fiercely devoted to her boys until the end, Zerelda died in 1911 at the age of eighty-six while on her way home from a visit to Frank.

Following Zerelda's death, Frank and Annie moved to the farm in Kearney. As Zerelda had once done, Frank greeted people when they arrived to tour the farm, and he told a few stories of his own. Frank died February 18, 1915. The reclusive Annie passed in 1944.

The James Farm itself, where many significant events in the outlaw's life occurred, eventually fell into ruins. Clay County purchased the farm in 1978 and began work to restore the property, creating the James Farm and Museum. It is open to the public and remains one of the oldest continually operated historic sites in Missouri, with an extensive collection of artifacts from the James family. The museum provides a fascinating look at life in Missouri before, during, and after the Civil War.

Author's Note

Why a quiet and deeply religious young woman like Zerelda Mimms would marry a man such as Jesse James—not only her first cousin but a bandit known throughout the country—is a question that long puzzled me. During my research, I found no easy answers. Some facts of Zee's life were a matter of public record and indisputable. Other sources gave conflicting accounts. Much remains a mystery, and under the circumstances, this isn't a surprise. Jesse and Zee worked hard not to leave behind a trail.

Within these constraints, Zee and the tumultuous times in which she lived came to life for me. In cases where no information existed or inconsistencies of fact were found, I imagined the lives and conversations of Jesse and Zee based on what I had learned about them. To help separate fact from fiction, the following explains some of the literary choices I made, and the reasoning behind those decisions.

In the novel, Jesse gives Zee a penny to seal their engagement. This is something he would likely have had in his possession at the time, and a gift he could easily give a young girl craving a tangible token of his affection. I crafted the story of him getting the penny from his father based on accounts claiming young Jesse had grown highly distraught at his father's departure. It made sense that a loving parent would devise some way to give comfort to his child, from which sprang the idea of the lucky penny.

Zee's visit to Jesse's mother, Zerelda, in January 1875, came early in her first pregnancy. Several sources speculated the visit occurred because of illness related to her condition. I found no reports of how long Zee stayed at the farm, but it seemed logical she would not have recovered overnight. This gave rise to the idea of her being present during the attack by Pinkerton agents on January 26, 1875. No existing evidence puts Zee at the scene, but it was the family's practice not to disclose any more information than necessary to authorities. Historians have noted a horse was stolen during the arrival of neighbors to help the Samuel family. If Zee had been at the farm, the possibility exists she could have been the one to take the animal and warn her husband of the tragedy. During her desperate ride, Zee shoots a man who means harm to her and Jesse. This scene was crafted based on an account by one of her Tennessee neighbors who claimed Zee showed him a gun and said she wouldn't hesitate to shoot anyone who threatened her family. I believe she would have done exactly what she said she'd do.

The family moved many times while in Tennessee, and according to sources may have even spent a year in Baltimore. However, since the details of each specific move had no bearing on the overall story, I chose to condense them.

Most of the characters in this book were truly a part of Zee's life. Some of them, notably William Locke, and a few of the Tennessee neighbors are fictional.

Finally, this novel is Zee's story, not Jesse's. According to some of Jesse's comrades, he did his best to keep his activities secret from his wife. Thus, most information on what he did likely came to her only through family, friends, and newspaper accounts. She would not have been aware of every move Jesse made or each crime he committed.

Although every effort has been made to be as accurate as possible, there were times when the author's imagination served the story.

Sources

The sources consulted by the author came largely from materials focused on Jesse, as there are few written records related specifically to Zee. I am grateful for the body of work others have created which helped guide and inform me on this journey.

The following publications provided the meat of my research for timelines, facts, and a feel for the era, although many other articles and anecdotal stories were reviewed. The following would provide a sound starting point for anyone who would like to read more about the life and times of the James family.

Jesse James was My Neighbor by Homer Croy
Shot All to Hell by Mark Lee Gardner
Jesse James, My Father, by Jesse James, Jr.
In the Shadow of Jesse James by Stella Frances James
The James Farm, It's People, Their Lives and Their Times by
    Martin Edward McGrane
Jesse James was His Name by William A. Settle, Jr.
Jesse James, Last Rebel of the Civil War by T. J. Stiles
Jesse James, The Life, Times and Treacherous Death of the Most Infamous Outlaw of All Time by Frank Triplett
Frank and Jesse James by Ted P. Yeatman

Reader's Guide

I love book clubs and would be happy to participate in discussions either in person (locally), or via Skype. Please email me at patricia.wahler@outlook.com for more information.

1. This story is told from Zee's point of view. Do her observations change or confirm your opinion about her husband? Why?

2. How does Zee's relationship with her parents evolve over time? Do you think this is typical of young people today?

3. Family and friends in the novel keep secrets from the outside world to present a unified front. Why do you suppose they remained silent and loyal even when they didn't approve of Frank's and Jesse's activities?

4. After the war, Jesse is determined to get revenge for the North's treatment of the South. Do you think most Southerners during Reconstruction agreed with this philosophy?

5. What events helped Zee to justify Jesse's behavior?

What events caused her to begin questioning the decisions he made?

6. In an effort to stop the economic impact in Missouri of the James gang, Governor Crittenden made an agreement that facilitated the murder of a private citizen. What do you think about his strategy? How did the agreement change the lives of Charlie and Bob Ford?

7. It appears likely Zee may have suffered from depression. Has the perception of mental health disorders improved since the nineteenth century or is it still, in some ways, the same?

8. Zee grows to blame herself for Jesse's activities and worries over what will ultimately happen to her family. Do you think she could have done something to change Jesse's behavior?

9. Zee's mother-in-law and aunt, Zerelda Cole James Simms Samuel remained an important influence throughout the life of Jesse James. Do you think this may have impacted upon his decisions and Zee's relationship with her husband?

10. One of this novel's themes is redemption. Was Zee able to come to terms with what happened during her marriage to Jesse? If so, how?

Acknowledgments

It truly does take a village to create a book, and there are many who helped guide me when the idea to write the story of Zee James first glimmered more than seven years ago.

I am grateful to writer friends who encouraged me—notably my esteemed colleagues in Coffee and Critique. Armed with red pens and clear observations, they always tell it like it is.

Thank you to Cassie Cox-Robertson at Joy Editing, who provided initial editing and feedback on the manuscript. I appreciate your input and sound advice.

I extend my deepest gratitude to friends and cherished loved ones who understood that last minute cancellations go with the territory when a deadline looms.

To the staff of Amphorae Publishing Group and Blank Slate Press, thank you for taking a chance on a debut author and birthing this book despite my countless questions, anxious moments, and tendency to be more than a little verbose in emails. A special thanks to Kristina Blank Makansi, who helped shape this story into a much stronger one, and Donna Essner, who supported the notion of giving Zee the chance to be heard.

For my family, what can I say? I'm more grateful for your love and support than you'll ever know.

About the Author

Pat Wahler is an award-winning author with fifteen stories in the popular *Chicken Soup for the Soul* series. Her work can also be found in *Cup of Comfort*, *Sasee Magazine*, *Storyteller Magazine* and other publications. She is inspired by the emotionally satisfying stories of historical women brought to life through fiction. Most recently, Pat co-authored a picture book, *Midnight the One-eyed Cat*, focused on disabilities and self esteem, due for release Fall 2018. *I am Mrs. Jesse James* is her first novel.

CPSIA information can be obtained
at www.ICGtesting.com
Printed in the USA
LVHW04s0237250818
587959LV00001B/1/P

9 781943 075461